CHRISSIE MANBY

Saying Goodbye to Tuesday

HODDER

First published in Great Britain in 2021 by Hodder & Stoughton
An Hachette UK company

1

Copyright © Chrissie Manby 2021

The right of Chrissie Manby to be identified as the Author
of the Work has been asserted by her in accordance with the
Copyright, Designs and Patents Act 1988.

A CIP catalogue record for this title is available from the British Library

Paperback ISBN 978 1 473 68297 9
eBook ISBN 978 1 473 68298 6

Typeset in Plantin Light by Palimpsest Book Production Limited,
Falkirk, Stirlingshire

Printed and bound in Great Britain by Clays Ltd, Elcograf S.p.A.

Hodder & Stoughton policy is to use papers that are natural, renewable
and recyclable products and made from wood grown in sustainable forests.
The logging and manufacturing processes are expected to conform to the
environmental regulations of the country of origin.

_u_ _r Chu_ _e_ _anby_

'This sassy a__ __li__ __ead will make you
laugh – a lot!'
Closer

'I've been a fan of Manby's writing for years and
thoroughly enjoyed this'
Daily Mail

'Perfect, unputdownable summer adventures'
Jenny Colgan

'Manby's novels are made for holidays'
Glamour

'Nothing short of brilliant'
Marie Claire

'Funny and inventive'
Company

'Destined to keep you up until the small hours'
Daily Mirror

'What a wonderfully lighthearted and uplifting novel'
Bloglovin

'Heartwarming . . . truly funny'
The Bookbag

'[This novel] was funny and emotional, it was
heartwarming, it was so genuine and realistic and it is a
MUST READ this autumn. Highly recommended!'

Also by Chrissie Manby

Flatmates
Second Prize
Deep Heat
Lizzie Jordan's Secret Life
Running Away From Richard
Getting Personal
Seven Sunny Days
Girl Meets Ape
Ready Or Not?
The Matchbreaker
Marrying for Money
Spa Wars
Crazy in Love
Getting Over Mr Right
Kate's Wedding
What I Did On My Holidays
Writing for Love (eBook only)
A Proper Family Holiday
A Proper Family Christmas
A Proper Family Adventure
A Wedding at Christmas
A Fairy Tale for Christmas
The Worst Case Scenario Cookery Club
Once in a Lifetime
Three Days in Florence

About the author

Chrissie Manby is the author of twenty-six romantic comedy
novels and a guide for aspiring writers, *Writing for Love*. She
was nominated for the Melissa Nathan Award for Comedy
Romance for *Getting Over Mr Right*. Raised in Gloucester,
Chrissie now lives in London.

You can follow her on Twitter @chrissiemanby or visit her
website to find out more: www.chrissiemanby.com

For Wren Violet Wigmore

This is not a love story. At least, it's not the usual kind of love story. Not the kind where 'boy meets girl and mayhem ensues'. This is about a deeper kind of love than that (though I promise some romance as well). It's about a love that knows no boundaries and is prepared to make any sacrifice.

It's about the love of a dog.

Meet Stupendo.

He's a very good boy.

Chapter One

The day I found out started just like any other. As the sun came up, Merle the blackbird sounded the first note of the dawn chorus. He was a little early in my view so I padded over to the window and ducked my head under the curtains to give him 'the look'. But Merle was facing away from me into next door's garden, and carried on singing regardless, so I went back to the bed, resting my chin on the mattress right next to my beloved Tuesday's sleeping face. Her eyebrows briefly knitted together but other than that, she didn't stir, so I settled down on the floor again and tried to ignore the noisy bird outside.

A little later the clock on Tuesday's bedside table started its own version of the dawn chorus. It was less tuneful than Merle's but it was a sound that I'd come to love, because if the blackbird didn't wake Tuesday up then the alarm clock always would. And I would be right there, ready with a cheery morning greeting and desperate for a wee. Tuesday would always get out of bed straight away, no matter how much she didn't want to, to let me out into the garden.

On this day, however, she did not get up when the clock started singing. Instead she silenced its trill by knocking it on to the floor, then sank back down into the pillows with a groan. I cocked my head at her. She didn't even look at me. I jumped up to put both front paws on the mattress. She put her forearm over her eyes.

'Seriously?' I complained. 'Come on, missus. Time to get up. Things to do.'

I was used to Tuesday trying to snatch some extra sleep – especially since William had come into the picture – but never without letting me out first. William would be waking up soon and I needed to get into the garden to check the perimeter fences and make sure the place was safe before he wanted to go outside. Who knew what might have happened during the night?

When Tuesday didn't respond to my looming right over her, with my tongue lolling within millimetres of her nose – a move that normally made her laugh – I sat back down on the carpet in confusion. Perhaps she was ill. I pressed my snout against her hand to check her temperature. She snatched her hand away from me and tucked it beneath her cheek.

'Tuesday?' I let out an exasperated wuff.

Still she ignored me, so I took myself on to the landing. When Tuesday appeared a little later, she walked right by me. I followed her into William's room. He was asleep in his cot and looked very comfortable so she let him snooze on. I trailed behind Tuesday as she tiptoed downstairs to the kitchen, careful not to wake William a moment sooner than she had to. At least she would open the back door now.

But she didn't. Instead Tuesday put the kettle on and stood at the sink, staring out into the garden where I should have been getting on with my morning's work.

Putting my paws up on to the draining board beside her and stretching to my full height, I could see the younger squirrels were on the bird table again. No amount of squirrel-proofing seemed to keep them off it. Meanwhile the old black cat, Caligula, was on top of the back fence watching them (as if he had the faintest hope of catching one). If I didn't get out there soon, the squirrels would be digging up Tuesday's plants to bury the peanuts they'd stolen. They'd already done for the geraniums in all the hanging baskets. I needed to warn them off. Caligula certainly wouldn't.

Tuesday sighed. 'Stupendo,' she said.

'That's my name.'

I wagged my tail to let her know I was listening. Always there. Always ready. Tuesday finally opened the back door and I sprang out on to the patio. She stood on the back step, with one of my toys in her hand. It was the bright green plastic sprout she'd bought me for Christmas. It smelled worse than a real sprout but if Tuesday wanted to play, I didn't want to appear unwilling.

'Throw it!' I said, feinting at her feet like a champion boxer. The human kind, not the dog.

Tuesday looked at the sprout.

'Throw it!' I gave a little yelp of excitement. Sometimes she would only pretend to throw the sprout at first and I would tear off down the garden before noticing it was still in her hand. Got me pretty much every time but if it made her smile . . .

But Tuesday did not pretend to bowl the sprout to the far end of the garden that morning. She didn't even throw it as far as the bird table. She just let it drop on to the patio right where she was standing, then turned and went back into the kitchen, closing the door firmly behind her and leaving me outside on my own.

I had no idea what I'd done to deserve this odd treatment and of course I was upset but I decided not to show it. Humans had their strange ways, I knew. I trotted across to the bird table with my tail held high. The young squirrels scattered with satisfying speed, eyes boggling out of their heads at my approach.

'Yeah,' I said. 'And don't come back. This is the *bird* table. It's for the *birds*.'

The squirrels chattered at me from the top of the holm oak. I gave them a sharp bark in response.

'Stupido?'

It was a moment before I realised that the old black cat – Caligula – was talking to me. He never talked to me unless he had to and vice versa. I certainly wasn't going to respond to him until he used my proper title.

'Stu*pendo*?' he tried again. I could hear the sarcasm in his voice.

'That's me,' I said, without turning to look at him. I carried on sniffing along the edge of the lawn. A female fox and a couple of hedgehogs had been by overnight. There was evidence, in the flattened grass, that the hedgehogs had been fighting. I wished I'd seen it.

'How can I help you?' I asked Caligula when I was ready.

'Stupendo, what are you doing here?' he responded.

'What are *you* doing here? I think you'll find this is my garden, *cat*.' I imbued that single syllable with as much disdain as I could manage.

'*Was* your garden,' Caligula said.

'*Is*,' I replied.

'*Was*,' Caligula insisted.

'What's with the word games, flat-face?'

Like a drop of jet-black oil, Caligula slid down the fence to the ground. He padded over to where I stood and sat down right beside me. It was the closest he'd ever come to me deliberately. He smelled of tinned tuna.

'You're not supposed to be here,' he told me.

'No, fish-breath, you're the one who's not supposed to be here.'

'Fish-breath? I should scratch your eyes out. But just this once I'm going to let it go, since you're clearly not in your right mind as well as not in the right place.'

'Eh?' Why did cats always have to speak in riddles?

'Stupendo, you're not supposed to be here because you're supposed to be somewhere else entirely. Some-where . . .' He sucked in his breath. 'I really don't know how I should put this.'

The tone with which Caligula was speaking now was unsettling. There was a softness to his voice that I'd never heard before. Not when he was talking to me, in any case. Then he lifted a paw as if he intended to pat me but thought better of it. All the same, the gentleness of the gesture alerted my suspicions still more.

'Why are you being so strange?' I asked.

'Oh dear.' Caligula shook his head. 'Are you telling me you really don't know?'

This time, he did touch me with his paw but quickly withdrew it again as though he'd been burned. As he did so, the squirrels came closer, watching me intently, and

Merle the blackbird landed on the fence, his gold-ringed eyes upon mine.

'Are you going to tell him?' Napoleon, the biggest squirrel, asked. He was called Napoleon on account of his always tucking up one front paw when he was sitting on his haunches.

'I suppose I'll have to,' Caligula said.

Merle fluttered down to the grass, putting himself right in Caligula's range. The cat and the blackbird shared an uneasy glance but it was clear that something was happening which meant the usual rules of engagement did not apply, and for the moment both the bird and the squirrels were safe within striking distance of Caligula's retractable claws.

'Stupendo.' Caligula took a deep breath. 'You're not supposed to be here because . . . well, because you're dead.'

Chapter Two

As Caligula's bombshell hit, Merle and the squirrels flinched.

'How else was I supposed to put it?' Caligula asked them.

'There are kinder ways,' said Merle, hopping closer and opening one wing as if to take me under it. 'Kinder words.'

'You could have said *deceased*,' suggested a squirrel.

'Departed?'

'Defunct?'

The squirrels were a wordy bunch.

While they argued about how best to have told me, I tried to take the situation in. Dead? That couldn't be right.

'Guys, hello? I'm not dead,' I piped up. 'I'm here. I'm standing right in front of you.' I wagged my tail to prove it.

'Well, yes. You *are* here but at the same time you're *not* here,' Merle explained.

'Tell him, Caligula,' said the smallest squirrel, whom everyone called Pipsqueak. 'Tell him what happened.'

'Do I have to?' the cat asked.

'Somebody does!'

'I can't stand it.' Pipsqueak's mother Primula covered her eyes and turned away.

'You were out in the street on your own,' Caligula began.

'I'm never in the street on my own,' I retorted.

'Well, you were on Sunday night. I don't know where you'd been or what you'd been up to but as you were crossing into Bracken Avenue from the junction with Walnut Road you were knocked flat by a speeding car.'

'Caligula!' Primula squeaked. 'Don't say "knocked flat" . . .'

'Well, he was, wasn't he?'

'Completely flat,' Napoleon agreed.

'The car was going *really* fast,' said Pipsqueak. 'I heard the screech of brakes.'

'You were killed at once,' said Merle. 'You didn't suffer. Tuesday ran out into the street when she heard the crash. The car was already gone but Tuesday held you as your spirit left your body. You weren't alone.'

'Why are you saying all this?' I asked.

Caligula had never been nice to me but Merle was always kind.

'Because it's true.'

Merle hopped across the lawn to a spot in the flower bed that edged the garden. I knew that flower bed like the back of my paw so I could see that the earth had recently been turned over next to the rosemary bush, which was one of my favourite spots for burying treasure. Merle pointed with his beak towards a large, flat pebble. There was something painted on it.

'Your name,' he explained. 'It's like a . . .'

'Gravestone,' Caligula supplied the word.

'Am I . . . ?' I gently rested a paw on the recently turned earth. I couldn't bring myself to say the words.

Merle closed his bright-ringed eyes. Pipsqueak pulled his extravagant tail over his face. Napoleon and the other squirrels followed suit.

'Yes,' said Caligula. 'You are . . . Well, most of you is anyway. The bits they could scrape up. But that's not the most important part of you, is it? Your earthly body?'

'I'll be the judge of that,' I said. I went to start digging. Merle hopped in my way.

'I wouldn't do that if I were you. Caligula's right. Don't think about what's down there, Stupendo. Look at this instead.' Merle tapped on the stone with his beak. 'Tuesday painted that for you. And here are all your favourite toys.'

Squeaky Pig stood guard over the mound. He was categorically *not* my favourite toy. I was always trying to silence him but his squeaker was indestructible. Next to Squeaky Pig was No-Longer-Squeaky-Sausage and Soon-Stopped-Squeaking-Minion and the stuffed Donald Trump that had always smelled too strange to play with. Scattered around the toys were several unshelled peanuts.

'From our family,' said Napoleon. 'In your honour.'

He'd pinched them off the bird table, I knew.

'Though now that you've seen them . . .' Napoleon eyed the peanuts hungrily.

'You can have them,' I replied.

The squirrels didn't waste any time.

Next to the stone was a sleek black feather that had been poked into the earth so it stood up like a flag.

'Is that from your tail?' I asked Merle.

He nodded.

'I didn't know what else to do.'

I felt my heart squeeze at such kindness.

'I didn't think you'd want half a mouse,' said Caligula.

'I didn't think you could *catch* a mouse,' I responded.

Caligula regarded his front left paw as he casually extended and retracted his claws.

I went back to looking at the stone. I couldn't read my name but I liked the shape of it. I liked the rainbow Tuesday had painted arching over it too.

'Anyway,' said Caligula, after we'd all shared a brief moment of contemplation. 'Now you know what happened, you can be on your way.'

'Where to?'

'To the other place. Where everybody is like you. They're all dead as a—'

Before Caligula could finish, Merle interrupted him, 'They're all faithful pets who've earned their place in the Rainbow Kingdom.'

Caligula rolled his eyes. 'The *Rainbow Kingdom*?'

Merle ignored him. 'You can cross over the Rainbow Bridge whenever you like, Stupendo. You should have crossed over already. It usually happens at once. All you have to do is say goodbye to this world. To us. To the garden. To Tuesday and William.'

How could I ever say goodbye to Tuesday and William?

Merle continued, 'You just close your eyes and say you're ready and everything will happen as it should. You just have to let go.'

I glanced back at the house. Tuesday was standing with her hands in the kitchen sink, staring out into the garden.

She looked in my direction but didn't seem to see me. Or any of the others, for that matter. I wagged my tail. I gave a cheery yip. I tried to pick up Squeaky Pig, thinking that perhaps for once his infernal squeal would come in useful for attracting Tuesday's attention. But I found I couldn't do it. My jaws closed on thin air.

Inside the house, Tuesday dried her hands, then she dabbed at her eyes with the tea towel. When I was a puppy, I used to steal the tea towels and race around the garden with them, hoping that Tuesday would catch the loose end for a game of tug-of-war.

'She's acting like she can't see me,' I said.

'Well, she can't.' Caligula shrugged.

'It's true,' said Pipsqueak. 'She can't see you at all.'

'But you lot can.'

Merle explained, 'Human beings aren't tuned into the different layers of the universe like we creatures are, Stupendo. They can't see sound or taste colour. They can't hear the vibration of the earth or smell a feeling on the wind. They spend their lives turning from nature. Most of them don't even know there's more than one dimension.'

'But . . . but . . .' I protested. 'How can I say goodbye if she can't see me? Tuesday!' I barked her name in vain.

Merle's eyes glistened. Pipsqueak's tail drooped. Even Caligula seemed quite pensive.

'You just have to say goodbye in your mind,' Merle said. 'Close your eyes. We're here for you. It won't hurt.'

I closed my eyes. I said, 'I'm ready.' Nothing happened.

'He's obviously not,' said Caligula. 'Ready, that is.'

The squirrels and Merle regarded me with concern.

'Look, you don't have to make your mind up now,' Merle told me. 'You can stay here for as long as you want. But she'll never know you're here. That's all.'

Tuesday turned away from the window and a cold shadow fell across my heart.

Chapter Three

After I found out I was dead, I just hung around the garden all day. I didn't know what to do with myself. I could tell my bird and animal friends didn't know what to do with me either. From time to time, one would pause in going about his or her business to ask me how I was feeling, but I knew they didn't really want me to elaborate. I would have thought it was obvious. I was completely devastated. I'd never felt so sad in my life. Or rather, my death.

Inside the house, Tuesday carried on with her day too. By standing on the garden bench, I could see into the kitchen. William woke up and Tuesday brought him downstairs. He sat in his high chair and banged a spoon on the tray while she made his breakfast. I loved having breakfast with William since he dropped at least every other spoonful. I thought hungrily of the porridge and toast soldiers that would be going to waste on the floor.

A few times, I forgot what Caligula and Merle had said about humans not being able to see or hear me, and I barked in an attempt to get Tuesday to open the back door. But though occasionally she gazed out into the garden, she always looked right through me. Her lovely brown eyes were sadder than I had ever seen them. Even when she was holding William and he reached out to 'boop' her nose, like he used to do mine, Tuesday's smile never quite took over her whole face.

In the afternoon, I thought my luck might be turning when Tuesday brought William out into the garden. I bounced around her feet barking with joy. But she didn't notice. Tuesday rolled out a rug on the grass and put William down to play on it while she hung up some washing. I stood right beside her as she put William's bedclothes on the line. I tried to pull on the end of one of the sheets but I couldn't seem to grasp it and Tuesday carried on as though I wasn't there.

With the washing flapping in the summer breeze, Tuesday spent a couple of minutes standing by the mound in the flower bed that I now knew was my grave. She crouched down and tidied up my old toys, putting them back in a row.

She smoothed the earth over my bones. Then she picked up the now empty peanut shells and all the feathers, including the magnificent black tail feather that Merle must have been missing quite badly, and put them in the garden waste bin. She had no idea they were a tribute to me.

Tuesday joined William on the blanket and I sat down on the grass nearby to watch them. Half-heartedly, Tuesday helped William fit wooden blocks into a puzzle. Then Tuesday lay down on her back and stared up at the sky until William started fussing to be taken back inside again. He was getting pretty good at walking but he still preferred to be picked up.

As Tuesday lifted William into her arms, he pointed towards the row of toys on my grave.

'Do . . .' he said. I knew he was trying to say 'dog'.

'You miss him too,' Tuesday translated.

They went inside, leaving me behind again. I wasn't fast enough to get through the door with them.

Eventually, Tuesday put William to bed and went into the living room to watch television. As it grew darker, she drew the curtains so I could no longer see her. I was still shut outside and I'm ashamed to say I had a little howl about it. Napoleon and Pipsqueak came and sat beside me for a while, but they didn't know how to make things better. They kept asking me if I wanted a peanut. I'd never really wanted a peanut – not since the first time I tried one and discovered how disappointing they were inside their brittle husks. I certainly didn't want one now.

Soon it was time for the squirrels to go home for the evening. They couldn't sit beside me in the dark. Merle led the local birds in their goodnight song. The swifts who came to stay on our street every summer made one last evening fly-past in formation as they headed to their nests. I knew that after sunset a whole new group of animals took over the garden, and the squirrels and small birds did not particularly want to meet the night shift. The bats were OK but there was an old dog fox who might eat a squirrel if he could catch one. I didn't know his name. None of the daytime regulars did. He came and went without talking to anyone, keeping his nose close to the floor as he slunk on by. Likewise, the owl, who was partial to a supper of small rodent, was a nameless stranger to the daytime crew. He couldn't have carried me off but I nevertheless found him frightening with his staring yellow eyes and wide white wings that made not the slightest sound as they flapped. He was more like a ghost than I was.

Only Caligula the cat and his feline kin could roam the garden at all hours with impunity. The fox and the owl saw him as an equal. He was, like them, a hunter by design, after all, even if I'd never seen him catch anything more than a loose feather when he thought no one was watching him play.

I heard the owl hoot as he left his roost and instinctively crept closer to the back door, trying to find comfort in the feeble circle of light cast by the glass panels. But it wasn't long before Tuesday turned the kitchen lights off, leaving me completely in the dark. As I sat alone on the patio sniffling with self-pity, I wondered how I would get through the night. I'd never spent the small hours outside on my own before and I'm sad to admit I was scared.

Chapter Four

Then

I need to tell you more about my early life on Bracken Avenue. I'll start right at the beginning, when I was just a pup.

The funny thing is, Tuesday thinks she chose me. She thinks that us ending up together was her decision, when in reality it was me that did the choosing. I knew from the moment she walked through the front door of Mandy's house that she was going to be mine. I just had to play it cool. While my brothers were all over Tuesday as soon as she came into the kitchen, I hung back, leaning against the dishwasher looking all nonchalant, waiting for her to come to me.

I was part of a surprise litter of four. Our mother, Rosa, was a pedigree black Labrador, who'd won several prizes as a young dog and was destined to mother great champions in her turn. It didn't quite work out like that. Our father, Neddy, was a brindled Staffordshire bull terrier, whose feckless owner kept him on a piece of string that wasn't strong enough to hold him when a likely female wandered by. When Neddy saw Rosa, it was love at first sight but, of course, the resulting

Labrador-Staffie puppies – we four boys – were a big problem for Mandy. At a time when every other dog was a 'cocka-poodle-something', Staffradors were not in any kind of demand.

Unable to keep us all for herself, much as she might have liked to, Mandy invited some of her friends to her house for a pizza one Friday night, hoping that a few bottles of wine would persuade at least one of them to commit to taking a puppy. Tuesday was one of the people who came along. But she didn't need wine to see my charms.

'What about that one? What's he called?' I heard her ask Mandy and I knew it was me she was talking about.

'Him? That's Stuart,' Mandy said. 'Stuart Little, after the mouse in the film, because he's the smallest.'

'He is so cute,' said Tuesday. 'Like a *leetle* furry cupcake.' And I was sure I was almost there. All I had to do was consolidate my position. While my brothers, Tyson, Derek and Boris, got into a fight over the remains of a shoe, I casually wandered across and sat down between Tuesday's feet, with my back against one of her shins. Then I gave her a coy look across my shoulder. It was a look that said, 'You can give me a scratch behind the ears if you like.'

'He is such a sweetheart!' Tuesday exclaimed, picking me straight up from the floor and plonking me on to her lap. I hadn't been expecting that and I have to admit the surprise made me have a small accident. Luckily Tuesday didn't seem to mind.

'These aren't my best jeans,' she told Mandy. Then she lifted me until I was level with her nose. 'Aren't you a lovely boy?' she said. 'Do you want to come home with me, Stuart Little?'

I wiggled my tail in a way that I hoped said, 'Tuesday, I can think of nothing better.'

I moved in with Tuesday three weeks later. I was only twelve weeks old but I knew at once that I had fallen on my feet. Tuesday's house on Bracken Avenue – number thirteen – had a garden straight out of any pup's wildest dreams. There were big shady trees to lounge under and a lawn just perfect for dashing about after a ball. I was Tuesday's first puppy and she'd really pushed the boat out to make sure I had everything I needed. Toys, bowls, bedding and the fanciest organic puppy food and treats that money could buy.

'Here you are, Stuart,' she said, setting me down gently on my plush new faux-fur bed in the corner of the kitchen.

'I won't be needing this,' I thought, as I made a show of trying to get comfy. Indeed, I only had to cry for a quarter of an hour that first night before Tuesday came downstairs to fetch me and carry me back to sleep in her room, which of course is where I'd wanted to be all along.

'I told myself I would not do this,' she said, as she lifted me on to her own bed and I cuddled up under the duvet. Tuesday kept saying that it was a 'one-off' and warning me that she would be a lot stricter once I had properly settled in, but I was pretty sure I would never have to sleep downstairs again.

'I promise I will look after you, Stuart Little,' she told me.

'I'm going to be the one looking after you,' I thought

as I licked the end of her nose. 'And please call me anything but Stuart Little.'

It didn't suit me. I was going to be big.

The following morning, as I performed a series of daring leaps on and off the sofa, she nicknamed me 'The Great Stupendo' and Stupendo was the name that stuck.

I had made the right choice. By Tuesday's side was where I was destined to be. I hardly missed my littermates at all now I had Tuesday to love (I especially didn't miss Boris, whose idea of fun was trying to fit my whole head in his enormous mouth). Tuesday was always ready with a treat or a tummy rub. She always forgave my little accidents. She laughed at all my doggy jokes and was delighted by my zoomies.

For the first few weeks I lived with Tuesday, before I had the last of my puppy vaccinations, I wasn't allowed out on to the street. That was when I got to know the other animals who lived on my patch. The squirrels had come to check me out on my first day at Bracken Avenue and since then they'd been baiting me from the safety of the trees every time I stepped into the garden. One day Napoleon threw a nut at my head while I was sniffing around the base of the holm oak. He pretended I was mistaken, of course, but after I jumped up the tree trunk and nearly caught his tail, the squirrels were slightly more respectful.

I met Caligula on my first day at number thirteen too. I didn't know much about cats at the time, or how much I was supposed to hate them, so I approached him just as I'd approached the squirrels and the birds – with a friendly smile and an open heart. Observing me from the top of the fence, Caligula groaned, 'That's all I need. A puppy. Is Tuesday dog-sitting or are you here to stay?'

'I'm here to stay,' I said proudly. 'I'm Stupendo. What's your name?'

'That's for me to know and you to find out.'

'Toby?' I started guessing. 'Cyril? Fred?'

'Enough with the puppyish enthusiasm.' Caligula stopped me. 'We're not going to be friends, you and I.' Then he slinked away. After he was gone, Napoleon the squirrel called me from the top of the bird table.

'His name is Caligula,' he said. 'He was named after an emperor of some sort. Like I am. You'll get used to him.'

Despite that inauspicious first meeting, I tried to make Caligula my friend. Every time I saw him, I greeted him with a polite 'wuff' and a wag of my tail, but I never got anything more than an eye-roll in return, so eventually I gave up and let Caligula keep himself to himself. Unless he set foot on the ground in my garden when I was out there too, in which case I was perfectly entitled to chase him off.

Fortunately, there were other, friendlier animals to meet. As soon as I had the last of my jabs and was allowed out into the world, Tuesday introduced me to the concept of walks. It wasn't long before the sound of the word 'walk' could send me into a frenzy of delight. After I knocked her favourite table lamp over with my tail in my enthusiasm to get outside, Tuesday took to spelling 'walk' out in an attempt to keep me calm until she got my lead on

– W-A-L-K – but it didn't take me long to understand that connection too.

The park soon became my favourite destination because there was always someone interesting to see there. Like Buster. Buster was an English bull terrier, who talked with a 'gangsta' accent. He told me I could be in his gang because I was part-Staffie. When I was a puppy, I thought Buster was really hard, though I soon came to learn that his 'crew' consisted of a cross-eyed French bulldog and a cockapoo who barked at his own tail. What's more, Buster had never been anywhere near a dogs home as he'd led me to believe. He got the scar on his nose not through fighting but through having tried to get the last baked bean out of a discarded tin.

Zephyr, on the other hand, had every right to play on her tough upbringing. Zephyr had been a racing grey-hound. A big success, I heard. But at the end of her career, those trophies seemed to count for nothing. Her owner, who had made so much money from her racing triumphs, had no compunction in dropping Zephyr off at the Greyhound Trust to be rehomed the day after her final race. Fortunately, she quickly found a new human family, but the weeks she spent in the kennels had definitely left a real scar.

Buster and Zephyr were very kind to me. Though they were several years older than I was, they were always willing to indulge my puppyish ways and have a quick game of chase or tag. I made other friends too, at the puppy training school that Tuesday enrolled me in when I was six months old.

I loved puppy training school, though Tuesday seemed

to find our Sunday afternoons there less exciting. She would get so exasperated when I didn't respond to her attempts to teach me to do really pointless things like sit still on one side of the children's football pitch while she took herself *and* the treats to the other.

'Stay!' she'd yell. 'Stay there! Stay, Stupendo! Stay!'

Why would I do that? Especially as it quickly became clear that the more I pretended not to understand what the trainer or Tuesday were asking me to do, the more treats I got when I finally *appeared* to cotton on. I was no fool. I knew what 'sit' and 'stay' meant. I may have graduated bottom of my class, but I guarantee you that I got more treats than any other dog there in the process. That's what I call intelligence.

On weekdays, Tuesday went to work. She was her own boss, a gardener, so she could take me with her in her smart green van. I was more than happy to sit in the sun while she mowed lawns, clipped hedges and dug up flower beds. I liked to do a bit of digging myself but though she laughed the first couple of times I tried to lend a paw, after I dug up a delicate rose bush she'd only just planted, Tuesday would put me off with a passable growl whenever I looked as though I was about to get stuck in. It was a bit annoying but all the same, I knew I was luckier than many other dogs, like Buster and Zephyr, who had to stay shut indoors while their humans were at work.

Some days though, Tuesday did stay at home designing new gardens on a big pad of paper on the dining room table. I helped however I could. Sometimes that was simply by placing a friendly paw on her knee to remind her to take her regular walk and snack breaks. Or should I say, *my* regular walk and snack breaks.

I was so happy in those puppy days. We both were.

'Stupendo,' Tuesday told me one quiet afternoon, 'you've brought the sun out in my life.'

It wasn't just that I had given her an excuse to go to the park. On the day she first met me, I heard Tuesday tell Mandy, my first human, the reason she'd decided to get a puppy.

Tuesday's mum had died six months earlier. 'When she was getting close to the end, she suggested I get a dog for some company,' Tuesday explained.

So I never met her – Tuesday's mum, Sarah – but I heard a lot about her through listening to Tuesday's conversations with her friends. Two years before I was born, Tuesday had moved back from a shared flat in London to her childhood home in Bracken Avenue to look after Sarah when she fell ill with cancer. When I arrived in the house, quite a lot of Sarah's stuff was still around. Including her slippers. They lived in the hallway, under the coatrack.

I'm ashamed to say that one day, when Tuesday left me at home on my own for the first time, I took those slippers into my daybed in the kitchen and chewed right through the toes. I'd never been in the house alone before. I was young and I was a little bit frightened. More than a little bit frightened. Without Tuesday the house seemed big and full of strange noises. Chewing the slippers distracted me until she got home again.

'Stuart Little!'

I knew by the fact that Tuesday had called me by my

old name and not Stupendo that I was in trouble. Her face, when she found me under the kitchen table, confirmed the worst. 'How could you?' she yelled.

Though of course Tuesday had shouted at me before – she'd shouted herself hoarse during puppy training – I knew this time was different. She wasn't just exasperated with me now; she was properly angry.

She snatched one of the slippers up. I was still holding on to the other. I mistakenly thought I might diffuse the situation by instigating a quick game of tug – I'd let her win – so I was shocked when Tuesday used the first slipper to give me a sharp tap on the bottom. I dropped the slipper I was still holding in surprise. Tuesday grabbed it and took both to her bedroom, where she stayed for what seemed like an age with the door firmly shut.

When Tuesday came downstairs again, I could see she had been crying. I'd been crying too. Howling. This was our first falling-out. I kept my ears down and looked up at her through my super-long eyelashes, which was an expression she usually found irresistible. It had worked when I chewed the leg of a dining chair and the corner of her second-favourite handbag. I didn't understand why Tuesday had merely shrugged when I ruined that lovely blue handbag, which was still quite new, but was so angry about a pair of old slippers.

Tuesday sat down on the floor beside me. She had both the slippers in her hands again. I gave them the side-eye.

'Here,' she said, offering me the one I'd chewed most enthusiastically. 'You can have them. I'm sorry, Stupendo. I shouldn't have got upset with you like that. They're just ratty old slippers but . . . having them there in the hall made it feel like Mum might come back one day. It was comforting. Silly, eh?'

I wished I could tell her that it wasn't silly at all. After all, the slippers had been a comfort to me while I was in the house on my own.

She continued, 'While I was upstairs, I thought I heard Mum's voice, saying, "Tuesday King, he's only a puppy" and I realised that if she'd been here, Mum would have found it really funny that you'd chewed her slippers up. She would have said it was a good excuse to go to Marks and Sparks and buy some new ones. She would have loved you, Stupendo. Like I do.'

'And I love you, Tuesday,' I told her with my eyes. She pulled me on to her lap for a cuddle and I licked her tears away.

Though the slippers were now officially mine, from that moment forward, I treated them with new reverence. I never chewed them again, though I occasionally gave the felted fabric a bit of a lick. If Tuesday thought her mum would have loved me, I knew I would have loved her in return. In my head, I promised Sarah that I would be loyal to her daughter and the people she loved forever. I would be loyal to my last breath.

Chapter Five

Now

Now here I was, stuck outside in the dark on my own, with Tuesday and William not even knowing I was still close by. I began to cry again – big, haunted howls – until Caligula popped up beside me as suddenly and unexpectedly as if he'd magicked himself out of thin air. He winced at my mournful singing.

'You're still here,' he said.

'Thank you, great master of stating the obvious,' I replied.

'Touchy. But then I suppose you have every right to be touchy, given the circumstances. It's not much fun finding out you're dead. Have you been out here all day, dog?'

I nodded. 'I did try to get through the door when Tuesday was taking the washing in but . . .'

Caligula slinked up to the French windows into the living room and tried to look through a small gap in the curtains. He turned back to me. 'Stupido, you do know you don't actually have to wait for someone to open a door to you now, don't you?'

'Don't call me Stupido.'

'Stup*ido*, Stup*endo*, whatever. Now that you're dead, you're no longer bound to the physical realm. You can go anywhere. You can do anything. You don't have to wait for a door to open because you can walk right through it.'

'Yeah, right,' I said.

'I'm serious. You don't need to be stuck out here. Just go inside. Think yourself in there.'

I didn't believe him. Though I had to admit that I'd noticed throughout the day a disturbing lack of ability to have any impact on earth, toys and other things, my paws still felt pretty solid to me. And I was on to that cat.

'Caligula, you just want me to try walking through a solid door so you can have a good laugh when I bang my head. Well, thanks but no thanks. As if I haven't already had a terrible day.'

'You think I would do that to you?' Caligula asked.

'I *know* you would.'

Caligula had form. When I was a puppy and didn't really understand how glass worked, Caligula delighted in lingering on the other side of the French windows to torment me. The number of times I'd gone haring across the living room floor in pursuit of him, only to crash into the glass and end up on my backside with my head spinning while he looked on from the safety of the garden. He thought it was hilarious. There was no reason why Caligula should stop pranking me now. I reminded him of his past crimes.

'Come on,' he said. 'It was funny how often you fell for it.'

'For you perhaps.'

'The squirrels laughed too.'

That hurt.

'Anyway, this time I am not planning any kind of evil trick, I swear on all my paws. I don't know why you haven't crossed over already – there's nothing left for you in this dimension – but if you want to stay here, sitting outside on the patio while Tuesday and William are in there,' he jerked his head towards the house, 'well, that is entirely your prerogative, I suppose.'

He started to walk away from me, towards the garden shed. As he went, he muttered, 'It really is true. You can't teach an old dog new tricks. Especially not a stupid one . . .'

'What?' I wuffed.

'You heard me,' Caligula said. He gave me a sly look over his shoulder. 'Stu*peedo*.'

Well, that was enough. Ordinarily, I was not quick to anger but Caligula had picked the exact wrong moment to tweak my tail. I was upset. I was *dead*. I thought I was facing an eternity alone on the patio. Caligula had gone too far. Without a growl of warning, I leaped in his direction, and coward that he was, Caligula fled straight for the shed roof with me in hot pursuit.

I realised too late that I was going too fast to be able to stop before I hit the shed door. I closed my eyes. I braced for impact. What a terrible way to end a terrible day. But . . .

'You OK in there, dog?'

I heard a voice from somewhere far above me. I shook my ears. I couldn't feel any obvious injuries. Opening my eyes in expectation of seeing a dog-shaped dent in the shed door, I was astonished to find that I was somewhere I had never been before. As my surroundings swam into focus, I asked the heavenly voice from on high, 'Is this the Rainbow Kingdom?'

It was pretty dingy if it was. And it smelled of dry grass, bagged compost and something else. Something musty and sweet. Something like rat pee.

'Am I in dog hell?' I stood up quickly.

'You're in the shed, Stupido,' came the voice from up above me.

It was Caligula.

'You ran straight through the door,' he explained.

'Whoa.'

I looked around me for a hole. Tuesday would be furious.

But there was no hole.

'Like I said,' Caligula purred through a small gap between the roof panels. 'You're not bound by the laws of physics any more. You can run through wood. You can float through brick walls. Now you know. Make the most of it.'

Then he was gone. I heard the sound of him landing heavily on the grass outside.

'Wait! Wait!' I yelled after him. 'Wait! You can't leave me in here!'

Caligula merely laughed in reply.

I howled and protested but he did not come back. I sat down again in the darkness. I really was in the shed. In the dim moonlight that came through the window, I could see the outlines of the lawnmower and Tuesday's bicycle, those compost bags and a pile of half-empty paint tins. And I could hear the sound of claws scrabbling in the corner. What was making that noise? I did not want to spend the night here. Not with an unseen companion.

'Bloody cat,' I muttered, trying to sound brave.

'He's not my favourite either,' said a small, sweet voice. 'But he is right, you know.'

I turned to find myself face to face with a female rat. I jumped in fright. An old reflex. In my experience, rats were not fond of dogs and vice versa. Still, I quickly composed myself.

'I won't hurt you,' she said, as though she could read my mind. Her clever eyes glittered as she regarded me with amusement. Her smile revealed two long yellow teeth that made me gulp.

'I need to get out of here,' I told her.

'You're not stuck in here, Stupendo. Not at all. It's like the evil cat said. Follow me.'

She headed for the bottom corner of the shed door. It was rotten from years of wet weather. A piece of wood had broken away, leaving a hole the perfect size for a rat flap. But not a dog flap.

'I can't even get my nose through there,' I complained.

'Just focus on my tail and think "outside".'

'I think you overestimate my powers of imagination.'

The rat sighed. She ran around behind me and positioned herself at the end of my tail. I looked back at her. 'What are you doing?'

She opened her mouth so that I could see all four of her sharp little incisors.

'Don't make me bite you.'

Well, I moved pretty swiftly after that. And a moment later, the rat and I were both outside in the garden. She must have gone through the hole and I'd . . . I'd run through the wooden shed panels.

'See? You just have to think yourself where you want to be. It's like magic.'

Somewhere nearby, the white owl called out. The little rat's whiskers twitched as she turned her nose skywards.

'Catch you later, dog.'

My new friend headed for the safety of a hedge. She disappeared so quickly, it was as though she had magicked herself away too.

Startled by the owl swooping low overhead, I made for the back door of the house. And this time I ran right through it without even thinking.

'I'm back! I'm back!' I barked in delight as I stood in the kitchen that was the heart of my home. 'I'm back! I'm back! I'm still here!'

No one responded because, of course, no one heard me. But I was inside and that was a start. I went straight upstairs to William's room. The door was ajar, so I didn't have to wish myself through it. My best boy was fast asleep with one little foot sticking out from beneath the covers. How I longed to give those perfect chubby toes a lick and have him giggle like he always did.

'Sweet dreams, William,' I told him.

Then I padded across the landing to check on Tuesday.

She was asleep too. I pressed my nose to her hand, though I knew now that she couldn't feel me touch her.

Still, she smiled in her dreams, and I felt sure that meant something.

'I'm still here, Tuesday. Reporting for duty. I'm not going anywhere. I'm still by your side.'

My heart yearned to see her open her eyes and look at me one more time. How could I ever say goodbye to Tuesday and cross the Rainbow Bridge? It was hard enough to say goodnight. As I gazed at Tuesday's face, loneliness washed over me like the waves that had taken me by surprise on my first ever trip to the beach.

'See you in the morning, Tuesday,' I said with my tail.

Then I chose a spot on the landing in which to pass the rest of the night, equidistant from my mistress and William, protecting them both, just like I always did, until Merle started singing and a new day dawned.

Chapter Six

Hearing Tuesday stir, I ran into her room to greet her. There was a moment or two as I rushed to say hello when I forgot what I'd learned the day before, only to be disappointed anew when Tuesday looked straight through me and carried on with her morning routine as if I weren't there. How could I have forgotten I was dead? I sank down on to the rug with my ears in full droop mode. My expressive ears used to make Tuesday laugh.

After she'd dressed, Tuesday gently woke William and lifted him from his cot. She didn't have time to sit and mope that morning. She needed to get William to nursery. I loved joining him and Tuesday on the walk there. William's nursery-mates were always pleased to see me and inevitably one of them would drop a snack. Biscuits, breadsticks, a lightly chewed piece of apple . . . I wasn't fussy. Picking William up again in the evenings was even better. I lived for the delight in his eyes when he saw me waiting for him at the gate. His sticky-faced hugs made my day.

Usually, William enjoyed going to nursery. He was a gregarious toddler who liked to be around other children almost as much as he liked being with dogs. That morning, however, he seemed restless. I watched from his bedroom doorway as Tuesday struggled to get him dressed for that day's outing. But I couldn't distract or comfort him as I wanted to. In the end, his distress became too uncomfortable to bear without being able to help, so I took myself downstairs to wait until he and Tuesday were ready to leave the house. Creeping from his room, I thought I heard him say, 'Do,' (the closest he could ever get to 'dog') as he waved a hand in my direction, but Merle had been quite clear that humans couldn't see me. I didn't allow myself to hope the wise old blackbird might have been wrong.

After Tuesday dropped William off, I accompanied her home again. She used the walk to phone a gardening client, Mrs Wilson. I liked Mrs Wilson very much. She always had a biscuit to share. Tuesday mowed Mrs Wilson's lawn for her once a week in the summer and tended to the roses that Mrs Wilson's husband had planted: a new bush each year for her birthday until the whole garden was full of colour and scent. Since her husband, Ted, had gone into a nursing home, Mrs Wilson couldn't manage the garden on her own. Tuesday did her best to make sure there was always something blooming so that Mrs Wilson always had something beautiful to take to Ted when she went to visit him.

'I'm sorry I had to let you down on Monday,' Tuesday told the old lady. 'I'm afraid Stupendo was in an accident on Sunday night. He was knocked over by a car. No. No, he didn't make it.'

With my superior dog's hearing, I could hear Mrs Wilson's dismay.

'I had no idea losing a pet could hurt so much,' Tuesday continued. 'I feel poleaxed. How did it happen? Well, he ran away that afternoon. At about nine o'clock in the evening, he was hit in the street right outside the house. He must have been on his way home.'

Mrs Wilson murmured her condolences.

'I know. Running away like that really wasn't like him at all . . .'

It really wasn't. I looked up at Tuesday, but of course she couldn't see me or my quizzical expression. Was that what had happened? I had no memory of it at all. It was very odd. The days leading up to my death were hazy too. The accident must have knocked them out of my head.

Tuesday ended her call to Mrs Wilson just as we were drawing close to the entrance to the park. I automatically turned to go in but Tuesday kept walking.

'No point in going there today,' she muttered to herself.

I stuck close by Tuesday all day. She caught up with some paperwork then drove to Mrs Wilson's to do the work she hadn't got done on Monday. At four o'clock, we picked up William. Again, he seemed out of sorts and Tuesday worried that he was coming down with something.

'Have you got what I had last week?' Tuesday asked him as she rested her hand on his forehead to check his temperature. William scrunched his face up and wriggled in her arms. He thrust his tiny fists towards the ground and again said, 'Do, do, do!'

'Sorry, sweet pea,' Tuesday told him. 'There is no dog any more.'

When William was in bed and Tuesday turned on the television, I went out into the garden by walking straight through the bottom panel of the back door. It was surprising how quickly I had become used to walking through doors, though I held my breath and closed my eyes every time I did so, just in case.

I had not seen Caligula all day. I'd been hoping I would. I wanted him to know that his dastardly trick to get me stuck in the shed hadn't worked. The squirrels hadn't seen him either. Neither had Merle. But as night fell, my old nemesis came slinking by again. When he saw me waiting for him, he stopped and settled on the top of the garden fence. He sat there purring to himself as though the narrow piece of wood was as comfortable as Tuesday's sofa.

'So you're out of the shed,' he observed. 'How long did it take you?'

'I was out of there the minute you left,' I lied.

'Good. I thought you'd be stuck until I came to fetch you.'

'How stupid do you think I am?'

'On a scale of *quite* to *very*?' he asked.

'Well . . . I'm not stupid in the least!' I complained. 'And you can apologise for saying I am whenever you want to.'

'May take a while,' said Caligula. 'But then, I suppose you do have all eternity . . .'

'Not funny,' I huffed.

'Look, it worked, didn't it? I called you stupid. You got upset and chased me. You ran straight through the side of the shed. It was a good thing. I'd never have persuaded you of your new superpowers otherwise. You should be thanking me.'

He closed his eyes and smiled to himself. He let his

tail dangle into my garden. His smug expression made
me want to grab it like a bell pull. But of course that
wouldn't work. I couldn't grab anything in my spirit state.

'Stu-*pee*-doh,' he purred.

But I could scare him.

I ran straight up the fence and barked in his face.

It took me a moment to let the fact sink in.

I'd run straight up the fence!

Caught off guard in a big way, Caligula toppled over
into next door's garden. He didn't even land on his feet.
Fortunately for him, however, he did land in the compost
heap. So a soft landing, if not an especially pleasant one.

'What the actual . . .'

Caligula struggled to right himself.

I looked down on him from the top of the fence.

'Not subject to the laws of physics any more, am I?'
I said triumphantly.

Caligula rolled from the compost heap on to the garden
path, stood up and shuddered to get some potato peelings
off his fur.

'That was uncalled for,' he complained. 'I might have
hurt myself.'

'Did you?'

'No.' He licked a paw and smoothed it over his pointed
ears. 'Of course not.'

'Well, you hurt my feelings. And they're the only part
of me that *can* still hurt,' I added, suddenly realising that
was the awful truth.

'Then I guess we're even,' said Caligula.

He clambered back up the fence and balanced upon it
so that we were nose to nose for an instant. He narrowed

his yellow eyes in a way that I knew was supposed to be intimidating before disappearing into the night.

Caligula left me standing on top of the fence alone.

It was the strangest sensation. I stood with all four paws in a row, like a cat in an Egyptian tomb painting. What was I going to do now? While Caligula was struggling to get out of the compost heap, the comedy of the spectacle had taken my mind off the fact that I was balancing six feet in the air on a strip of wood not quite as wide as my nose. Now that Caligula was gone again, I felt my confidence deserting me too. I wobbled and, inevitably, I fell. But I did not fall as I expected to. I did not hit the ground with a thump, or even make it that far. Instead, my fall was strangely slow and stately and, just like a cat, I found I had the time to right myself. I stopped within a paw's reach of the ground, floating in mid-air.

'You can go anywhere,' said Caligula's voice in my head.

I doggy-paddled through space.

Perhaps I really could.

Tuesday and William were safely in bed. There was only one other place I wanted to be.

Running straight through the closed side gate to my garden, I headed for number twenty-four on the opposite side of the street. Growing closer, I sniffed the air. Zena, *my* Zena, lived here.

Chapter Seven

I loved Tuesday and William above everyone and everything, but if I had a third favourite being in the world, it was Zena. She was, as it happened, the only other dog on Bracken Avenue, but what a dog she was. I'll never forget the first time I saw her.

I'd been living with Tuesday for about a year and a half at the time. She and I were on our way back from the park. I was sniffing around a lamp post and adding my own comments when I looked up and there she was.

Majestic and elegant with glossy black fur and ginger highlights, her brown-eyed gaze imperious as she looked straight ahead, nose held high. I could only let my mouth flop open and my foolish tongue loll in awe as the German Shepherd of my dreams walked right by me without so much as a sideways glance in my direction. Her human – a tall man with a confident stride – didn't look at me or at Tuesday either.

'Stuck up,' I decided, to defend my lightly bruised ego. They were both stuck up. Him and her. All the other dogs and their humans in the neighbourhood acknowledged each other in the street, even if it was just with a nod. I felt stung that we'd been ignored, on both my own and on Tuesday's behalf. But it wasn't long before I found out what had really happened that afternoon.

The very next day, Tuesday and I were at the park again. I was taking advantage of her being distracted by her phone to roll in some top-grade fox poo when I became aware of the fast-approaching sound of a bell.

'Hey!'

The wearer of the bell stopped right next to me. I finished rolling and righted myself and there she was. The stuck-up German Shepherd.

'I wanted to introduce myself,' she said. 'I'm Zena.'

'Stupendo,' I said.

'Good name . . . I also wanted to say that I'm sorry I had to ignore you when we met in the street yesterday afternoon. I don't like to appear rude, especially not to another dog, but when I'm working I'm meant to ignore everything and everybody unless my Andrew says otherwise.'

Zena glanced back towards the bench where her human – the tall man with the fast stride – was sitting alone. Like Tuesday, he was deeply involved with his phone and ignoring the busy world around him. Zena continued, 'When I've got the harness on, I'm working with him and I have to keep my focus. When I've got this bell on,' she shook her ears so that the little bell tinkled and she sounded like Christmas, 'I can talk to whoever I want.'

And that included me. She flopped down on to the grass beside me.

'What's with the bell?' I asked. I'd never seen a dog with a bell before. Cats, yes, but never a dog.

'It's so Andrew can hear where I am when he needs to get me back into harness. He can't see me. He's blind.'

My mouth dropped open. 'Are you a guide dog?' I asked.

She nodded. 'I am indeed.'

I'd heard about guide dogs – there was a plastic one with a slit in his head outside the corner shop – but Zena was the first real one I'd met.

'You must be really clever.'

Zena dipped her eyes modestly. 'Oh, it's not so difficult,' she said. 'Well, actually,' she corrected herself, 'it can be very difficult but I've had a lot of training.'

'Is it true you can go anywhere?' I asked. 'Supermarkets? Restaurants?'

Zena nodded again.

'The butcher's?'

'Yep. Was in there just this morning in fact.'

'No way.'

'Guide dogs can go everywhere humans can. It's the law. When I'm in my harness, I've got a free pass.'

'You are living the life.'

'It's not so bad,' she agreed.

Zena sniffed delicately at my flanks then.

'Fox poo?' she asked.

'Yes. There's loads of it here today. I can show you the best place . . .'

Zena shook her head. 'I'm not supposed to roll in the smelly stuff even when I'm off harness. We might have to go straight from the park to a meeting and Andrew would not be happy if I came back from my free run smelling of *Eau D'Ordure.*'

'Tuesday won't be happy either,' I said. 'But I couldn't resist! I've never smelled anything like it.'

'You'll get a bath,' Zena warned me.

'But it will have been worth it.'

Zena laughed. It felt good to have amused her.

At the top of the hill, Zena's Andrew was standing up from the bench. I could hear him calling her. She pricked up her elegant ears. 'I'd better go. I'll see you again soon, I hope.'

Zena went to Andrew the first time she heard her name. She didn't muck around like I would when Tuesday called me. When Tuesday yelled my name, I liked to wait until her pitch reached 'utterly desperate' before I took any notice. It was too much fun to do otherwise. I could actually hear Tuesday calling me as I watched Zena bound back up the hill but I waited until I'd heard Tuesday shout at least eight or nine times more before I sauntered up to be put on my lead.

Tuesday recoiled as she reached down towards my collar.

'Oh no! Stupendo! You stink! What on earth have you been rolling in? You filthy, filthy dog.'

Tuesday never appreciated the lengths I went to when it came to hunting camouflage.

When we got back home, Tuesday opened the side gate and put me straight out into the back garden rather than let me walk through the house as she usually did. Zena was right. I did get a bath. What's more, it was a bath with the special shampoo that would make me smell like a freshly bathed human baby for days. I wouldn't be able to stand myself. But for a brief moment I'd smelled exactly as I wanted to and, what's more, I'd made Zena smile.

Zena. Her name sounded like music to my floppy ears. I hoped it wouldn't be too long before I saw her again.

After that first day, even if she was wearing her harness, Zena would always at least nod in my direction but my Tuesday and Zena's Andrew never exchanged a word. In the park, Andrew would always sit on one of the benches at the top of the big lawn, well away from the other dog people. He kept himself apart, making business calls or using voice technology to read and send emails from his phone until it was time to go home again. Tuesday didn't always hang out with the other dog people either but her favourite bench was nearer the rosebeds and the bandstand. It was just about as far from Andrew's bench as she could get.

If we passed in the street, Tuesday would look down at her shoes as Zena and Andrew went by. Every time I'd think perhaps she was building up the courage to say something but she never did. Not even hello. Not even when I tried to hint that she should engage by wagging my tail until it was in danger of a sprain.

Humans are the weirdest creatures on earth. Is there any other animal on the planet that fails to acknowledge another of its own kind when they pass in close proximity? Cats always greet each other. Squirrels do. Even hedgehogs do, though usually with a muttered curse. Dogs would *never* pass a brother or sister by without a proper greeting. That's why it had been so strange to me that Zena kept her eyes straight ahead the first time I'd met her when she was in harness.

When we were in the park together, Zena and I would sometimes talk about it – that human thing of pretending other humans didn't exist. She explained to me that her Andrew didn't talk to many people at all. Occasionally, someone would come up to him and ask about Zena and try to start a chat that way.

'. . . but Andrew is of the view that people who ask about me aren't really interested in getting to know *him*, so he says he's not interested in getting to know them either.'

'Tuesday's shy,' I said. Though that didn't seem quite right. She wasn't shy with anybody else at the park. Just Andrew. Sometimes walking close by him would even make her blush. Applying my canine logic to the way she reacted, I would say that Andrew affected her in the same way that I was affected by Zena.

Now I crept up to the living room window of number twenty-four and looked in. Thankfully, Andrew had not drawn the curtains for the night yet.

Zena was asleep on the rug in front of the fireplace. Her paws twitched. She was running in her dreams. Was she chasing squirrels like we used to chase them together at the park? Those were some great times, though of course we never caught one. That wasn't really the point of the game.

Sitting on the sofa, Andrew was working on some papers, even though it was late. I knew that he read with his fingers instead of his eyes like the other humans did.

Braille, Zena called it. Andrew was always reading. He had an important job. Zena took him to a lot of meetings, where she sat under a table and resisted temptation when people tried to slip her a biscuit. The very idea of resisting a biscuit was completely alien to me. It must have taken a lot of training for Zena to find such resolve.

Anyway my heart might not have been pumping blood around my body any more but all the same I felt it flutter when I saw my favourite German Shepherd lying on that rug, fast asleep after what must have been a busy day. I was mesmerised by her beauty. I longed to talk to her and tell her what had been going on. Perhaps she knew something about my accident. For a moment, I considered walking straight into her house and waking her up. But that didn't seem right. She probably had a day of hard work ahead of her. She needed her sleep. So with a deep sigh, I wished her a silent goodnight and turned for home.

Chapter Eight

Then

With her mum gone, Tuesday didn't have much in the way of family nearby. Her father had moved to Spain with his new wife. Tuesday had a half-brother, Henry, much younger, who lived in Spain too. Though she spoke to her father on the phone from time to time, they didn't have the best of relationships. Occasionally, their conversations got quite heated, with Tuesday reminding her father that while it was great that he wanted to offer her moral support now her mum had died, it wouldn't make up for all the years he *hadn't* been there for her throughout her childhood. Still, he did keep trying and sometimes I thought Tuesday might be softening. There was even talk of his coming to visit. I was keen to meet him.

In the meantime, Tuesday did have some good friends. I had a soft spot for Mandy, of course, since she was the first human I met, but Emily was my favourite. She was what you would call Tuesday's best friend. They'd known each other since they were at school and were as close as any sisters.

Emily always looked out for Tuesday, just as she had

when they were little girls. I once heard them talking about their first day at junior school, when three boys in their class teased Tuesday for being named after a day of the week (her mum had liked the Rolling Stones' song 'Ruby Tuesday'. Tuesday was actually born on a Wednesday). The boys pushed Tuesday to tears. Emily waded in on Tuesday's side.

There was a photograph of Tuesday and Emily pinned on the fridge from when they were very young. They hadn't changed much, as far as I could tell. Tuesday was the quieter of the two. Emily was a joker – she'd tried to make it as a stand-up comic before she became a physiotherapist – but she never made jokes about Tuesday. She was Tuesday's biggest fan and most steadfast supporter.

Emily was a big fan of mine too. She was the first of Tuesday's friends to meet me when I arrived at Bracken Avenue. She brought me a squeaky rubber Minion toy as a 'welcome' gift. It took me twenty minutes to kill the squeak but after that, it was perfect. Whenever she came over, Emily would scoop me up on to her lap and 'boop' me on the nose. Until I got too big to scoop and boop, that is. It didn't take long for me to grow into the dog my big puppy paws suggested I'd be, even if I had been the smallest of my litter. I was half-Labrador, half-Staffie, after all. There were no small dogs in my lineage.

Even when she could no longer pick me up without saying 'ooof', Emily would still give me plenty of fuss and talk to me in the silly soppy voice I adored. It made me wriggle like my tail had a mind of its own. What's more, if Tuesday and Emily were eating while I was around, Emily would always slip me a titbit or two. Then she'd wink and say, 'Don't tell.' Tuesday would act outraged if she caught us, saying I was not allowed to eat from the table and Emily was teaching me bad habits. In fact, that rule about not begging from the table was only for show when guests were around. Likewise the one about not drinking from the toilet bowl. When we were home alone, just the two of us, Tuesday could never resist my best puppy gaze. Sometimes she even turned a blind eye to my licking the plates clean when she left the dishwasher door open.

Even though Emily was the very best sort of friend, she was of the opinion that Tuesday needed more people in her life. Specifically, a mate – or a 'boyfriend', to use the human term. I learned that Tuesday hadn't had a boyfriend since she moved from London to look after her mother.

'This town isn't exactly full of eligible bachelors,' Tuesday complained one evening.

'But you haven't even tried,' Emily insisted.

She showed Tuesday her phone, on to which she had downloaded Tinder, which I understood to be like a Kennel Club register.

'Come on,' said Emily. 'Just have a look.'

Tuesday and Emily huddled close together on the sofa while Emily flicked her thumb back and forth across the screen of her mobile. Whatever it was they were looking at inspired much cackling and hooting. They reminded me of the squirrels getting drunk on rotten plums at the end of summer. You would not believe how lairy those squirrels could get on fermented fruit. And don't even get me started on the dangers of a drunken hedgehog.

But I was very happy that Tuesday and Emily were so distracted. Before settling down to play with Emily's phone, they'd prepared themselves a healthy supply of snacks, which they'd loaded on to a tray. Tuesday would have made sure that the tray was out of my reach but it was Emily who carried it into the living room that night and she made the rookie mistake of putting it on the low coffee table.

I could not believe my luck. The coffee table put those snacks on the exact same level as my nose. I could have gone for a smash and grab but I decided to take it slowly. Nonchalantly, I sat down sideways on to the table, making it look as though I just wanted to be closer to the fire (which wasn't even lit, it being summer). Then, slowly – so slowly that from moment to moment it looked as though I wasn't moving at all – I tipped my head so that my tongue was within lolling distance of the tray. And when I was sure that Tuesday and Emily were looking anywhere but in my direction, I snaffled a sausage roll from the plate like a frog whipping a fly from the sky. And then another. And then another. And another.

It was one of my best stealth raids ever. Tuesday and Emily did not see a thing. I only stopped after six sausage rolls because I simultaneously hoovered up a hair (one of my own) and it made me cough.

Still, Tuesday and Emily did not suspect what I'd been up to even then. When I started spluttering, Tuesday just called me out to the kitchen for a bowl of water, which I gratefully drank. Those snacks were very salty.

'Have we really eaten all those sausage rolls?' Tuesday asked Emily as she passed her the half-empty plate. 'It was meant to be a family pack. What a rip-off.'

'You see, this is the problem,' said Emily. 'It's why I can never lose weight. I don't even notice what I'm eating half the time.'

'Me neither,' said Tuesday. 'More wine?'

'Lots more wine,' I agreed, with a burp.

Zena was very impressed when I regaled her with my tale of sausage roll snaffling. She was interested too when I told her that Emily was trying to persuade Tuesday to find a mate.

'Humans are much happier when they have each other,' Zena agreed. 'It takes the pressure off us dogs and, if they choose the right one, means twice as much fussing.'

That sounded pretty good to me.

'I wish Andrew would find another human to love,' she mused. Her Andrew was, as usual, sitting on his own on the bench at the top of the big lawn, while she enjoyed her free run. Tuesday too was in her habitual spot on the bench by the rosebeds. She'd brought a ball to throw for me but was totally absorbed in her phone. I didn't mind too much. While talking to Zena, I'd caught the whiff of fresh fox poo on the air. When I rolled in it, Tuesday would have only herself to blame.

'I won't even ask if you're interested,' I said to Zena.

'Alas, no,' Zena replied.

After Andrew called Zena back to him, I made a beeline for that fox mess and rolled in it to my heart's content. It cost me another bath but it was worth it to have that twenty-minute walk home when I smelled absolutely wonderful.

Over the next few days, I tried my paw at a spot of matchmaking. There were always plenty of men at the park, walking with their own dogs or exercising children. I could easily engineer a few meetings.

I tried Buster's owner first, but while he seemed very happy to meet Tuesday, she didn't seem quite so excited to talk to him.

'Buster's owner is old enough to be Tuesday's grand-father,' Zena explained.

Zephyr the greyhound's owner was a good-looking chap and of course it was a foregone conclusion that he liked dogs. When Tuesday let me off the lead one afternoon, I ran straight in his direction and stayed there when she tried to call me back so that she had to join us. I thought my ruse worked pretty well. They started talking and seemed to get on and I definitely liked him. He had pockets full of snacks. But when I told her that I was trying to find Tuesday a mate, Zephyr told me, 'My human is already married. To a man.'

Emily was also on the case. She set Tuesday up on a couple of blind dates. The first was with someone Emily knew from the gym. I went along to their meeting at a café, though alas, I couldn't join them inside. I thought the guy was alright. He said hello when we met outside, then, when he and Tuesday came out of the café again, he slipped me a piece of ham saved from his sandwich, which was a good sign as to how any future relationship between him and me might pan out. I was prepared to give him the opportunity to impress me further.

'He was sweet,' Tuesday concluded when Emily called to see how the date had gone. 'But I want to be with someone who pays as much attention to the muscles between his ears as his biceps.'

'There are no muscles between your ears, Miss Pretentious.'

Either way, the gym fan did not get a second date, which was a shame. I wish I'd been able to plead his case. It's not everyone who'll save you a bit of their sandwich.

Then Emily tried to fix Tuesday up with the man who looked after her car.

'He is so hot, Tuesday. If I thought he was interested in me, I totally would . . .'

'That,' said Tuesday, 'is probably not a great recommendation. You and I have never, ever fancied the same men. It's how we've managed to stay friends for so long.'

'True,' Emily agreed. 'But I'm not giving up on finding the perfect man for you.'

'Why can't you just let me try to find someone I want to get to know *organically*?' Tuesday suggested. 'I'll know the right one when I see him.'

But would she? I shared Emily's exasperation. It seemed as though Tuesday was impossible to please. However, if brainy was her type, then perhaps I could think of someone.

'Why don't we see if we can get Tuesday and Andrew to talk to each other?' I suggested to Zena at last.

'I don't know. Andrew can be quite . . . prickly,' Zena warned me.

'Like a hedgehog?'

'Exactly like a hedgehog,' Zena agreed.

You have to understand that we weren't talking about hedgehogs' actual spikes here, but the fact that they tend to have combative personalities to go with their appearance. I suppose if you can't even cuddle up to your own family lest they accidentally take your eye out, it must make you pretty grumpy.

'But it's worth a try,' Zena concluded.

The very next day, I saw Zena and Andrew as we were leaving the post office. Spotting me and Tuesday at the same time as I spotted her, Zena quickened her pace. I heard Andrew tell her to slow down but for once Zena took no notice. As a result, she and Andrew arrived at the zebra crossing at the exact same time as Tuesday and I did. And what's more, the green man had just stopped flashing. The timing was perfect. We would all have to wait while the cars took their turn.

Zena and I gave each other a little nod of complicity. This was our big chance. Andrew stood with his hand under the crossing's control box, feeling for the special spinning rod that would tell him when it was safe to walk (Zena had told me all about it). Tuesday smiled down at Zena who grinned back up at her.

'Hello,' Tuesday said, almost in a whisper. She was talking to Zena rather than to Andrew but it was a start. Tuesday transferred both her shopping bags and my lead to one hand, then she leaned towards Zena and scratched her on the top of the head. Zena shuffled closer to enjoy the scratch further. Tuesday looked up at Andrew and I knew she was about to try to break the ice with him at last. And that's when it all went horribly wrong.

'What do you think you're doing?' Andrew snapped.

'I'm, er . . . I'm just saying hello to your dog.'

'Well, I'd rather you didn't,' he said. 'Can't you see she's in harness? When she's got that harness on, she's working. You should never distract a working guide dog. You might put them and their owner in danger.'

'I was just . . . I only patted her on the head.'

'She might pull me out into the traffic to follow you.'

'I'm sorry, I'm not going to walk into traffic . . .' Tuesday said, but her apology fell on deaf ears.

'Did you give her anything to eat?' Andrew asked.

'No. No, I didn't.'

'Are you sure?'

'Of course I am.'

'Because I thought I heard a crisp packet . . .'

'You didn't. It was probably my shopping bag.'

'If you fed my dog anything, then at least have the decency to tell me what you gave her.'

'I didn't feed her! I promise!'

Zena and I shared a worried glance. This was not the 'meet-cute' we had intended.

'If she gets food poisoning, it might mean that I can't go to work for days, do you understand that?'

'I did *not* feed your dog. I just made the mistake of giving her a little scratch between the ears when she looked at me, and for that, I am very, very sorry. As I said.'

'As you should be. People like you have no idea . . .'

'People like me?'

'Yes. People who think they have the right to touch any

animal they come across without considering the consequences. Zena is *not* a pet. She's my eyes when she's working. She's part of me. You wouldn't pat a random stranger on the head at the bus stop, would you?'

Tuesday's mouth dropped open as she struggled to respond. 'I just—' she began. 'I was only . . .'

'Save it for someone who cares,' Andrew snapped. He shook his head in a pitying way. 'This is what I have to put up with every day of my life. Idiots. Idiots everywhere.'

'Wow. Being blind obviously doesn't make you any less of an arse,' Tuesday said then. Quietly but not quietly enough. Andrew turned his face towards her. His expression was as cold and hard as stone.

'I beg your pardon?' he said.

Zena's eyes boggled out of her head, as did mine. Tuesday blushed from head to toe. But Andrew didn't wait to hear any more. The traffic had stopped now and the green man was flashing and beeping.

'Zena, forward,' Andrew commanded. With a desperate backwards glance at me, Zena did as she was told and crossed the road. What else could she do? Tuesday was still flushing a furious red as she watched Andrew walk away, muttering as he went.

'I only gave his dog a quick pat,' Tuesday said to me, in the absence of there being anyone else to complain to. 'There was absolutely no need for him to have a go at me like that, was there?' All the same, I could tell that Tuesday was hurt by Andrew's reaction and shocked by her own outburst in response.

So much for that grand matchmaking plan.

★　★　★

I didn't get to see Zena for a while after that. Tuesday changed the direction of our walks for the next few days. Though she told me it was because she thought I would enjoy a change of scene – 'Lots of new smells, Stupendo!' – I knew she was really trying to avoid bumping into Andrew again. From time to time, when she thought I wasn't listening, I heard her berating herself.

'Why did I have to say that?'

Tuesday was so ashamed of losing her cool and in such an awful way that she didn't even tell Emily what had happened and she ordinarily told Emily everything. This time I was her only witness and confidante.

'Do you think I'm a bad person, Stupendo?' she asked me.

Of course I didn't. I licked her hands to let her know. But I *would* start to think she was a bad person if her outburst at the crossing meant that I never got to go to the park again. Or see Zena. The thought made me very sad indeed. And it could be so easily dealt with. When we dogs offend each other, we are always quick to make amends. We have a sort of ritual dance for it. Why couldn't Tuesday and Andrew do something like that, then we could all get on as normal? No permanent harm done.

I thought not for the first time that if humans could recognise their faults and admit to them in the way we animals do, the world would be a much better place.

Chapter Nine

Now

Two days after I found out I was dead, I felt a little calmer about my situation. At least now I knew I didn't have to stay outside howling all the time. Being able to come and go entirely as I pleased was such a novelty that it almost felt like a treat.

I lay on the doormat in the kitchen, watching Tuesday and William go about their usual morning routine. Tuesday sorted a pile of washing while William ate his breakfast. I was delighted when William dropped half a banana from his high chair until I remembered that it didn't matter whether I got there before Tuesday noticed any more. I couldn't eat it. I wondered how long it would take before I stopped wanting food.

After breakfast, Tuesday changed William into some clean clothes and loaded him into his pushchair. I trotted alongside them as she took him to the playground in the park. While Tuesday pushed William on the swings, I caught up with a few familiar faces. Buster and Zephyr bounded over as soon as they saw me.

'Stupendo, my main man,' said Buster.

'Little Stu.' Zephyr brought her nose close to mine and asked, full of concern, 'How are you?'

I told them both that death wasn't as bad as I'd expected and that there were even some bonuses to being stuck between the Rainbow Kingdom and the earthly realm. 'Watch this,' I said, leaping deftly on to the top of a bin and balancing there on one paw. Then I got down and walked right through the trunk of a tree.

'No door is closed to me now.'

'Wow,' said Buster. 'Like, you could steal food from anywhere. Like, you could just walk into the supermarket and take all the sausages.'

'Yeah. Except I can no longer eat.'

Zephyr commiserated when I said I could no longer be seen by my humans either.

'Yet I can't bring myself to leave them behind,' I said. 'Even if I can't go to the Rainbow Kingdom until I do.'

'You're missing out on a lot of heavenly snacks, man,' said Buster.

'I've heard that. But I just can't go. Have you ever seen this happen before?' I asked my friends. 'I mean, have you ever known another animal to not pass straight on when they died? Why am I still here?'

'You must have done something terrible,' Buster suggested.

'He's joking,' Zephyr said quickly. 'But I've never met another ghost animal, it's true. Everyone else just disappeared within moments of leaving their earthly body.'

'Then why haven't I? I did exactly what Merle said I

should. I closed my eyes and said I was ready but . . .
here I am. Have I got unfinished business?'

Even as I said it, I wondered what kind of 'business'
the average dog had anyway.

'I suppose I'd like to know how I died,' I added.

'You were . . .' Buster began.

'Flattened. I know. But who was driving the car? Did
they hit me deliberately?'

'I'm sure it was an accident,' said Zephyr. 'As to why
you're still here, I don't know . . . It's very, very strange.'

'Perhaps you've got a purpose,' said Buster, pronouncing
the word 'poi-puss' like a New York gangster. 'You've just
got to find it.'

'Have you guys seen Zena lately?' I asked then to change
the subject, not mentioning that I'd gazed at her through
the window of number twenty-four the previous night. 'I
heard she was quite upset about me getting killed . . .'
I was fishing.

Zephyr and Buster shared a glance.

Then Zephyr caught the scent of something or someone
familiar. I followed the direction of her nose and there
was Zena, tumbling across the grass towards us with her
free run bell ringing. Until she suddenly stopped – as
though taking fright at something – and turned on her
tail. Had she seen me? She must have seen me. In fact,
I was sure she had.

'Zena!' I barked but she did not stop running in the
opposite direction and I couldn't seem to catch up with
her. And then, glancing over at the playground, I saw
that Tuesday had spotted Andrew too. As had William.
He was pointing in Andrew's direction and shouting

something that sounded quite close to 'Drew, drew, drew!' Tuesday quickly lifted William out of the swing and strapped him into his pram then left the park at top speed, without acknowledging Andrew or my doggy friend.

I was utterly dumbfounded.

'Zena saw me, didn't she?' I questioned Buster and Zephyr when I got back to them. 'And then she ran away.'

'Andrew must have called her back,' said Buster.

'Yes. That will be what happened,' Zephyr agreed. 'He must have called her. We just didn't hear it.'

We all of us knew that wasn't true. We were dogs. We could hear the sound of someone opening a crisp packet half a park away. Of course we would have heard Andrew calling Zena back to his side. Zena had run away from me and Tuesday in turn had run away from Andrew.

Chapter Ten

As darkness fell, Caligula came back again. I saw him from William's bedroom window. I floated down into the garden, making him jump when I landed on top of the shed roof beside him. He pretended that I hadn't taken him by surprise.

'You again,' he said by way of greeting. 'Why are you still hanging around?'

'That's what I want to find out. I think I must need to know how I died, Caligula. I can't remember anything that happened in the days leading up to my death. I want to ask you some questions.'

'Me? I can't help you. I don't know what happened. I only saw the aftermath.' He winced at the memory. 'Flat as a pancake.'

I ignored that. 'But maybe one of the night animals does know what went on. You could introduce me. Or the humans.'

'The humans?' Caligula scoffed.

'You get around, don't you? I thought you might have heard something.'

'Most of the humans round here have got a lot more to think about than a random squashed dog.'

Random squashed dog. That hurt. I could tell I wasn't

going to get anywhere with him. 'Fine,' I said. 'I suppose I shouldn't have expected you to want to help me.'

'You got that right.'

He turned to go, slipping down from the shed roof on to the top of the fence in that strange liquid way he had. I stayed where I was for a while, wondering what I should do next.

I decided to follow him.

Given that he considered himself to be a master of stealth, I was astonished at how easy it was for me to track Caligula at quite a short distance without him noticing I was there. As he waddled down the centre of the road, with no care as to whether a car might come by, I stayed in the shadow of the hedges and fences that edged the gardens on the odd side of Bracken Avenue. Then suddenly, Caligula darted to the other side of the street and into the front garden of number twenty-four. Zena's house.

Caligula scaled the side gate. I waited a moment before I walked straight through it. Silent as a cat (though a much more intelligent cat than Caligula), I positioned myself on top of the shed, while my nemesis settled down in a spot in the middle of the lawn and gave a quiet yowl. Moments later, Andrew opened the back door and Zena trotted out. Andrew left the door ajar so that Zena could let herself back in and returned to working on his laptop.

'I'm here,' Caligula whispered.

Zena joined him in the middle of the grass. She sat down next to him, so that they were both looking in the same direction, back towards the house, keeping an eye out for Andrew. I was immediately struck by how comfortable they seemed with each other, as if they had met in the garden like this many times before. I had no idea that they even knew each other. Why wasn't Zena chasing Caligula off her patch? They were sitting very close for sworn enemies, which is surely what cats and dogs are?

'He's still here,' Caligula said.

Zena closed her eyes tightly. 'I know. I can't bear it. Why won't he just go over?'

Caligula shrugged. 'I have no idea. We told him what he had to do. Me and Merle and the squirrels.'

Were they talking about me?

'He's staying for a reason,' Zena concluded.

'He told me tonight that he wants to find out how he died.'

They *were* talking about me!

'Noooo.' Zena lay down with her head between her paws.

Caligula made a strange chirping noise that almost sounded like sympathy. 'It was an accident. He will accept that in the end and then I'm sure he'll pass straight over.'

'But it wasn't an accident,' said Zena, with sudden passion. 'You know it, Caligula, and so do I. It was my fault, wasn't it? It wouldn't have happened if it wasn't for me.'

Caligula shook his head firmly. 'You cannot blame yourself,' he said. 'If you're going to go down that route, then you might as well blame Andrew.'

Shocked by what I was hearing, I couldn't help but gasp, making both Zena and Caligula suddenly prick up their ears and look in my direction. Before they could see me, I spirited myself into the garden of number twenty-two, but I stayed close to the fence, listening hard.

'What was that?' Zena asked.

'Nothing,' Caligula said, calming her. 'Or maybe just a rat.'

Then Andrew was on the doorstep, calling Zena back inside. Before she went in, Caligula whispered to her, 'I promise I will sort this out.'

I did not wait to see where Caligula went next but scurried home. Back at number thirteen, I lay down on the landing and tried to make sense of what I'd heard that night and how it fitted with what Tuesday had said to Mrs Wilson and what the other animals had already told me. I'd run away. I'd been hit by a car when I was on my way home. And somehow Zena was involved . . . and Caligula was in on it?

I couldn't believe it. I dare not. But those last few days of my life were still a blank. Why was it that the distant past seemed so much clearer? So many things were bubbling up again. Could I find an answer there?

Chapter Eleven

Then

About a week after the disastrous incident with Andrew and Zena at the pedestrian crossing, Tuesday invited Emily over to binge-watch *Fleabag*, which disappointingly contained no actual information on fleas. That said, I didn't really care what was happening on screen because Emily and Tuesday were eating supper off their laps on the sofa and my focus was entirely on whether any food might be dropped. Alas, they were both being frustratingly tidy eaters. I could usually rely on Emily at least to drop a chip or two. Deliberately, if I gazed at her hard enough.

'You seem distracted,' Emily said to Tuesday at the end of one episode.

I could tell it was on the tip of Tuesday's tongue to tell Emily what had happened with Andrew and Zena but, though Tuesday had told Emily some pretty embarrassing stuff in the past, this time she chose not to. Instead she said, 'I don't know. I suppose I've been thinking about Mum quite a bit lately. It's coming up for the second anniversary . . .'

'Oh, Tuesday!' Emily grasped both of Tuesday's hands

between hers. 'How could I have forgotten! You know if you ever want to talk about your mum, I'm all ears.'

'I know you are, lovely Em. But you've heard enough sad stuff from me. I only want to talk about the good times with you. I've joined an online group for cancer carers where I can talk about everything else. I wish I'd joined up sooner, everyone in the group has been through the same thing – caring for someone twenty-four-seven at the end – so we all get it. I thought it would be depressing but it helps.'

'Do they have real life meet-ups too?' Emily asked.

'I'm going to one next week.' Tuesday paused for a moment before she added, 'There's someone from the chat room I really want to meet in the flesh.'

As she said that, Tuesday nonchalantly speared a piece of chicken that I had hoped might be coming my way.

Emily raised her eyebrows and her eyes sparkled with mischief. 'Is this someone a man?'

Tuesday nodded.

'Tell me more.'

Ugh. I braced myself for a load of mushy talk. So as Tuesday began to fill Emily in on the details of her virtual flirtation, I may have accidentally-on-purpose sat down quite heavily against Emily's leg so that finally a chip fell off her plate and landed right in front of my nose.

The person Tuesday really wanted to meet was Kenton. Kenton Harding. I met him at the same time she did. The first 'in real life' gathering for the carers' support group was at the Moon Under Water, a pub by the river that allowed dogs in, so Tuesday took me along too.

The Moon Under Water was one of my favourite places.
They had a jar full of dog treats on the bar and I always
made it my mission to get at least three on any visit. One
memorable night, I managed to wangle six by making my
best 'haven't had a thing to eat all day' eyes at each of
the bar staff in turn. I'd have made it seven but Tuesday
cottoned on and told the manager the vet had warned
her to watch my weight.

'So no more snacks, please, no matter how sadly he
looks at you . . .'

'I get it,' said the manager. 'He's part Labrador, isn't
he? I had a Labrador once. They're so greedy, they'll eat
anything.'

I was outraged by the slur. Eat anything? Not true. I
categorically will not eat Brussels sprouts.

Tuesday explained as much. 'You can't trick him. He'll
never eat a sprout. Not even if it's covered in gravy.
Though he will eat horse manure,' she added.

Anyway, I could tell that Tuesday was a little nervous
as we headed for the pub that summer night. She kept
telling me to slow down. I was walking no faster than
normal but she was tottering along at a snail's pace. Slower
than a snail's pace. She was wearing ridiculous shoes. I've
never understood that about human females. Why would
you ever want to impede your ability to zoom?

'There's no need to hurry,' she told me. 'You're not
getting any bar treats tonight.'

I chuckled to myself. 'That's what you think, missus.'

Several members of the online group were already at
the pub when we arrived. They'd taken a table outside

overlooking the river. When Tuesday joined them, one of the men asked what she'd like to drink and returned with both her drink – a gin and tonic – and a bowl of water for me. Even better, as he put my bowl down on the floor, he pulled a couple of treats from his pocket. Having been told by Tuesday that I wasn't supposed to have any snacks, he subtly placed them in the shadow of the water bowl while she was distracted. Result! I wolfed them down. I was two treats up and I hadn't even had to pull my 'starving puppy' face. I hoped this chap was Kenton.

Alas, he wasn't Kenton. Kenton arrived a whole hour after everyone else, during which time Tuesday shredded two beer mats and checked her reflection in the screen of her phone ninety-hundred times.

I noticed Kenton before the rest of the group did. He stood at the door to the pub's terrace, pushing back his floppy brown hair from his face in a way that I knew was meant to look casual but which was carefully intended to draw attention. I could read human body language better than most humans did.

When Kenton and I were finally properly introduced – after he'd shaken hands with all the humans – I did my best to impress. I stood up but kept all four paws firmly on the floor and wagged my tail instead of jumping all over him. I certainly didn't stick my nose in the crotch of his trousers as I might have done on a less formal occasion. All the same, I could tell at once that Kenton was not a dog person. He didn't lean down to pat me or try to make my better acquaintance as the others had. His smile was more wary than warm.

'Ah well,' I thought, as I settled back down at Tuesday's feet. 'Can't win 'em all.' There were plenty of other people at the gathering that night who couldn't get enough of my canine charm. I ended up getting five more secret treats from the bar and the best part of a jumbo bag of pork scratchings that someone knocked on to the floor after a half-pint of cider too many. Pork scratchings . . . Now there's a snack worth snaffling. I threw up twice on the way back home but it was worth it. Tuesday seemed to have had a good time too.

The following day, I saw Zena at the park for the first time since the crossing incident. She was impressed by my pub treat count.

'And pork scratchings,' she sighed. 'What I wouldn't give for a bag of those.' She lamented once again that a guide dog's treats were strictly limited to make sure she didn't get unwell. 'I'm grateful for a carrot,' she said.

Then I told her about Kenton and how Tuesday had hoped he might turn out to be a romantic interest.

'But he's not a dog person,' I concluded. 'So hopefully that's the end of that.'

'Not a dog person? But everybody loves you, Stupendo,' Zena assured me. 'If you have to see him a second time, he'll come round, I'm sure.'

'Do you think Andrew would come round? To Tuesday? If they were to meet again,' I asked.

Zena looked doubtful. 'He was really angry after that disaster at the crossing,' she admitted. 'He even tweeted about it.'

I knew about Twitter. Emily was a fan.

'Andrew has quite a big following,' Zena said. 'And they all agreed that Tuesday was out of line, calling him an arse like that.'

'It was out of character,' I said in Tuesday's defence.

'I'm sure it was, but Andrew doesn't know that,' Zena pointed out.

'And Andrew did call her an idiot.'

'That was a little harsh. Perhaps if Tuesday were to make the first move?'

Zena and I both looked over at Tuesday, who, looking up from her phone for the first time in twenty minutes, suddenly noticed that I was with my guide-dog friend. She quickly scanned the field for Andrew and, spotting him on his usual bench, called me back to her.

'Come on, Stupendo. We've got to go. Now! Stupendo! Come on! Come!'

'I guess that means she won't be making the first move to patch things up,' I said. 'Humans!'

Zena agreed. She looked back at Andrew. He had his phone pressed to his ear and was frowning as he paced back and forth.

'I just want him to be happy. I want him to be able to trust somebody other than me.'

I understood. We dogs, we can tell a friend from a foe within seconds. Human beings, however, often get it wrong and get hurt as a result. Then they don't want to take the risk again. Trust is a difficult thing for humans.

As far as I was concerned, Kenton had not passed the first-meeting test but later that same week, he called Tuesday up and I could tell by the way Tuesday twisted her hair and laughed her 'tinkling' laugh that her interest in the man was only increasing.

On the night of their second meeting, I watched as she put on her make-up with extra care. I was excited by the prospect of another night down the pub. If Tuesday was distracted by Kenton, I would easily be able to persuade someone to slip me a snack or ten. But then I learned that Tuesday wasn't going to be taking me with her.

'Sorry, Stupendo,' she said. 'We're going to a posh restaurant tonight. No dogs allowed, I'm afraid.'

I was disappointed, of course. Whenever Tuesday picked a restaurant to visit with her friends, she always chose one I could go along to. I was an essential part of the gang. Emily in particular would have been disappointed if I didn't show up on a 'girls' night'. But I understood that not everyone was as excited about sharing a meal with a dog as Emily was – I knew from talking to Zena that some people got upset to see a *guide dog* in a restaurant, let alone a civilian mutt like me – and even if Kenton hadn't considered me that day, I knew I should be pleased that he'd asked Tuesday to go out again. The invitation seemed to have made her really happy. Giddy, even.

She asked me how I thought she looked as she was leaving the house.

'Will I do?' she said.

To me, Tuesday was always beautiful because, as every dog knows, beauty is nothing to do with surface considerations. It's the way people *are* and not the way people *look* that decides whether they are lovely or not. When I looked at Tuesday's face, I saw her kindness and her generosity and her gentle sense of humour, not her shimmery lipstick and her perfect flicky eyeliner. She looked as good to me first thing in the morning, with her eyes all puffy, as she did after hours in the bathroom obliterating her perfectly nice natural smell with synthetic flower scents. She glowed with goodness. All the same, I wished in that moment that I could tell her in her own language that she looked beautiful in the superficial way human beings are so hung up upon. I settled for wagging my tail.

'Thanks, Stupendo. I'll be back soon,' she told me. She held my face in her hands and kissed the end of my nose, leaving a smudge of her pink lipstick upon it. The taste made me sneeze.

'Be. A. Good. Boy,' she added.

'I'm always a good boy,' my tail wag said.

As soon as Tuesday closed the door behind her, I padded into the sitting room and settled down on the sofa, which wasn't strictly 'good boy' behaviour, I know.

As usual, Tuesday left the radio on to keep me company. I wished, not for the first time, that I had some way of telling her I actually preferred it when the radio *wasn't* playing and I could hear what was going on in the rest of the house and on the street outside instead. Still, after an hour or so a good tune came over the airwaves and I had a little roll on my back on the scratchy hall rug. Then I stood at the French windows that led from the living room into the garden for a while to see what I could see.

To a human eye, the garden would probably have looked deserted but a dog sees with all of his senses. Even through the glass I could smell that the old fox had been by recently. I could hear the snuffling of a small hedgehog in the flower bed. I heard the quiet hoot of the owl in the distance. I saw the yellow flash of a cat's eyes – not Caligula's – as he briefly glanced in my direction before carrying on along the wall to next door's garden. Pleased to see that the strange cat had decided not to stop on my patch, I went back to the sofa for a snooze. The smell of Tuesday's perfume on the cushions was comforting. All was well. I hoped she was having a good time even if I couldn't be there with her.

Chapter Twelve

When Tuesday came home after that first evening alone with Kenton, I could tell she'd had more to drink than she usually would. She fumbled with her key in the front door and almost tripped over me when I greeted her in the hallway. She sat on the bottom of the stairs to take off her high-heeled boots, which she did with great difficulty, and told me all about her evening. I did my best to look interested, while surreptitiously checking her pockets for snacks. Maybe she'd brought something home for me? She hadn't. She was all about Kenton.

'Kenton is amazing, Stupendo. He's even nicer than I remembered. He's such a good guy. He's funny and thoughtful and compassionate. He works as a property developer but he's not one of those selfish rich people making a fortune by pricing everyone else out of the market. He's big on affordable homes. And sustainability.'

'Mm-hmm,' I said. I checked Tuesday's handbag. Perhaps she'd hidden some titbits in there? No such luck.

'He thinks about things really deeply. He's caring. He really wants to make a difference in the world. I have never met anyone like him, Stupendo. Never . . .'

Had I been able to talk, I would have said, 'I think you

may have had one too many.' But I wagged my tail to let her know I thought it all sounded very exciting and I was glad to see her so happy, even if I wasn't the reason. I couldn't be jealous of anyone who made Tuesday smile, could I? I only ever had her best interests at heart. When she let me out into the garden, I checked the perimeter fences one more time to ensure that nothing was amiss before we went to sleep. Protecting Tuesday was always my number-one priority.

The following day – a Sunday – Emily came over for brunch and Tuesday went through the whole date story again. I was slightly distracted from hearing Emily's responses by the food she and Tuesday balanced on their laps as they sat on the sofa. Tuesday was gushing. Emily was, for her, admirably measured in her response.

'He sounds great,' she said. 'But remember that everyone is on their best behaviour on a first date.'

I pricked up my ears.

'Emily, he's lovely,' Tuesday said. 'He was his fiancée's carer for two years before she died. He's not the type to play games. He's got just as much to lose as I have emotionally. I think I may be in love.' I could tell Emily was alarmed when she realised that Tuesday was only half-joking.

Emily forced a laugh. 'Don't go throwing your heart beneath his feet just yet. Let him keep working to impress you for a little while longer.'

'Good advice,' I thought. I wanted to add, 'Make sure he works to impress me too.'

'Always remember,' Emily concluded, 'what you need

is a man who looks at you the way your dog does. Even when you feel like dreck.'

Tuesday looked at me then. I gazed back at her with my best melted chocolate, 'you're the only girl in the world' eyes. My best 'give me a snack and we'll forget all about your leaving me home alone last night' eyes.

'Nobody could ever look at me like Stupendo does,' Tuesday told Emily. 'Especially when he wants a treat. Cupboard love.' She ruffled my ears. She'd rumbled me. 'You're not having anything, Stupendo,' she said. 'You know what the vet said about watching your diet.' But after she'd loaded the plates into the dishwasher – without letting me lick them first because Emily was looking – she did let me have a Dentastix. Not my favourite treat as treats go – it basically being an edible toothbrush – but better than a Brussels sprout.

As if he'd heard Tuesday and Emily's conversation, Kenton did do his utmost to impress Tuesday for at least a little while. Over the next few weeks, she went out more often than I had ever known her to go out in all my time on Bracken Avenue. To my disappointment, most of those outings with Kenton – in fact nearly all of them – were to places where I could not join them. More fancy restaurants, the theatre, the cinema . . . He pulled out all the stops. There was only one occasion when she took me along. We were back at the pub, with the rest of the online cancer carers' group for their monthly meeting. After giving me a fleeting pat on the head, Kenton mostly ignored me. Luckily, my friend the purveyor of illicit snacks was there, though he only managed to slip me five biscuits and there were no pork scratchings this time.

'I promise I'll stay in tomorrow,' Tuesday told me as she went out yet again the following day. I'm afraid I was so upset that I turned my nose away when she came in for a kiss. She returned home that night with a doggy bag containing a bit of steak, which I did appreciate, but not as much as I appreciated having her around. Lolling on the sofa was not the same without her, even if I did get to stretch out and use all the cushions. So I was pleased to hear that she was going to be staying in the following night, until I worked out that she was only going to be staying in because we were going to have a guest.

When I met him at the front door, Kenton rebuffed my friendly welcome by actively shoving me away.

'I don't want to get hair on these trousers,' he said.

Evidently, Kenton's trousers were expensive. Tuesday told Kenton she understood his concerns absolutely and would take extra measures to make him comfortable. Since they would be eating in the dining room – unused for eating in my living memory except on the Day of the Sprouts (which you humans call 'Christmas') – me and my hairs would stay in the kitchen.

While Tuesday was in there doing the cooking, it wasn't so bad, but I really resented being shut in the kitchen while she and Kenton sat first in the dining room and then the living room, drinking wine and talking nonsense until the early hours. It was almost better when they went out to the places where I couldn't join them. At least then I got to watch the night-time goings-on in the garden through the French windows. Even if I stood on my hind paws, it was hard to see out of the kitchen window. I was especially disgruntled when I heard a hedgehog fight erupt somewhere out there in the darkness. I would have liked to have watched it. You have never seen anything like a pair of hedgehogs going into battle over something revolting like half a dead slug. I'd have to get the squirrels to tell me how it turned out.

I was more than a little grumpy when Kenton finally went home and Tuesday let me out into the hall again. While she carried the washing up through to the kitchen sink, I sulked at the bottom of the stairs until it was time for bed.

'I had such a great night,' she told me. 'Kenton is really special.'

I responded with a quiet but, I thought, eloquent 'hmmmph'.

The second time Kenton came over, I knew what was coming and didn't bother to greet him at the door when he arrived. I just took myself off to the kitchen and hung out there until he was gone again.

I'm ashamed to say that when he came over for dinner a third time and I found myself stuck in the kitchen once more, I may have stolen some chicken bones wrapped in silver foil out of the bin, which Tuesday had failed to properly close. I ate the bones *and* the foil. When she realised what I'd done, Tuesday had to take me to the emergency vet. It wasn't much fun to have to have a laxative injection but at least I'd cut short her romantic evening which was a small silver-foiled lining.

'It's worse than having a child,' I heard Kenton say as Tuesday bundled me into the back of the car and promised to call him next day. Alas, it didn't put him off. He was back at number thirteen the following night. And the night after. And Tuesday made sure that the kitchen bin lid was firmly closed every time.

Soon Kenton Harding became a more or less permanent fixture at 13 Bracken Avenue. He stayed over several times a week and when he was in the house, I was banished from his sight. If he was in the sitting room, then I had to be in the kitchen. If he was in the kitchen, I had to go into the dining room or even sit outside in the garden. I was definitely not allowed in the bedroom while Kenton was around. His smart 'property developer' suits and my tendency to shed hair like a dandelion clock sheds seeds did not mix.

I'm glad to say I wasn't banished in the same way on those rare occasions when Kenton wasn't there. On those nights when Kenton had somewhere else to be, I was allowed to sleep in my usual place on Tuesday's mattress and she just hoovered like a crazy person three times the following morning. I quite enjoyed it when Tuesday went on a mad vacuuming spree. Chasing the hoover was a great game. From time to time she even let me catch it.

For the most part, life was still good. I knew I was a lucky dog. I had a comfortable bed to sleep on. I had a lovely garden to play in. I got two nice walks a day and all the love I could handle. At least, I did when Kenton wasn't around . . . I could only hope that Tuesday would get bored of him sooner or later, like Emily was always getting bored of her boyfriends. She'd had three in the time I had known her. Then everything would be absolutely perfect again. Just Tuesday and me once more.

Unfortunately, that day did not come.

Four months after Tuesday and Kenton first met, he moved into our house.

Chapter Thirteen

Kenton was coming to the end of the lease on his flat and he said it seemed ridiculous for him to continue paying rent there when he spent so much time at Tuesday's place anyway. Tuesday agreed it would be better for both of them if Kenton was at number thirteen full-time, helping with the bills. 'But what about Stupendo?' she asked.

'As long as you keep him out of all the rooms I need to use, I'm sure everything will be fine,' Kenton said.

Tuesday agreed. Though, as far as I could see, there wasn't a room in the house that Kenton didn't 'need' to use. Was I going to end up living in the shed?

I suppose I should have been grateful that he didn't go so far as to ask Tuesday to choose between us. Zephyr had told me plenty of fur-raising stories about the dogs home. I knew what could happen when even the most devoted dog person ended up falling in love with someone who did not like dogs at all.

I just had to keep my head down, that's what Zephyr told me. I knew there wasn't much point in my trying to win Kenton over – he just wasn't a dog man – but it was still possible that once he and Tuesday were together on a more permanent basis, one or the other of them would decide they were happier single after all. It had all happened very quickly. They didn't really know each other yet.

I wasn't the only one with concerns.

'Isn't it a bit fast?' Emily asked when Tuesday told her what was happening.

'Aren't you the one who's always telling me that when you know, you know . . .' Tuesday countered. 'And the minute I met Kenton, I knew.'

'I know,' said Emily. 'But . . .'

'But what?'

The moment I saw Kenton, I knew exactly what I thought about him as well, but I also knew that my company was not enough for my beloved Tuesday. I was just a dog and Tuesday was a young, beautiful human who needed company of her own kind. Though she was my everything, I couldn't hope to be the same for her so I resolved to be as grown-up about the whole thing as I could be.

'Guard your heart, Tuesday,' warned Emily. 'Guard your heart.'

It was hard, having to stay out of the kitchen and the living room if Kenton wanted to be in there. It was especially horrible never being able to go upstairs any more. I missed being able to stand on Tuesday's bed and have a bird's-eye view of the garden. And despite my efforts not to get in his way, Kenton complained about me all the time. He said I made the place smell, though he broke wind at least as much as I did, if not more. I know for a fact he tried to blame some of his on me. And there really was nothing I could do about the amount of hair I shed in the average day. Labradors and Staffies shed. We just do. Kenton shed quite a bit of hair himself. I knew that worried him, actually. I'd seen him trying to use a hand mirror to look at the back of his head.

There was a small silver lining to Kenton's presence, in that Tuesday took to brushing my coat every day in an attempt to lessen the amount of hair I left around the house and over Kenton's fancy clothes. First thing each morning, Tuesday would sit on the back step and I would sit between her knees, while she brushed me all over. I loved to look out over the garden while she smoothed down my ears in the softest way possible. It became my favourite moment of the day. A moment when it was just me and Tuesday again and I could forget that I was having to share her.

Frustrated as I was by the new regime, after a month or so, Tuesday told Emily that she was very happy to have Kenton around and that cohabiting was 'wonderful'.

'It's been so easy,' Tuesday said. 'Kenton fits right into my life, just like I always hoped someone would.'

Though it seemed to me that Tuesday was fitting her life *around* Kenton. She no longer left her new garden designs spread out across the dining room table like she used to because Kenton had told her he might need to use the table himself as his own office. He never did, though, I noticed.

Likewise, Tuesday didn't let me lick the dishes clean any more but took them straight from the table to the dishwasher and always made sure the heavy door was shut. She picked up her clothes from the bedroom floor rather than leave them around for me to snooze on. She straightened the shoes in the hallway every time she passed.

'I wish you'd get rid of those tatty old slippers,' Kenton said, when he came in as she was putting them into the row.

Those tatty old slippers! He was talking about the slippers that had once belonged to Tuesday's mum and which now belonged to me. How could Kenton even suggest throwing those precious things away? He knew, didn't he, the story behind the well-chewed pink mules? I thought Tuesday would remind him, and that would be that, but she didn't, and half an hour after Kenton raised the matter, the slippers were gone.

'I'll get you some new toys,' Tuesday whispered to me as I watched with despair as she came back from the bin with the scent of those much-loved slippers still on her empty hands. They weren't toys, I wanted to tell her. Not to either of us. They were a totem. A symbol of our love and understanding of each other.

And they weren't the last thing to go. Every week, Kenton turned his nose up at something different. He didn't like the artwork on the living room walls. "Too John Lewis'. The blanket that covered the sofa was too scratchy. 'Can't you get something in real wool?' He thought the rug in front of the fire – my favourite rug – looked a bit cheap. 'Perhaps it was nice when it was new but I doubt it.' The contents of Tuesday's wardrobe met with his disapproval too.

He didn't have to say anything overt. He'd just ask,

'Are you wearing that?' and Tuesday would respond by running back upstairs to change. The offending outfit would find its way to the charity shop bag a day or two later. Thus, little by little he made his mark on Tuesday's house, her personal appearance and our lives. I kept hoping that he would finally go too far and she'd throw him out just as she'd thrown out the green winter coat that she'd been so fond of before she heard him singing in a Kermit the Frog voice as she buttoned it up. But as the nights grew longer, I resigned myself to the fact that Tuesday wasn't getting tired of Kenton at all. In fact, with every week that passed, she seemed to be working harder for his affections than ever. She changed her hair. She started wearing pink polish on her nails, though polished nails were a total waste of time for someone who worked as a gardener. She looked into getting braces for her teeth. She wanted to be perfect for him. She wanted him to stay.

Soon it was December. I knew that Tuesday was excited as the end of the year drew close. She loved Christmas and this one was set to be particularly good. She told Emily that she would be pulling out all the stops to make it special.

'For Kenton. It's our first Christmas as a couple.'

'Don't spend too much money on his present,' Emily said flatly.

Tuesday did spend too much money on his Christmas present. Of course she did. She bought him a beautiful new leather weekend bag.

She spent a lot of time and money on decorating the

house too. Kenton, she explained to Emily, hadn't had a decent Christmas since before his dead fiancée fell ill. Also, he had been working much too hard and she wanted to make everything easy for him. 'Magical.'

Three weeks before Christmas, Tuesday brought home a vast Christmas tree. We had a small falling-out when I went to pee on it while it was leaning against the outside wall next to the front door. How was I supposed to know there were trees and there were *trees*? The previous Christmas, Tuesday had decorated the living room with a fake tree, in which I'd had no interest at all. But this one smelled of all the gloriousness of the forest and the animals that lived there. Of course I wanted to add my own notes.

I resisted. And I was glad that I did. When Tuesday had finished decorating it, the tree was supernaturally beautiful. I had never seen anything like it. Delicately, I touched one of the new glass baubles on the lower branches with my nose and watched it rock to and fro on its ribbon, turning my reflection into something weird and wonderful as it did so. I was transfixed as I watched my nose grow big and small and big again.

Tuesday could not wait for Kenton to get back from his important meeting that evening. At six o'clock, she started preparing a special Advent dinner. She was cooking lamb tagine. His favourite. She'd also splashed out on a bottle of wine. As she uncorked the bottle to let it 'breathe', I could smell a whole world in the wisp of scent – hot summer days and autumnal mornings – that escaped with the cork. Obviously, I wasn't a drinker myself but I could still appreciate a fine bouquet.

Two hours later, dinner was ready but there was no sign of Kenton. Tuesday sent him a text. No response. Another hour and she sent him another message. Still no response.

She covered the dinner with tin foil and screwed the cork back into the top of the bottle of wine. She phoned him. No reply. She phoned Emily.

'Do you think I should call round the hospitals?'

'It's three weeks before Christmas,' Emily said. 'He'll have been invited to have an impromptu drink with some friends.'

'Without telling me? He wouldn't . . .'

He had. Kenton came home at midnight. The lamb tagine had long since dried out and was spoiled. I felt sorry for Tuesday though secretly happy for myself, since it meant all the more for me. I didn't mind a bit of dry couscous.

When he came into the kitchen, Tuesday tried to extract an apology from Kenton in a very feeble way.

'I made a special dinner,' she pointed out.

'Won't it keep?' Kenton asked.

'Not really. You might have phoned me. Or texted?'

'It was a spontaneous thing. We went straight from the meeting. There wasn't a chance to get my phone out without appearing rude.'

'All night?'

'All night.'

Kenton said he was tired. He didn't want anything to eat anyway. He didn't even want to join Tuesday in the living room for a nightcap in front of the newly decorated Christmas tree. He just wanted to go to bed.

Tuesday didn't push it. She sat down at the kitchen

table, composing and deleting texts to Emily, while Kenton brushed his teeth. I listened as he came out of the bathroom and crossed the landing to the bedroom, closing the door behind him. Moments later, the bedroom door reopened and Kenton shouted down the stairs.

'That bloody dog's been in here, hasn't he?'

Tuesday raced from the kitchen to the hallway.

'What, love?'

'I said the dog's been in here. My Gucci sweater is covered in hair.'

'I promise Stupendo hasn't been in the bedroom,' Tuesday told him.

That wasn't strictly true, but Tuesday wasn't to know I'd been in there for a couple of hours while she was at the supermarket that afternoon. And that Gucci cashmere was very comfy.

Kenton shook the sweater at her.

'You promised, Tuesday, that you would do everything you could to make it work with me and Stupendo under the same roof.'

'He hasn't been up here.'

Tuesday was at the top of the stairs now and Kenton had gone back into the bedroom but I could still hear his muffled complaints.

'Since you don't seem to want to put me first, I think it's time we called it a day, don't you? I can't live like this a minute longer.'

'Kenton! Please. It's late. You're tired. Why don't we sleep in the spare room? Just for tonight. I know Stupendo hasn't been in there. Then tomorrow morning, I'll vacuum everything and change the sheets and . . .'

'You sleep in the spare room,' said Kenton, closing the bedroom door in Tuesday's face.

Tuesday didn't sleep at all that night. I knew because I could hear her pacing the spare room floor. I was staying downstairs in the kitchen, out of the way. Kenton didn't emerge from the bedroom before Tuesday had to go to work the following morning. I went with her to Mrs Wilson's. By the time we got back at lunchtime, Kenton was gone. So was his stuff. He didn't even leave a note.

All that afternoon, Tuesday tried to get hold of Kenton but he did not return her calls, her texts or her emails. Tuesday grew increasingly upset. So much so that she forgot to feed me at teatime. I was very glad when Emily came over at the end of her work day and noticed that my bowl was empty and for once I was genuinely hungry.

Emily listened patiently as Tuesday ran through the events of the previous evening over and over until eventually, she said, 'You know it wasn't actually about your letting Stupendo into the bedroom, don't you? He hasn't really let it bother him for all the months he's been here before. Kenton was looking for a reason to start a fight so that he could leave. He's been planning it. He wanted to leave and he couldn't find a way to tell you.'

'So he blamed it on Stupendo?'

'Yes. He made you think you had to choose. I'm glad Stupendo won. Kenton must have known Stupendo would and he'd be off scot-free.'

'He didn't even give me time to come up with a solution,' Tuesday complained.

Emily's eyes widened. 'Tuesday, please don't tell me

that you could ever come up with a solution other than having that idiot move out.'

'Stupendo would be easy to—'

Emily waved her hands in front of Tuesday's face to stop her mid-sentence. 'Do not say what I think you are going to say! There is a special place in hell for people who aren't loyal to their dogs.'

Well said, Emily. I was glad she'd interrupted Tuesday so I could tell myself that the last word of the sentence was most definitely, one hundred per cent *not* going to be 'rehome'. She would *never* have done that to me.

'It doesn't matter what you think you could have done to make him stay, Kenton was already leaving,' Emily insisted. 'He probably didn't want to have to buy you a Christmas present.'

'Emily!'

'OK, maybe that was a little harsh. But you know what it's like. Christmas is a big deal. It piles on the pressure in any relationship. In a relationship where one person isn't as committed as the other . . .'

'But we *were* talking about further commitment,' Tuesday interrupted. 'We'd been talking about putting him on the deeds to the house so he could raise the loan he needed to set up his own business. If that isn't commitment . . .'

'You what?'

'I don't know why I was hesitating. I was wondering if there was another way for me to guarantee the money without risking our house, but he must have thought I wasn't committed to him! I should have just done it, shouldn't I?'

Emily covered her face with her hands.

'Oh Tuesday. Thank goodness you didn't.'

'But I ruined everything.'

'You ruined nothing. Let him go.'

Never were wiser words spoken.

As it was, Tuesday had no choice but to let Kenton go. Twenty-four hours after he left, he had blocked her calls and texts to his mobile. Her emails were bounced back from his Gmail account. Then he changed his phone number and when Tuesday called the company she thought he'd worked for, they told her that he hadn't been an employee there for at least three months.

'Which explains why he was so keen to move in back in September,' Emily observed. 'He couldn't afford to keep his own flat because he wasn't working.'

The more Emily said, the worse Kenton sounded. Still Tuesday longed to 'just talk to him' though she had no means of getting hold of him at all. She didn't know where he'd gone to. It suddenly struck her that she'd never met any of his friends in the brief time they'd been together. He hadn't wanted to spend much time with her friends either (which had not gone unnoticed by Emily). He'd said that he liked being alone with her best. He'd never been on Facebook, or Twitter or Instagram. He'd always said that social media was for idiots. He'd even left the cancer carers' support group after that second meeting we attended together. He had effectively vanished.

'He's ghosted me,' Tuesday concluded after a week.

'Good,' said Emily. 'It will make it all the easier to get over him.'

There was very little likelihood that Kenton would be coming back for the one unusually (for him) scruffy T-shirt he'd left behind.

'So you might as well chuck it out,' Emily said.

Tuesday reluctantly agreed.

Emily and I had a brief but very satisfying game of tug-of-war in the garden before the T-shirt finally ripped in two and was banished to the bin. As I raced around the garden afterwards, I felt triumphant. My Christmas had come early.

Chapter Fourteen

B ut Christmas was going to be difficult for Tuesday and that made me sad.

So that Tuesday and I didn't have to be alone on Christmas Day, Emily invited us to join her at her parents' house on the edge of town for the whole holiday. Emily's mum and dad were always glad to see Tuesday, having known her for so many years, and, fortunately, they were just as keen on me. I knew that Emily's dad, Bob, and I would get on the minute he crouched down to say hello. I could tell he was a dog person. I liked him even more when he took me out for a walk in the fields at the back of the house while Tuesday settled in. I loved the familiarity of the park but it was a real treat to be out in the wild. Well, the nearly wild. Fox poo seemed very boring compared to cow pats. Now they *really* were worth getting a bath over.

My instinct that Bob would be a soft touch when it came to giving me treats was right too. On Christmas Day I stood beside him as he carved the turkey and he dropped every tenth piece he carved straight into my open mouth. By the time everyone sat down for Christmas dinner, I was already completely stuffed. I found myself a comfortable spot under the dining table and had a little snooze, until I heard the humans shout as one, 'Stupendo!' I came round to the sound of Tuesday apologising on my behalf.

'I don't know what to say. It's so disgusting . . .'

Apparently I'd broken wind in my sleep and the resulting stink had everyone at the table burying their noses in their napkins. Nudged by Tuesday, I slunk out into the coolness of the hall, looking suitably shamefaced.

Once everyone had calmed down, I sneaked back in to check the floor for any droppages between the turkey and the pudding. It was quite disappointing. A few peas and a sprout. I didn't bother with that, of course.

Fortunately, there were leftovers aplenty on the plates the humans carried into the kitchen and, ignoring the potential for more toxic fumes, Bob assembled a whole Staffrador-sized meal of them in my bowl, complete with stuffing. He did try to sneak a sprout in, having been told by Tuesday that I wouldn't touch them, but I spotted it early and, having licked it clean of gravy, left it neatly beside my bowl on the black and white kitchen floor tiles.

Bob handed Tuesday a pound coin when he saw it. It seemed they'd made a bet.

When the washing up was done, I followed Bob into the living room. As we stepped through the door, he made an audible parp of his own. He winked at me and whispered, 'I'm afraid I'm going to blame this one on you.'

Normally, I would have been offended but after all the food he'd given me that day, I was only too happy to cover for him.

*   *   *

At the end of the evening, I joined Tuesday and Emily in Emily's childhood bedroom, which hadn't been changed since she left home more than a decade earlier. They were sleeping in Emily's old bunk beds. Tuesday on the bottom. Emily on the top. I had a pile of blankets on the floor by the radiator.

'Thanks for inviting us for Christmas,' said Tuesday.

'I know it isn't what you planned.'

'It's been lovely all the same.'

I agreed.

There was silence for a moment before Tuesday said, 'I wonder where Kenton is tonight.'

Emily groaned. 'Who cares?'

'You know,' Tuesday continued, 'I really thought life was starting to come together when he moved in. Now here I am in a single bunk bed aged thirty-two. Could I be a bigger loser?'

'Hang on. I'm in a bunk bed too. And I'm six months older than you are.'

'Yeah, but . . . these are your childhood bunk beds so . . .'

'Stop digging,' Emily said, laughing. 'I'm glad Kenton's gone because I got to have my best friend – and my favourite dog – beside me on Christmas Day. It will get easier, Tuesday. One day you will look back and be glad Kenton left when he did, before you got any more involved. I never liked the way he talked to you or the way he criticised the way your house looked or what you wore. I bet he made comments about your body too, didn't he? Negative ones.'

Tuesday didn't deny it.

'You were still vulnerable from losing your mum when

you met him and I think he took advantage of that. Perhaps,' she added darkly, 'your vulnerability was exactly what he was looking for.'

Tuesday had refused to talk any more about the fact that Kenton had wanted her to sign half her house over to him. So Emily was gentle and avoided suggesting that Tuesday's money had attracted Kenton too. 'He moved in much too fast because it suited him. You'll soon start thinking he did you a favour by moving out just as quickly. Isn't that right, Stupendo?'

I thumped my tail against the floor to let her know I was definitely in agreement.

'I've got the feeling that next year is going to be a good one for both of us.'

'I hope you're right,' Tuesday sighed.

'I know I am. Hang on . . . I've got something to show you.'

Emily swung her legs over the side of her bunk and lowered herself down to the floor. She went to her old wardrobe and reached down a shoebox from the top shelf. She sat down on the floor next to Tuesday and me and opened the box up. Out wafted a concoction of ancient dust and teenage perfume that tickled my nose.

'Remember this?'

'Your box of secrets!'

Emily took out two envelopes. One was marked with her name. The other with Tuesday's.

'You kept them?'

'Our letters to the future? Of course I did. Let's see how we've got on. Mine first.'

Emily read her letter out loud.

'New Year's Eve, 1999. Dear Universe, by the time I am twenty-one, I want to drive a red Ford Ka, live in a flat in London and have a job as a supermodel. I will be engaged to Robbie Williams.'

Emily pulled a face. 'Hmm. Still waiting on all four counts. I should have made a blood sacrifice. Let's see how you did.' She read Tuesday's letter out too. 'Dear Universe, by the time I am twenty-one, I would like to have a moped, a job as a landscape gardener and a dog. I would also like to be married to Ronan Keating, the lead singer from Boyzone.'

'I got the job and the dog,' Tuesday conceded.

'You asked much more politely than I did. But Ronan Keating? We really always did have different taste in men.'

Emily passed Tuesday a handful of photographs from those distant days. 'Look at our hair. Weren't we lovely? And we had no idea . . .'

The old photographs made Emily laugh but Tuesday was getting tearful. 'There was so much to look forward to when we were twelve.'

'There is still so much to look forward to, idiot. You're thirty-two, not ninety.'

I agreed. I pressed my nose against Tuesday's wet face to remind her that she still had me, for a start. If I had anything to do with it, the next twelve months would be full of adventure. There were so many walks to take. Places to see. Great smells to roll in.

'Ignore me. I don't know why I'm so emotional,' Tuesday said.

'Group hug?' suggested Emily. She included me in the huddle and I happily let both of them wrap their arms around me. Unfortunately, they squeezed me a little bit too hard and I might have let out a small fart. OK. Maybe it was a big fart. A big Christmas turkey with all the trimmings (except sprouts) fart.

Not my fault! I said with my eyes.

'Stupendo!' my two favourite ladies groaned.

In the week between Christmas and New Year, Tuesday seemed to be feeling better about the Kenton situation. She took me on long walks every day. There was one wonderful moment when we almost caught up with Zena and Andrew going into the park, but though Tuesday looked as though she might be about to say something this time, she didn't. Instead, she shook her head to herself and quickly dragged me in the opposite direction.

'Least said, soonest mended, right, Stupendo? He probably doesn't even remember what happened at the crossing. He probably has an argument with a different person every day of the week. We don't need that kind of energy.'

When Zena was off harness, she joined me in the middle of the grass and told me about her Christmas.

'It felt just like any other day. Andrew refused every invitation that came our way,' she said. 'Wouldn't even go to his mum's. He spent the afternoon working. I didn't get so much as a sprout.'

'You could have had one of mine. I can't believe you like sprouts.'

'I can't believe you don't. How was your Christmas?'

'Tuesday spent a good part of it crying because Kenton's gone for good.'

'Then at least you'll have a very happy New Year,' said Zena.

I was sure that we would.

On New Year's Eve, Tuesday and Emily made plans to go clubbing. I had a feeling I wouldn't be invited when I saw Tuesday getting dressed up – she was not putting on her usual 'pub clothes' – but for once I didn't mind that she would be leaving me at home while she went out. I knew Emily would take care of her and hoped that an evening of dancing and time spent with friends would fill her with happiness. I would make the most of having the sofa to myself.

Tuesday rolled in at two o'clock in the morning, drunk as the proverbial skunk (I don't know why skunks have a reputation as being big drinkers). She was singing 'I Will Survive' as she tumbled through the door. That was always a reliable sign that she'd had a good night. Or a big one at least.

She held my head in her hands and kissed the end of my nose. Her kiss smelled of booze and a burger. When she released my head and sat down on the stairs to wrestle her shoes off, I set about checking her handbag in case she'd brought half the burger home. Emily had done that once, after a couple of drinks too many. She was furious with herself when she discovered that she'd absent-mindedly put the burger in her favourite bag to take a call on her mobile, but I was delighted to help her clean up the mess.

'Stupendo, you are the only male I'll ever need in my life,' Tuesday told me. 'Human men are rubbish. I'm never going to bother with one again.'

Tuesday climbed the stairs unsteadily. She made it to her bedroom safely, thank goodness, but she didn't even change into her pyjamas before she rolled into bed. She had also forgotten to let me out into the garden. I crossed my legs for as long as I could but had a small accident as night turned into day and Tuesday snored through the first dawn chorus of the year.

When Tuesday finally woke up, she looked very unwell indeed.

'I'm never drinking again,' she said.

I made a contrite face when she came downstairs and noticed the puddle by the back door but fortunately she understood that it wasn't my fault.

'I'm sorry, Stupendo,' she said instead. 'I neglected you. And it's not the first time. I neglected you so much because of that stupid man. It won't happen again.'

'I won't hold it against you,' I assured her with a wag. 'If you could just let me out into the garden as a matter of some urgency . . .'

Tuesday opened the back door and I made a dash for it. Moments later, she leaned out through the door herself and threw up all over the patio.

'Don't eat it!' Tuesday yelled at me as I watched the cocktail-coloured splatter cover the paving slabs. As if I would. Well, I suppose there was that one time . . . but that day I just stared at Tuesday as she sank down on to the back step with her hands over her mouth and tried to stop a second bout of vomiting.

She called her best friend. 'Emily, I think my drink must have been spiked.'

Emily responded by telling her, 'No, Tuesday. You've got a hangover. It was New Year's Eve. We had two bottles of prosecco and three piña coladas each. I did suggest we stop at one cocktail but you insisted . . . You said, "Let's start this year as we mean to go on." Then you asked me if I wanted to be in a romantic relationship with you as well as being your best friend.'

'Oh.'

'Of course I can't think of any woman I admire more but . . .'

'So you don't think anyone roofied me?'

'I think we both just got very, very drunk.'

Tuesday accepted the explanation but even then, I sensed that it wasn't the full story.

When Tuesday's 'hangover' went into its third day, we both started to worry. There was no way she could still blame the urge to be sick on New Year's Eve's excesses.

'Stomach bug?' Emily suggested. 'Food poisoning?'

'I haven't eaten anything.'

'Do you have any other symptoms? Temperature?'

'Nothing. I just wake up feeling nauseous and feel that way until lunchtime. It gets a bit better in the afternoons.'

'Oh. My. God,' said Emily. 'It's not just the mornings, is it?'

Emily and I sat on the landing outside the bathroom while Tuesday peed on a stick. When she came out of the bathroom, Tuesday was as white as the plastic from which the stick was made, apart from two bright pink spots on her cheeks that happened to match the pink of the message in the magic stick's window.

'Is it?' Emily asked. 'Are you?'

Tuesday sat down heavily on the top stair.

'I am.'

Somehow I'd already known.

Chapter Fifteen

'I've got to tell Kenton,' Tuesday announced after a while.

'Are you sure it's his?'

'It's either his or the Immaculate Conception, and I didn't notice any archangels hanging around this Christmas Eve. Emily, how could you suggest any differently? You know I loved him. I haven't even so much as glanced at anyone else since I met him.'

But though Emily agreed that, technically, Kenton had a right to know he was going to be a father, how Tuesday would let him know was far from obvious. Kenton had done a very good job of disappearing at the beginning of December. Tuesday had already exhausted every obvious avenue in her attempts to track him down so that now that she really needed to talk to him, she knew there was no chance.

'Not unless I hire a private detective.'

'Do not hire a private detective.'

Emily had Tuesday sit on the sofa while she made hot chocolate with squirty cream on top to help her get over the shock. I couldn't have the hot chocolate but I had some of the cream. Emily may have squirted it straight on to the end of my nose while Tuesday was distracted.

'What can I do, Em? What can I do?'

'It will be OK,' Emily told her over and over.

'But I'm all on my own!'

'You're not on your own. You never will be. You've got me. You've got Stupendo.'

I wagged my tail at the sound of my name. Whatever Tuesday needed me for, I was ready.

With Emily gone home for the night, Tuesday went into the living room and switched on the television. I padded in after her and lay down on the rug in front of the sofa until Tuesday patted the space on the sofa beside her. It was the space that always used to be mine before Kenton and his horror of dog hair spoiled everything. I tilted my head to make sure I'd understood the invitation.

'Come on, Stupendo. Jump up. If you want to.'

I didn't need to be asked twice. I settled into my old spot with my head in Tuesday's lap. She stroked my ears. I think it made both of us feel better.

'It's just you and me again, Stupendo,' she said. 'Just you and me. And the baby. Are you up for it? Having a little brother or sister?'

Of course I was up for it. I could have howled for joy! But knowing that Tuesday was in a reflective mood, I looked up at her with my best sympathetic gaze and hoped she could see that I was taking it all suitably seriously. 'We'll get through this together,' I told her with my eyes.

A visit to the doctor confirmed that Tuesday was already about twelve weeks pregnant when she found out. She told Emily that she'd never been 'regular', whatever that meant, so hadn't been concerned when she skipped her period in October and November. Emily thought it was bad luck that she'd discovered the situation so late but Tuesday said that it was a good thing, since it would make it much easier for her to decide what to do. And what she was going to do was have the baby. The doctor recommended that Tuesday have a scan right away. Emily went with her.

After the scan, Tuesday and Emily came back to number thirteen smelling of hospital and Caffè Nero (they'd stopped off for a coffee on the way home but, disappointingly, bought no biscotti). Tuesday showed me a piece of paper, upon which was printed a picture that didn't make a lot of sense to me.

'This is the baby's head,' she explained. 'And there's its heart. We heard its heartbeat, Stupendo. It's happening.'

I already knew that. Whenever I lay my head against Tuesday's stomach, I could already hear that second smaller heart, ticking in time with her own. I didn't need a stethoscope.

'It all feels so much more real now,' Tuesday told Emily as they sat at the kitchen table with the print-out of the baby scan between them. 'I'm going to give the baby a name. Until he or she is born and then I can choose something that really suits them.'

'So what will this temporary name be?' Emily asked.

'Sparrow,' she said. 'One of the smallest birds in the garden.'

One of the toughest too, despite their diminutive size. I approved.

'Well,' said Emily. 'When I said that I thought this year

was going to be different for you, this wasn't exactly what I had in mind.'

'But it's good,' Tuesday reassured her. 'It's really good.'

Pretty soon after the scan, Tuesday stopped being sick in the mornings and life went back to being more or less normal for a while. As the worst of the winter faded into the past, Tuesday had lots of work to do again, getting her clients' gardens tidied up for the growing season ahead. I accompanied her, of course, making the most of the weak spring sunshine whenever I could. Some of Tuesday's clients were worried that she was taking on too much now that she was pregnant but Tuesday explained that she actually felt stronger than ever. Once the morning sickness passed, Tuesday started thriving.

'I'm pregnant, not ill,' she'd remind anyone who disagreed.

She waited until she was six months pregnant to tell her father what was going on. When she did, he was pleased but concerned for her too.

'So, you're going to be a single mother,' he said.

'And?'

'Well, it's not ideal, is it?'

'You're telling me? The daughter you left behind. I know what it's like to grow up in a single-parent household, Dad. It's hard. But I also know that having one parent who dedicates themselves to your happiness and loves you with all their heart is just as good as having two parents who are disengaged because they're too busy arguing with each other.'

Tuesday's dad conceded that the years when he was

still married to her mother had not been good for any of them. And he couldn't deny he hadn't always been there for her since.

'But I want to be there for you now,' he told her. 'I want to be a good granddad. Whatever you need. Money, whatever, anything. I could even be there . . . you know, at the birth.'

'I'll be just fine,' Tuesday said firmly.

I checked her face to see if the words matched what she was feeling. I wasn't sure they did. Whatever, the conversation didn't end well. Though it had been over twenty-five years since her dad walked out, Tuesday still felt the pain very keenly, and nothing he could say would take that away.

Meanwhile, life was changing for Emily too. The previous year had been almost as disappointing for Emily as it had been for Tuesday. Emily hated the private medical company she worked for and her personal life had been less exciting than she hoped. Her adventures in Tinderland had been bruising. But in January, Emily had left her job to go freelance and swiped right on Elvis. He was not her usual type but their first date was such a success that it ended with both of them ceremoniously removing all the dating apps from their phones and making a pact to give whatever it was they felt for each other a proper chance to thrive.

Tuesday liked Elvis and so did I. He was a true dog person and as such he was utterly incapable of denying a heartfelt plea for a snack. Or even a half-heartfelt plea. Though Tuesday had explained at length that the vet wanted me on a diet, when I turned on 'the look', Elvis could deny me nothing. He was the softest touch I had ever known.

He was also always up for a good old play-fight. Tuesday used to play-fight with me too but as Baby Sparrow grew inside her, I knew I had to treat her with more delicacy and gentleness. When we were out and about, I was constantly alert to danger, making it clear to anyone who got too close that Tuesday had her own canine bodyguard. I even did my best not to pull too hard when we were on a walk. Sometimes I forgot, in my excitement to get to the park, but most times I did manage it.

Zena actually commented, 'Stupendo, I'm beginning to think you could have been a guide dog.'

I was pleased with that. Zena had told me about her time at guide dog training school. She and her colleagues were the elite of the canine world. That she thought I might have what it took to be a guide dog filled me with pride.

As Tuesday reached the last few weeks of her pregnancy, the baby bump got so big I began to wonder if she was having a litter of six. Suddenly she was very tired all the time and got out of breath quickly. I wished I were a donkey rather than a dog as she huffed and puffed on the way back from the shops. But though I did my best to communicate to her that I wanted to do whatever I could to help – I could probably even carry the shopping bags if she rigged up some kind of harness – she didn't understand what I was trying to say.

Though Kenton was gone and we no longer had to

worry about the house being covered in dog hair, Tuesday
still took a moment or two to groom me every day. When
I lay my head against her belly now, I could feel the baby
moving. Once, he kicked me right in the ear. I was sure
he was a 'he' quite early on. I don't know how. Call it
canine intuition.

Tuesday talked to Emily every day. Emily also came
round whenever she could and accompanied Tuesday to
her doctor's appointments (unlike Zena, I was not
allowed inside a hospital, no matter how important I was
to Tuesday's mental health and well-being). I learned
that Emily was going to be Tuesday's birthing partner.
Two weeks before Baby Sparrow was due, they were
practising breathing at the kitchen table. They dissolved
into laughter when they noticed that I was panting along
with them.

'Perhaps Stupendo should go into the birthing suite
with you after all,' Emily suggested. 'He's got the panting
thing down pat.'

If there's one thing a dog is good at, it's panting.

'Where's he going to go when you give birth?' Emily
asked. 'We can't just leave him here. You don't know how
long you'll be in labour for. It could be days. Like with
Nicki's first.'

'Don't remind me,' said Tuesday. Emily's sister Nicki
had been in labour for nearly a week with her first baby.
At least that's how she told it.

My two favourite humans came up with a plan that,
when the moment came, Emily would get Elvis to drive
her over in his car. They would pick me and Tuesday up
and, while Emily and Tuesday were at the hospital, I would

hang out with Elvis at his house. It sounded like a good plan. There were no rules at Elvis's place. Not a single piece of soft furnishing was out of bounds. So I was delighted. But suddenly Tuesday looked sad. When she saw that Emily and I were both studying her face, she plastered on a smile but it was unconvincing.

'I know it's not how you wanted it to be,' said Emily. 'Having me in the delivery room instead of . . .' Emily would not say the 'K word'.

'It's OK,' she said. 'It's a great plan. Can you imagine how Kenton would have been in the birthing suite? All that mess and the screaming. He would have hated it and I would have spent all my time worrying that he was hating it when I should have been panting. No, I really don't miss Kenton at all. And he clearly doesn't miss me.'

More than six months had passed since Kenton walked out. Six months without so much as a text. I can't tell you how relieved I was that he'd at least had the decency not to string Tuesday along.

'I've got you. I've got Stupendo.'

I lay my head on her knee. 'And I've got you,' I told her with my eyes.

'If only Stupendo were human,' Emily said. 'He'd make someone a great husband.'

A week later, I was asleep on the bedroom floor when Tuesday woke with a start. She sat up in bed with a swear word. I hadn't heard her swear for a while. She'd made an effort to stop while Kenton was living with us. He didn't think it was 'ladylike'. Anyway, as soon as I heard her swearing, I rushed to her side.

'It's OK,' she said. 'Nothing's happening. It's too early. Braxton Hicks.'

I had no idea what she meant but I allowed myself to be calmed by the quiet authority with which she spoke. We settled down for an extra half hour of snoozing.

Since Tuesday's bump had got as big as a beach ball, she hadn't sat down on the back step to groom me. Instead, she would sit on the bench in the garden. That's where we headed after breakfast. It was a beautiful early July day. Much warmer than usual. As Tuesday gently brushed my ears, I watched the newest crew of blackbird fledglings preparing for their first flight. I gave Caligula, who was sitting on top of the neighbour's shed, the side-eye, to let him know that if he tried anything funny, I had him in my sights and would be on him in a heartbeat. Caligula raised his eyebrows at me and soon left for a different garden.

About five minutes in, Tuesday paused in her brushing and clutched at her belly. She swore again. I sat to attention immediately and put my paw on her knee as I looked deep into her face.

'What can I do?' I asked silently.

Her eyes were squeezed tightly shut. I knew she was really in pain this time. I whimpered in sympathy. She stood up carefully. A wet patch spread across the back of her skirt.

'It's OK, Stupendo. It's OK. I know what I'm supposed to do now. It's going to be just fine. This happens thousands of times a day all over the world. No reason why I can't do it too.'

She started panting as she and Emily had done at the

kitchen table. I joined in. As she moved inside the house, Tuesday called Emily on her mobile, but she didn't get beyond a first word before another contraction made her bend double.

'Emily!'

Tuesday dropped the phone on the kitchen floor.

I barked into the receiver to underline the seriousness of the moment.

From out of the phone came Emily's voice, all tinny. 'Hold on, babe. We're on our way.'

With the reassurance that Emily was on her way, Tuesday sat down on the kitchen floor with her back against the fridge-freezer. Then she lay down, with her knees in the air. I licked her face, which was the best way to say 'I'm here for you' under the circumstances. The only way, really.

All the time, the contractions were getting closer and closer together. Tuesday panted like her life depended on it. I panted too and ran frantically from the kitchen to the front door and back again, eager to hear the arrival of reinforcements.

'Come on! Come on!'

Tuesday and I were both willing Emily to be there as quickly as she could.

When Emily let herself into the house with the spare key, I jumped and whined. Elvis was right behind her.

'Good boy, Stupendo. Just like Lassie,' Elvis said.

'Get me to the effing hospital!' Tuesday shrieked from her place on the kitchen floor.

'I think it's too late,' said Emily, when she saw what progress had been made during her absence. 'The baby's already crowning in a serious way. When my sister got to this stage with her second, it only took another two minutes. Just push!'

'What?'

'Push! No time to get you into the car now.'

Elvis grabbed the back of a chair and had to sit down. Suddenly, he did not look well at all.

'Bloody useless,' Emily berated him. 'Go upstairs. Get some towels. And . . . and . . . hot water! And call an ambulance while you're at it! Quick!'

Emily and I stayed by Tuesday's side. Tuesday put her hand on my back and grasped at my fur. And one of my puppy fat rolls. I flinched a bit but understood why she needed to do it and I wanted to help however I could. Tuesday panted. Emily panted. I panted. I panted like I had never panted before.

'You're doing fine, you're doing fine,' Emily said again and again, as Tuesday strained with the contractions. Though I could tell from the adrenaline I smelled in the air that Emily wasn't at all sure that was the truth and neither was I.

But the baby was born just half an hour after Emily and Elvis arrived. Emily gasped as she took his little head and shoulders in her hands to guide him and he was suddenly out in the world. A brand-new human being. Elvis was still faffing around upstairs in search of towels – deliberately, I suspected – so Emily carefully guided the baby out on to her favourite denim jacket, which she had placed on the floor in lieu of the towels that Elvis was too slow to find.

'Show me!' Tuesday pleaded. 'What did I have?'

Emily lifted the baby on to Tuesday's breast. Tuesday was crying. Emily was crying too. The baby let out a fine, big-lunged wail. I stood guard over all of them.

'You've had a boy,' said Emily. 'And he's perfect.'

He really, really was.

Chapter Sixteen

The ambulance arrived within moments of the birth and Emily and Elvis stood back as the paramedics took over, dealing with the umbilical cord and the placenta. Emily and Elvis took me out into the garden to wait with them. I didn't make it easy. They had to drag me by the collar to get me out there. I didn't want to leave Tuesday and the new baby alone for a second.

'You really looked after her, didn't you, Stupendo?' Emily said, as we stood beside the back door. I stared at that door, willing it to open so I could get back on guarding duty.

'You're a braver man than I am, doggo,' said Elvis as he offered me half of the granola bar he'd just found in his pocket.

It'll give you an idea of how seriously I took my duty to Tuesday and the new baby that I gave that granola bar only the merest sniff.

Tuesday and the baby were taken to the hospital by ambulance for a check-up. Emily and Elvis stuck around at number thirteen for the rest of the day. They cleaned up the kitchen and got the house ready for Tuesday's return. They stocked the fridge and made sure I had enough kibble to last a month. Elvis even got out the lawnmower at Emily's behest and tidied up the lawn. I knew it had bothered Tuesday to see it get so scruffy while she felt too big to do it herself.

Though I understood Tuesday was in safe hands, I couldn't settle until she was home. I paced the garden, waiting for her and the baby's return. Elvis took me for a walk but as soon as he let me off my lead, I ran straight back in the direction of Bracken Avenue, cutting our outing short. I had bigger things on my mind that day than a potter around the park.

Late in the afternoon, Emily got a call saying they could pick Tuesday and the baby up from the hospital. She and Elvis didn't take me with them in the car. I waited anxiously by the front door until they got back. Elvis came in first and took hold of my collar to stop me from jumping up. As if I would! Tuesday had Baby Sparrow in her arms. He was wrapped in a soft white blanket. She sat down on the bottom stair and called me over. Gently, she moved the blanket out of the way so that I could see the baby's face. I gazed at him in adoration. He was perfect in every way. I wished I had the words to tell Tuesday how happy seeing him made me.

The story of the baby's arrival went into the local newspaper a few days later. 'Hero dog saves the day in maternity emergency.' It wasn't quite true – Emily did all the really hard work of being a birthing partner while I just panted – but it made a good story. A photographer was despatched to take a photograph of me, Tuesday and the baby sitting on the garden bench where her contractions had started. The story caused quite a stir. When it appeared online, lots of people shared it on social media as an example of much-needed good news in a difficult time (humans are always having a difficult time, it seems to me) and several well-wishers sent boxes of dog treats to the newspaper's office to be passed on to me, which was exciting. Unfortunately, Tuesday told the newspaper editor that I was on a diet so the edible treats had best be sent straight to the local dog rescue charity. Most of the toys too went to the homeless dogs. But after another photo shoot during which I was allowed to choose my favourite from the big pile of donated squeaky toys, I came home with another squeaky Minion to replace the last one, which I'd comprehensively wrecked. I liked his face.

Now that she had met him, Tuesday decided that her son wasn't a 'Sparrow' after all. He was indeed quite a bruiser, weighing in at more than nine pounds. Instead Tuesday called him 'William Stuart'. William because that was her grandfather's name and Stuart in honour of me.

'Because secretly, it's William Stupendo,' she confessed to Emily.

William Stupendo was a living miracle. I loved him from the moment I saw him, just as I loved his mother. Whenever I was allowed to, I gently pressed my nose to his downy soft cheek and breathed in his delicious baby scent. He smelled like family. When he was just two weeks old, I licked the top of his head as he lay on his changing mat and he smiled his first smile. Emily noticed and pointed it out.

'He's too young. It's just wind,' Tuesday said.

But I knew it was a smile. A smile for me.

★　★　★

William Stupendo, as I liked to think of him, quickly turned our lives upside down. Tuesday and I were soon exhausted from lack of sleep but nevertheless, many of my happiest memories are from those earliest days right after Tuesday brought William home from the hospital. We all slept together in the same room and when William cried in the middle of the night, I would usually hear him first and gently nudge Tuesday with my nose to let her know that he was awake. Then I would do my best to entertain him while Tuesday shook herself into wakefulness and climbed out of bed.

I always joined Tuesday for the night feeds. She would sit on the floor with her back to the bed, with William at her breast. I would lay my head in her lap to let her know that they were both safe and protected.

'I'm so glad I have you keeping me company,' she'd tell me. She thought William seemed to settle more quickly when I was around. Sometimes, his chubby little hands would seek out my head. Having my ears twisted or even turned inside out was a small price to pay for knowing that William was glad to have me there.

Tuesday didn't have time to groom me any more but that was OK too. I understood that there were more important things to do now than worry about dog hair on the sofa. There are always more important things to worry about than dog hair on a sofa. Had Kenton known that (and been prepared for the odd sneezing fit) he could have been part of this joy. He did not know what he was missing.

When William was three months old, Tuesday decided it was time that he was christened. She chose Emily and Elvis to be William's godparents.

'And you, Stupendo, are going to be the dog-father.'

Tuesday arranged for the ceremony to take place at the church where she herself had been christened more than thirty years before. It was to be a small affair. Tuesday's father was invited but said he couldn't make it from Spain at such short notice (and to be fair to him, Tuesday did give him very short notice). I could tell Tuesday was disappointed by that but on the day of the christening itself she was excited as she dressed William in the little blue suit that Emily and Elvis had bought for him. I approved of the christening outfit. It included a bow tie with a print of dachshunds on it. A silly-looking breed, in my opinion, but a sort of dog all the same. I'm sure Emily had looked for a tie with Labradors or Staffies on it first.

The vicar, who was a dog lover herself, let me attend the service. When Tuesday carried William up to the font, I was right behind. Elvis held my lead. I sat when the vicar told me to and lifted my paw to show I was paying attention and agreeing when Emily and Elvis promised to renounce the devil and be positive influences in little William's life. Of course I would renounce the devil too. Whatever that meant.

'And be a good boy,' the vicar added when I took my vows.

Wasn't I always?

At the party afterwards, everyone wanted to tell me what an excellent dog I'd been when William was born. It was lovely to have so much attention. Almost as much as William was getting!

When the christening cake was brought in, I'll admit I

got a little distracted, hoping that someone might slip me a piece. I'd already worked out who were the softest touches in the room – the vicar was one of them – and had done quite well on canapés and sandwiches. But in the end, I didn't need to beg for a piece of cake because Emily revealed that she had made me one of my very own. As she put it down on the floor for me, she explained to Tuesday that she'd made it from a dog-friendly recipe that was low in sugar and high in fibre but nonetheless still delicious, in my view. She told me directly that the icing on top said 'Dog-Father', but by that point, I'd already eaten as far as 'ther'. It was a nice thought.

That Christmas, William's first and my fourth, was the sort of Christmas that Tuesday had always hoped for. This time I knew not to pee on the tree when it was brought into the house. Once Tuesday had decorated it, with the help of Elvis and Emily, I showed William the delight of gently nudging a bauble so that he could see his own little nose grow bigger and smaller in its curves. I kept him amused for hours that way.

Christmas lunch was at our house, with Emily and Elvis in attendance. There was a tense moment when Emily and Elvis argued over who should carve the turkey. Thankfully, Elvis won. He wasn't very good at it, as Emily had suspected, but I knew it would be better for me. Just as I'd done the year before, when Emily's father was in charge, I made sure that every tenth piece Elvis carved went straight into my mouth.

William had his own Christmas dinner, puréed. Tuesday was persuaded by Emily to purée the sprouts separately.

'I've read that sprouts taste different to children,' she said. 'Really bitter. He might not like them.'

I was secretly gratified when William had the same reaction to sprouts as I did, spitting out his first mouthful of sprout purée right on to Elvis's Christmas jumper. Tuesday and Emily had cunningly delegated Christmas feeding duty to him.

That New Year's Eve Tuesday spent at home with me and William. I didn't think either Tuesday or I would be able to stay awake until midnight, but at ten o'clock, Emily and Elvis arrived with a bottle of champagne. They'd been planning to spend the night out on the town, 'but decided we'd have a much better time with William and Stupendo,' as Elvis said. I was delighted. They'd also brought snacks.

Emily reminded Tuesday of the Christmas night, in Emily's childhood bedroom, when they'd looked at old letters and photographs and wished for a different sort of year ahead.

'As it certainly turned out to be.'

'Very different,' Tuesday agreed.

'What are you going to wish for this year?' Emily asked.

'Much more of the same sort of surprising happiness,' Tuesday said.

I thumped my tail on the floor in agreement. To happiness, indeed.

The other dogs at the park loved William. One February afternoon, as Tuesday sat on the bench with William beside her in his pushchair, I brought Zena across to meet him. Andrew was busy on his phone, as was Tuesday. Andrew's expression was fixed in its usual frown.

When William saw Zena he stretched his fat little hands out towards her in delight and giggled as she gently licked his fingers.

'It'll be nice when he's big enough to play with you properly,' Zena said to me.

'Human babies are a bit slow to get going,' I concurred. When I was eight months old, I could have run for miles. William still couldn't stand without assistance.

But it wasn't long after that afternoon in the park before William started to crawl and then to try to walk. He had a smart little trolley on wheels full of wooden bricks that Emily had bought him to help him find his balance but it turned out that he preferred to use me instead. Occasionally, he grabbed a handful of fur just a little too hard as he used me to haul himself to his feet, but I didn't mind. I was proud to be able to help him get up and take those early steps.

I remember the first time it happened. Tuesday had been changing William on his mat on the living room floor when she realised that a pan was boiling over in the kitchen. She got up to deal with it, leaving William on his back. I was sitting nearby. With a determined expression on his sweet face, he rolled towards me and hauled himself up, draping his arms over my back so that when I stood – slowly, very slowly – William was suddenly standing too.

Tuesday's mouth dropped open in delighted surprise when she came back into the living room and saw us. I took a step forward. William duly took a step sideways. I did it again. William did likewise.

'You're . . . you're walking!' Tuesday said to her son.

William giggled. My favourite sound.

'You're walking! Oh my goodness.' When William lost his grip on me and landed on his bottom, Tuesday picked him up and danced him around the room. I danced along with them.

Emily confirmed that at just nine months old, William was a prodigy, well advanced of other children his age. I could not have been more proud.

Every day after that, William and I went a little further. I could feel him holding on to me less tightly as his confidence grew. Until one day, while he and I were out in the garden, he let go of me altogether and took three steady and determined steps completely on his own.

The squirrels and the blackbirds chattered their approval. Even Caligula, who had been watching from the top of the fence, was moved to mutter, 'Nice work, human bean.'

We were such a great team, William, Tuesday and I. I had never been so happy. I didn't even mind when William got his first teeth and used my ears for chewing practice. I was as happy as any dog who ever walked the earth to be that little boy's dog-father. I thought it would last forever.

Now, sitting on the floor of William's bedroom as a dead dog, watching him sleep, I felt angry enough to howl at the thought of the future joys that had been cruelly snatched away from us by my untimely death. In life, I had not been an angry sort of dog at all. I took it for granted that the people and other animals I knew were good at heart and that ultimately everything worked out for the best. I was even grateful to Kenton. Though he had not made my life easier and he had made Tuesday doubt herself in so many ways, without him there would have been no William.

Yes, it used to be that I could see the silver lining in every cloud, but hearing Caligula and Zena talking in the garden had shaken me to the bones. The whole of the next day, I replayed what I had heard and tried to make sense of it. I felt so terribly alone.

Chapter Seventeen

Now

Caligula didn't look as though he had anything particularly heavy on his mind when he ventured into my garden that evening and settled down in his usual spot on the shed roof. I saw him from my place on William's windowsill. I stayed out of sight behind the curtain while I summoned all the energy I needed for a truly impressive feat of teleportation. I closed my eyes tightly and wished myself right in front of him. As I materialised at the end of his nose, Caligula's fur stood out in terrified spikes like the fur on a cat in a cartoon.

'Stop doing that,' he said, barely keeping the edge of fright out of his voice. 'I'm not as young as I was. You could give me a heart attack.'

He backed up. I loomed over him. He backed up again. I moved so that I was still just an inch from his face, growling all the time.

'What is wrong with you?' he asked me as he tucked in his chin to get just a little more space from me. 'You were never this mad when you were alive.'

'When I was alive, I thought I could trust all the animals

around here to ultimately be honest and kind. Even you, Caligula. Even you. But now I know differently.'

'What?'

Caligula pretended he didn't have a clue what I was talking about.

'I suppose it was stupid of me ever to take the word of a cat . . . I followed you last night,' I told him. 'I followed you to number twenty-four and I saw you and Zena in the garden. To think I considered her a trusted friend when really she's my killer!'

Caligula raised his chin and looked away from me. 'So it *was* you. I thought it might be. And you heard . . .'

'*Everything*,' I said.

'Well you can't have done,' said Caligula. 'Because if you had, you wouldn't be playing the tough dog with me now. And you would know what you're saying about Zena is ridiculous.'

'She said she killed me!'

'She said it was her *fault*. Which it wasn't, by the way. How would she have done it? I know guide dogs have pretty impressive skills, but so far as I know, they are not taught to drive. And Andrew doesn't drive either, for obvious reasons.'

'But she said . . .'

'Dogs,' Caligula tutted. 'You're like beginners at chess who can only think three moves ahead. You and Zena. Zena thinks she killed you because the car that hit you was a taxi that had just brought Andrew home, and Andrew was in a taxi because Zena was not feeling well enough to work. And she was not well enough to work because she ate something she shouldn't have.'

'Zena never eats anything she shouldn't!'

Caligula just raised his eyebrows at that.

'Not usually anyway,' I admitted.

'Well, she did this time. And there you have it. She ate something she found on the side of the road, she got sick, she had to have a night off. Andrew had to go out anyway so he took his white cane and ordered a taxi. The taxi that brought him back is the one that flattened you.'

'But . . .'

'That doesn't mean Zena killed you, right? And that's what I keep telling her. Now she thinks you're hanging around in limbo to have your revenge. I told her that's ridiculous. I told her that you were never the vengeful type. Though now I'm not so sure.'

I still loomed over him.

'Could you please take just one step back? I have personal space issues.'

I sat down, giving Caligula space to breathe at last. He gave me a small smile. It was almost fond.

'So as I said, I've told Zena she's crazy to blame herself for your being knocked over. At worst, it was an unfortunate coincidence. But perhaps you should tell her yourself.'

'How can I? She ran away from me in the park.'

'We'll visit her at home,' Caligula said. 'I'll go ahead. Tell her that you come in peace.'

Was I ready for that?

Caligula read my mind. 'It wasn't her fault, Stupendo. Or Andrew's. As you said yourself when we broke the news to you that you were dead the other morning, you were never usually outside on your own.'

Then did that mean it was my fault?

'It was an accident!' Caligula went on. 'And no, I still don't know why you haven't passed over the Rainbow Bridge. Your decision, I suppose. You just love Tuesday too much or something like that. Come on. Let's see Zena.'

My anger was already fading into something . . . something fluffier. Zena was my favourite dog in the world. Caligula was right that there was no obvious reason why she had turned murderess.

'She had no motive,' said Caligula, seemingly reading my mind once more. 'And no means.'

When we got to number twenty-four, Caligula went ahead, as he'd suggested. I watched from the shadows as he went up to the French windows that led on to the living room. Zena was sleeping in her usual place on the rug in front of the fire. Caligula put his paw on the glass. Even with my supersonic hearing, I didn't hear him make a noise, but all the same, Zena suddenly sat up and trotted over to the window as if summoned by name.

'Stupendo?' Caligula called me over at the same time. I saw Zena start at the sight of me but Caligula reassured her. 'It's OK. I've told him everything. He just wants to talk.'

'It's true,' I said. 'I just want to talk to you.'

Visibly relaxing, Zena pressed her nose against the glass and I did the same from the other side. As we both stepped back again, I noticed with dismay that her nose had left a little heart-shaped smudge in condensation. Mine had not.

'Oh, Stu,' she said. 'I'm so, so sorry.'

Zena persuaded Andrew that she needed to go outside and he obliged so that, unknown to him, Zena could meet me and Caligula in the garden. For the first minute, I couldn't get a word in edgewise. Zena's apologies kept tumbling out. She had, as I suspected, run away from me in the park that day because she really did believe she had caused my death.

'It was an accident,' Caligula said.

'But it was an accident that would never have happened. If I had been with Andrew, we would have been on the bus . . . If only I hadn't eaten that dog treat I found on the street at the top of your driveway. But it was such a tiny thing. I didn't think it would do any harm. I'm so ashamed of myself. Stupendo, have you ever known me to just pick up something on the street and eat it? I don't know what I was thinking. Well, if I'm honest, I was in a mood. After what happened at your house that afternoon.'

'What happened that afternoon?'

'You don't remember?'

'I don't remember anything.' I was about to ask Zena to fill me in but Andrew was on the back step, calling her back inside.

'I've got to go. Come back soon and I'll tell you everything I know.'

She pressed her nose to mine again – or rather, held her nose towards mine – and shivered.

Caligula made a gagging sound at our small show of affection.

'Furball,' he muttered when I glared at him.

Chapter Eighteen

I was frustrated that we'd had such a brief window of time to talk to Zena, especially as our conversation had left me even more confused than before.

'What happened the afternoon of the day I died? What happened at my house?' I asked Caligula. 'You must know.'

'I don't do afternoons,' he said. Presumably he meant in the way that some people don't do mornings.

'Why can't I remember?'

'You always had a pretty bad memory. I could do that trick with the French windows three times in a row some days. Like a goldfish . . .'

I glared at him. He had the grace to look a little ashamed.

'Look, come for a walk,' he said. 'I could use the company. And if you stop thinking so hard about the day you died for a while, then perhaps more of the details will come back to you. That's what I find works for me.'

What did I have to lose? Tuesday and William were asleep. Zena too had to go to bed. We set off on what Caligula explained was his regular nightly circuit.

I followed Caligula to number seventeen – Mary Brown's house, he informed me. We stood on a windowsill and looked into a kitchen that was very different from the one at Tuesday's house. Tuesday's kitchen had fairly new cabinets. Here at number seventeen, everything looked old, though it was spotlessly clean. At a table, bleached and worn like driftwood from years of careful scrubbing, Mary Brown sat with her knitting.

Now that I was able to get closer, I recognised Mary. I'd seen her in her front garden on many occasions. The front garden of number seventeen was beautiful. Like Tuesday, Mary had green fingers. Every spring her flower beds were full of flowers every colour of the rainbow and some besides. The bees and the butterflies loved her.

I'd seen Mary often as Tuesday and I headed out for a walk and yet we'd never really stopped to talk to her. Tuesday would say hello if Mary was looking in her direction, and vice versa, but the conversation never went any further than that. I don't know why. One of those human things. As a result, I knew nothing much about her. Unlike Caligula. He seemed to know quite a bit.

Mary was knitting a small hat. A child's hat.

'For her grandson Toby,' said Caligula. 'Who lives on the other side of the world.'

'How do you know?' I asked.

'She talks about him, of course.'

'To you?'

'Why's that so surprising? I'm a good listener. And I *observe*. There are pictures on the mantelpiece, see? One of Mary getting married back in the day, another of her and her husband with two little girls, and a much newer one of her standing on a beach with a little boy in her arms. She wishes he lived closer.'

Just then Mary got up to change the channel on the

radio, which was also on the mantelpiece. While she was standing there, she kissed her fingertips and pressed kisses to all three photographs. She wiped the picture of herself and the little boy with the sleeve of her cardigan and smiled a smile that was both happy and sad at the same time. I'd seen Tuesday smile the same way when she kissed William goodnight sometimes. I felt a little pinch in my heart at the thought of it.

'I drop by most days,' Caligula told me. 'She feeds me. The good stuff. Out of a pouch, not a tin. Sometimes she even gives me fresh salmon. Sushi quality.'

As though she'd heard us on the windowsill, Mary looked up in our direction. She beamed.

'Can she see me?' I asked. I wagged my tail enthusi-astically.

'No. No one can see you, Stupendo. Like I said. No humans. But she can definitely see me.' Caligula put his paw on the windowpane and gave a little mew. It was a plaintive mew that suggested, 'I haven't been fed in days.'

Mary opened the back door and leaned out.

'What are you doing out so late, Mr Boots?' she asked my feline friend. 'And why won't you use your cat flap?'

'More fun not to,' Caligula told me with a purr.

He jumped down from the windowsill and wound his way around Mary's legs in a very attentive manner.

'I've got something for you,' she said. 'Wait there, Bootsie.'

'Tell anyone she calls me Bootsie and I will kill you,' Caligula told me.

'I'm already dead,' I reminded him.

'Though funnily enough, Caligula means "Little Boot" in Latin.'

'How do you know this stuff?' I asked.

'Perhaps this isn't my first time around the sun.'

He was trying to be mysterious. I didn't rise to it.

Mary couldn't hear us. She carried on talking to Caligula alone, 'I saved this specially. You like this, don't you, Bootsie-poo?'

Mary had returned to the back door with a piece of smoked salmon. Caligula wolfed it down while Mary reminded him of his manners. When she'd gone back inside, I reminded him of his manners too.

'You might have saved me some.'

Caligula gave me the side-eye. 'You're really not getting the hang of this being dead thing, are you?'

The next house Caligula took me to was occupied by three young women. That night, only one was home.

'My favourite,' said Caligula. He told me her name was Zoe. He explained that, like Mary, Zoe fed Caligula whenever she saw him.

'She calls me Gorgeous George.'

But Zoe did not notice her Gorgeous George on her bedroom windowsill that evening. She was trying on clothes in front of a long mirror, turning this way and that, frowning as she caught sight of herself at what she obviously thought were unflattering angles.

'It's a bit late to be going out,' I observed.

'Oh, she never goes out,' said Caligula. 'She just gets dressed up like she's off to a ball, puts her make-up on and then does this for hours and hours and hours . . .' Caligula tipped his head towards the window.

Seeming satisfied with the way she looked at last, Zoe

applied another slick of lip gloss then posed in front of the looking glass and snapped a couple of photographs. She inspected and deleted them, then fluffed up her hair and posed again for a new set.

'She's never happy with the pictures she takes. She's never happy with herself. She's an "influencer",' Caligula explained. 'Or rather, that's what she wants to be. She's actually a temp at the council's refuse and recycling department. Her real life bores her rigid, so she posts pictures of herself in what she's wearing to impress people she'll never meet. Tomorrow she'll take the clothes back to the shop for a refund and start again.'

'Sounds like hard work,' I said. I was glad that the only thing I had to do to look good was wake up and shake my ears. Tuesday did once try to dress me up but I let her know pretty quickly that it wasn't my idea of fun, running down to the bottom of the garden and ripping to shreds the stupid elf hat she was expecting me to wear for Christmas. No dog was ever improved by a hat.

Caligula agreed. 'Zoe bought me an outfit once. Needless to say I didn't let her get anywhere near me with the thing. I'm afraid I might even have scratched her to make my point. Though only lightly. But as soon as she turned her back for a second, I peed on that cat dress like my life depended on it. I know she was disappointed but a cat's got to maintain his elegance and dignity.'

'Absolutely,' I concurred.

Just then Caligula's eyes bulged from his head and he hacked up a furball. I politely looked away.

Chapter Nineteen

After we left Zoe's house, we carried on down the street all the way to number thirty-one.

'This is Derren,' said Caligula as we looked in on the occupant there. 'Like Zoe, he never goes out.'

The dining room of number thirty-one had been converted into an office. Derren was glued to a screen, like so many humans seemed to be most of the time, but he wasn't watching anything exciting. At least, not so far as I could see. Still, he stared intently as a stream of figures poured down the page. Occasionally, he looked at another smaller screen, which showed a picture of lines. Sometimes, the lines made him nod, sometimes the lines made him frown. They all looked the same to me.

'During the day, he's always on the phone and he does a lot of shouting,' Caligula explained. 'He's a trader and I gather shouting's an important part of the job.'

The larger screen, neglected for a few minutes while Derren went to make himself a cup of instant coffee, suddenly showed a picture of Caligula on his back with his white belly flash on show.

'That's you!'

'Of course it is, I live here. Officially.'

This was the place where Caligula was Caligula.

'How embarrassing that he insists on using that picture. Not my best angle, as Zoe would understand. But we'd better go. Derren will be looking for me soon. Keeps trying to make me wear a satellite collar so he knows where I am at all times.'

'So, let me get this straight: you have three different people who think you belong to them?'

'A cat *belongs* to nobody, Stupendo. Belonging is a dog thing. Dogs have owners. Cats make beneficial alliances. I get food and warmth and the human beings get my company. When I feel like it. It works both ways.'

We stayed outside Derren's house for a little while longer. I noticed there was a big plastic mat on the floor in one corner of the room, covered in what looked like brightly coloured toys. Buttons.

'What's that?'

'Oh. *That.*' Caligula rolled his eyes. 'That is my AAC device.'

I had no idea what he meant.

'It stands for Augmented and Alternative Communication. Those buttons – when I press them – make a sound. A word. In human. Derren is trying to teach me to communicate with him. I communicate with him all the time, of course, but he has a limited grasp of cat.

'He saw a video online. An American speech therapist taught her dog to talk with a board just like that. Derren thought he would see if the same method might work on me. He got the buttons a couple of months ago. Now, before he does anything, like get me a treat or open the door to the living room, he tells me what he's going to do by pressing the appropriate button. Food. Outside. Bed. That kind of thing. The idea being I'll learn to associate the word with the action – as if I haven't already worked it out – and in turn be able to press the correct button to ask for the things I need.'

'That's really cool.'

I could think of nothing better than being able to talk human and be understood.

'It would be cool if he ever took any notice of me when I do talk,' said Caligula. 'But whenever I press "hungry", he just looks at me and tells me I can't be. What is the point of giving me a means to communicate with him in his own language if he's not going to take me at my word when I do? Still, it's better than when he tries to speak my language. You have never heard such a terrible sound. All that yowling.'

'But that's what cat sounds like, isn't it?' I said. Dangerously.

Caligula looked at me with pity. 'Do you think all your barks sound the same, Stupido?'

'Well, obviously not. There are different barks for different occasions.'

'It's exactly the same for cats. The language of my people is a complicated and beautiful thing. It is not *yowling*. It's nuanced and musical. To hear it mangled on the tongue of a human being is one of the most painful experiences a cat ever has to endure.' He squinted his big yellow eyes. Just the thought of it seemed to pain him.

'So, it's lucky that he's teaching you human,' I suggested.

'Here's hoping that one day soon he'll provide me with the buttons I need to tell him "for the love of all that is

holy, please don't speak my sacred tongue ever again".
Want to come in and have a nose?' Caligula asked me
then.

'Of course,' I said.

'You can watch me talk to him. Should be fun.'

Caligula pushed his way through the cat flap, letting it
swing back into my face as he did so. Fortunately, I didn't
have a three-dimensional face to hit any more. The flap
whooshed straight through my ghostly muzzle, which was
disconcerting but didn't hurt. I followed Caligula into the
dining room. He announced his arrival with a short yowl.
Hearing that, Derren yowled back and I understood at
once why it was so painful to Caligula's ears.

'You see,' Caligula muttered to me in an aside. 'I said,
"I'm back, *Patron*. Break out the treats." He thinks he
said, "Hello, Caligula." What he actually said was, "Come
any closer and I'll scratch your eyes out."'

'He said all that in one yowl?'

'As I told you, the feline language is infinitely complicated and complex.'

I blinked. It certainly was.

Caligula headed for the soundboard and surveyed the
coloured buttons.

'Now what shall I say tonight?' he asked himself.

Derren was watching eagerly. It was strange indeed to
be standing right behind Caligula and yet not have Derren
glance in my direction. Not even when I wagged my tail
at him. Not even when I gave a little yip.

'What are you doing?' Caligula asked me when I yipped.

'Testing that humans definitely can't see or hear me,'
I said.

'They definitely can't hear or see you,' Caligula confirmed. 'Derren can barely see me. He's ruined his eyesight, staring at that screen all day.'

In any case, Derren was too interested in getting Caligula to talk to him via the soundboard to notice anything else at all. While Caligula hesitated, Derren used the board to speak first, pressing three buttons in quick succession.

'Inside? Bed? Happy?'

He said the words out loud as he pressed them.

Caligula took another moment to walk around the buttons before he pressed, 'No. Inside. Food. Want.'

'Let's see what he makes of that,' Caligula said to me.

Derren pressed, 'Food. No.'

'What?' Caligula was outraged. 'I want something to eat. Really, I couldn't have been clearer. Could I have been any clearer, Stupendo?'

'No, Caligula,' I had to agree.

'Food,' he pressed again. 'Yes. Food. Yes.'

Derren spoke to Caligula in human language, without pressing the buttons this time. 'No way, Caligula. You know what the vet said. One meal a day until you're back at your fighting weight. You're not really hungry. You could live off your fat reserves for a month.'

'If only there were a button for "arsehole".' Caligula tried again. 'Food. Yes. Want.'

Derren shook his finger and pressed 'Bed' to underline the gesture.

Then Caligula tried a look I had not seen before. He made his eyes as big and round as the marbles I'd once swallowed in the children's playground at the park. (That was a mistake. Tuesday had to take me for an X-ray. Luckily, the vet decided there was no need to operate but the next three poos were challenging, to say the least.) Anyway, I guessed that Caligula was trying to look appealing, or perhaps just pathetic. Whichever would work best to bend Derren to his will. But Derren was not to be persuaded.

'Come on, Caligula,' he said. 'You'll feel much better when you've shifted that belly and you're not so *rotund*.'

'Rotund!' I sniggered. Caligula shot me a look. Derren saw the look, if not its target. He suddenly stood up, looking worried.

'What's there?' he asked. 'I can't see anything. There's nothing there. Caligula, I wish you would stop trying to freak me out like that, looking into space like you're seeing a ghost.'

Caligula gave me another look that said, 'See?'

'I know you're just pretending something's there to upset me.' Derren tried one more phrase on the sound-board. 'Bed. Happy?' Then he patted a soft fake-fur-covered cushion that was presumably meant to be where Caligula spent the night.

'I don't know how I'll ever make him understand that I am never going to sleep on that thing,' Caligula told me. 'Why would I? It smells weird and makes crunchy sounds when I sit on it.'

I gave the cushion a sniff. Caligula was right. It smelled of the plastic bag it must have once been packaged in.

'Bed?' Derren tried once more. Plaintively.

'Nope. Let's go,' Caligula said to me.

Then he turned his back on Derren, lifting his tail

towards him in a gesture that I knew to be full of disrespect. He'd done it to me enough times. Caligula tossed another yowl over his shoulder as he made his way to the cat flap. Derren yowled in return.

'Oh, for crying out loud,' said Caligula, when we were both in the garden again.

'What did he say that time?' I asked. 'What did you say?'

'I said, "Later, loser." I think he thinks he said, "Good night." What he actually said was, "In two weeks' time it will be the start of sardine season."'

'Will it?' I asked. 'I was always partial to a sardine.'

'What do you think? Of course it's not sardine season.'

It didn't seem that obvious to me.

'Derren wouldn't even know a sardine from a sprat. He has no idea what he's saying. He's just stringing any old words together. It's so insulting!'

Derren leaned out of his back door and yowled again, presumably in a last-ditch attempt to persuade Caligula to come back.

'And what was that?' I wanted to know.

Caligula stiffened his tail. 'You do not want to know. But put it this way: if I thought he actually knew what he'd said, Derren and every last member of his family would be dead by morning. And I am not a bit *rotund*. This – this "belly" is my primordial pouch. It protects my internal organs in battle. Rotund! I should smother him while he sleeps . . .'

Caligula came with me back to number thirteen. We sat together on the roof of the shed as I ran through everything I could remember in the run up to my death. My memories stopped tantalisingly short. A few days short at least.

I was bemoaning my luck when, glancing down towards the patio, I saw the unmistakeable shape of a rat. My rat! The one who had helped me escape the shed after Caligula tricked me in there.

'Hey!' I shouted. 'Hey! Little rat!'

Caligula slowly turned to see who I was talking to. When he saw the little rat himself, his face was suddenly serious.

The rat stopped and looked up at us. Her eyes glittered in the light from the moon. But she didn't seem to want to talk. I don't suppose my being with Caligula helped. She turned and scurried away.

'How do you know that rat?' Caligula asked.

'She helped me get out of the shed.'

'On the day we told you that you were dead?'

I nodded.

'Thing is, Stupendo – that little rat is dead too. She died the same day as you did.'

'I thought no one knew of another animal who hadn't passed straight over to the Rainbow Kingdom?'

'Until this very minute, that was true.'

'Then I need to talk to her!' I said. 'I need to find out why she hasn't gone over either. Perhaps we can help one another!'

I scrambled down from the shed roof but the little rat had long since disappeared.

Caligula jumped down beside me. He looked thoughtful.

'Stupendo, I think if you want to know why you died,

you need to know why you were outside in the first place. That's where the answer lies.'

'But I told you, I don't remember anything about that day.'

'Then start with what you do remember. Go back as far as you can. That's what a human detective would do.'

I wasn't used to Caligula talking to me like this. As if I were an equal.

'Everything that happens in life is the result of a long series of tiny choices that nudge us in one direction or another,' he mused. 'Goodnight, Stupendo. And good luck.'

He hadn't even called me Stupido! He must be serious.

'Goodnight.'

Chapter Twenty

Back back back . . . Was that where I would find the answers? Returned to my sentry post in William's bedroom, I thought back as far as I could.

In those early days as a family of three, Tuesday and I made an excellent parenting team. I could smell a wet nappy from three streets away and let Tuesday know accordingly. I made sure that any baby food spillages were swiftly cleared away and would even lick William's face and hands clean after he'd finished eating to save Tuesday having to find the wipes (I liked to think of myself as the eco alternative). Whenever William cried, I stuck my wet nose against his soft cheek and he would always stop for a moment or two and consider whether he was actually upset. He usually wasn't. In fact, I soon began to suspect that William had cottoned on that crying was the best way to get my attention if I was otherwise occupied.

Between us, Tuesday and I had William's every need covered. Except that we still needed money to buy food and keep the roof over our heads. Unfortunately, money was one thing that I couldn't help with.

'I've got to go back to work,' Tuesday told Emily when William was about ten months old.

Tuesday had taken a step back from her gardening business two months before William was born. It was just too much for her to be digging and trimming and lugging plant pots and dead branches when she was so heavily pregnant. Then, after William arrived, of course she needed to focus entirely on him. Tuesday's regular clients had reacted with understanding when she told them that she would need to take maternity leave, but the fact is that their grass did not stop growing while Tuesday wasn't working. Lawns needed mowing. Hedges still needed to be shaped. Roses needed to be pruned and new flowers planted for the spring. Thus when Tuesday was ready to go back to work, having found William a place with an old school friend who had a nursery nearby, she discovered that her list of clients was much depleted. They'd found alternative options.

Tuesday needed to start advertising to build up her client base again. One evening, I amused William in his bouncer chair while Tuesday created a new flyer for her business. She'd found in the past that it was the most successful way to get new work. The people who most needed help with the gardening tended to be older and were less likely to find her on the internet. Using flyers also meant that Tuesday could target more local work so that travel costs didn't eat into our already tight budget.

The following day Tuesday had copies of the flyer printed and we set about distributing them. It was hard work. Tuesday discovered that many of our neighbours had unfriendly letter boxes that nipped at the end of her fingers. She called Emily to complain.

'Why don't you stick some in shop windows?' Emily suggested. That was how she had advertised her new physiotherapy business since she'd set up on her own. Emily told Tuesday which places she thought had the most footfall.

One of the shops on the list was SuperSave, the local minimart with the guide dog collection box outside. Tuesday tied me to the dog loop while she went inside to ask if she could put one of her flyers in the window.

I hated being tied up outside shops. As a younger dog, I made my annoyance clear. If it didn't work to make Tuesday hurry back to me, it would at least attract the attention of a passer-by who might slip me a snack to make up for my distress. I'd got some good treats outside SuperSave in my time, using this method. Bits of sandwiches and crisps. Even a whole sausage roll once. The kid cried when I grabbed it after he dropped it on the floor but the three-second rule applied. If he couldn't pick it up within three seconds, then it was officially mine. His mother wouldn't have let him eat it anyway.

There was however one unfortunate occasion when another child dropped a piece of bubble gum while talking to me and I snuffled it up before he had time to say, 'Noooo! Don't eat that!'

I swallowed the gum without chewing and it probably would have gone through my system without causing any ill effect but the child's mother told Tuesday what had happened and Tuesday, not knowing what bubble gum might do to a young dog, took me straight from SuperSave to the vet.

'You again?' the vet said when he saw me. Thank goodness Tuesday had taken out insurance. 'Stupendo, you need to be more discerning about what you eat.'

I didn't know what the vet was on about. I was very discerning. By that age I'd already discerned that I didn't like sprouts.

Anyway, this time, while I waited for Tuesday and William, the only person to pass by on the street was a young woman who was so engrossed in her phone screen that she almost tripped over me. Having sniffed all around the dog ring and discovered nothing new on the canine grapevine, I sat down again and began the warm-up for a whimper. What was taking Tuesday so long? But just as I was about to begin the first verse of the song that Tuesday so hated to hear, I caught a familiar scent on the air.

Zena!

She and Andrew were walking towards me. I hadn't seen Zena for a while. I almost wagged my tail off to let her know how pleased I was to see her.

Because she was on her harness, Zena could only nod in recognition as she and Andrew carried on into SuperSave. I hoped they were dropping in on their way to the park and that Zena and I could have a proper conversation there later on. I thought that was where we were headed next.

What I didn't know at this point was that, having arranged with the store manager that her flyer would be displayed on the board in the window, Tuesday had decided she might as well pick up some shopping. We needed the usual things – milk, eggs, bread.

Andrew, too, was shopping for essentials. Zena led him to a shop assistant who guided Andrew to the items he needed. Once Andrew had all his shopping, he asked the assistant to walk him in the direction of the cashiers. Tuesday was already in a queue. Zena joined it. Pulling my lead to its fullest length, I could see them from the door.

'Look at that,' said the shop assistant who had helped Andrew find his milk and veg. 'Your dog chose the shortest queue. She's very clever.'

Indeed she was. Zena had chosen to stand right behind Tuesday.

As I watched, Zena gently nudged Tuesday on the back of the leg. Tuesday tried to ignore her. Zena nudged her again. William strained to turn round in his pushchair and said, 'Do, do, do!', which I knew was short for 'dog'. He was pointing at Zena as he said it. Zena gave a little whine.

'Zena, what's the matter?' Andrew asked her. 'You're being really strange today.'

'I'm not doing anything to encourage her,' Tuesday said quickly.

'I'm sorry. Are you talking to me?'

'Your dog keeps nudging me like she wants me to stroke her or something but I swear I'm not doing anything to make her do that. I can see she's got her harness on. I'm just standing here with my baby waiting to pay for my shopping.'

'Do I know you?'

'No,' Tuesday lied. 'But I understand that you should never distract a working guide dog and so I want you to know that I'm just standing here minding my own business while your dog keeps nudging the back of my legs with her nose.'

'Zena.' Andrew pulled her back a little. 'Stop bothering the other customers.'

The cashier had finished ringing up the shopping of the person ahead of Tuesday. Tuesday piled everything from her own basket on to the conveyor belt and hopped from foot to foot as the cashier slowly, ever so slowly, passed each item across the scanner.

'I'm in a bit of a hurry,' she said to the cashier. It didn't make any difference at all. The cashier moved at her usual glacial speed. And then, when the shopping had all been packed away, the first card Tuesday tried to use wouldn't work.

'Sorry, sorry,' she muttered as she tried another one. Why was everything taking so long?

Then, just as she was about to get away . . .

'Hang on,' said Andrew. 'I remember now. I *do* know you. I recognise your voice. You're the woman from the pedestrian crossing, aren't you? The one who called me an arse.'

The cashier was agog. 'I read about that on Twitter! I follow you and your dog,' she explained to Andrew. She turned back to Tuesday and fixed her with a glare. 'Unbelievable. So you're the one who called him an arse, eh?'

'Yes,' said Tuesday. 'I did. And I'm very sorry for having done so. It's not like me at all, but if you'll forgive me for saying so, he was *being* an arse.'

'How so?' The cashier wanted to know more.

'We were standing at the crossing and I made the simple mistake of patting his dog on the head when she looked at me, and he talked to me like I was an idiot. All he had to say was, "Please don't pet my dog while she's working," but he went on and on about it and, as anyone can see – well, as you and I can see – that guide dog is not entirely blameless in all this! It's *she* who won't leave *me* alone!'

The cashier looked from Tuesday to Zena and back again.

'But you called him an arse, right?'

'Yes, I did!' Tuesday exclaimed. 'And it won't happen again, but when people act like arses they should expect that from time to time other people will call them out on it. So there.'

Before Andrew could jump in, Tuesday grabbed her bags and fled from the shop. She was so discombobulated that she almost forgot that she and William had brought me out with them, even though she had to walk right by me.

I barked at her to come back and untie me.

'Come on, Stupendo. Let's get out of here,' she said.

As we walked away at high speed, I looked back over my shoulder at Zena, who was guiding Andrew out of the shop door. Like me, she was utterly confused by the way another chance meeting between Tuesday and Andrew had managed to unfold so badly.

For the rest of the day, Tuesday was in the same sort of strange mood she'd been in after the original incident at the crossing back before William was born. It was clear to me that she hadn't wanted to get into another argument with Andrew, and the same probably went for him too.

In which case, why hadn't they just apologised to each other and laughed the whole thing off? Everyone would have been so much happier. Humans! Sometimes hedge-hogs were easier to understand.

Once Tuesday had distributed the flyers, all we could do was wait for a call. And wait. And wait. And wait. In the meantime, Tuesday paid some attention to our own garden, adding more pretty flowers for the bees and the butterflies. I knew to be extra respectful to the bees, having made the mistake of chasing – and catching – one, when I was just a pup. My nose swelled up and I looked like a Shar Pei for days. Butterflies were less dangerous, of course, but I didn't chase them either. I just liked to watch them going about their fluttery business, as I marvelled that they'd once been caterpillars. I would never have believed it if Merle and the squirrels hadn't told me what had happened to a caterpillar I befriended one spring. I thought he'd ghosted me.

Then Tuesday *did* get a call about a garden renovation and, even better, it was from someone who lived on our street. She told Emily all about it.

'He's just moved into the house with the cherry tree in the front garden. The one where Mr Harris used to live. You know, Mr Harris. His daughter Kelly was in the sixth form when we started secondary school.'

I remembered Mr Harris. He had a Volvo. Once, when I was very young, Tuesday walked me past his house and Mr Harris shot out backwards from the driveway in his car, not noticing we were right behind him. Tuesday and I had to jump into a hedge to save our lives.

Mr Harris was mortified when he realised what had happened. He apologised profusely. After that, we never saw him in his car again, and six months later his daughter came to move him into an assisted living complex. They had to sell his house and the car to pay for his flat there.

While the house remained empty pending new owner-ship, the garden, of which Mr Harris had been so proud, had grown wild and unruly. Every time we went out for a walk, Tuesday would insist that we stop to look and she would tut at the sight of the weeds choking the roses. She thought it was a terrible shame. She'd even once suggested to Emily that they go round under cover of darkness and try to tidy it up.

'What's the point?' Emily said. 'Whoever buys the house will almost certainly tarmac over that front lawn so they've got enough off-road parking for two cars.'

Tuesday had to agree that Emily had a point. Since the council had become more strict about street parking permits, our front garden was one of very few on Bracken Avenue that hadn't already been converted into a car park.

'It will be awful if someone cuts that cherry tree down,' Tuesday sighed. Every year it heralded the arrival of spring with its beautiful blossom, petals dusting the floor like snowflakes as they fell. I agreed. It was a truly exceptional tree.

But now the house had been bought and the future of the tree hung in the balance.

'What do they want you to do?' Emily asked. 'Clear the weeds and cut the tree down ready for the hardcore to go in?'

'I hope not,' said Tuesday. 'I'll refuse to be involved if

that's the case. I'm a gardener, not a builder's mate, and
to cut that cherry down would be a crime. Not to mention
a bit beyond me, working on my own. I'm going round
tomorrow for a meeting. I suppose I'll take a proper look
at the space and get an idea of what might be possible.
Gauge the sort of budget they have in mind and see what
I can do with that.'

'Don't sell yourself short,' Emily reminded her.

It was agreed that William would spend the following
morning – a Saturday – with Emily and Elvis while
Tuesday and I went to see the garden. If the new owners
of the house didn't seem keen on having a dog about, she
could always run back over the road and leave me at
number thirteen for a while. But Tuesday hoped they
wouldn't mind me being there, because when people did
like dogs, my presence was a useful ice-breaker.

That evening, Tuesday prepared everything she would
need for the first meeting at Mr Harris's old house. She
had a folder full of photographs of previous projects. She
went through them now, pulling together a selection that
she thought would be particularly interesting; gardens of
what she estimated to be a similar size. She then went on
to the internet and found plants that she thought might
thrive in such a garden. It was on the opposite side of
the street to our house so would get the sun at different
times of day – more in the morning than in the evening,
as we did. Tuesday printed off pictures of plants that
could thrive in the shade.

And then, of course, there was the cherry tree in the
front garden. It needed just a bit of a haircut to keep it

looking its best year after year. It was such a wonderful tree, thought Tuesday, such a showstopper in the spring, that the rest of the front garden could be left fairly simple. It didn't need anything else. Tuesday would just weed out the flower beds that already bordered the path and perhaps replace some of the roses.

I could tell Tuesday was excited to be getting back to work and relieved too at the prospect of being able to make some money again.

'You'd be within your rights to ask Kenton for money, you know,' Emily had once suggested to her. 'We might not have been able to track him down but I'm sure social services could.'

'No,' said Tuesday firmly. 'When Kenton left, he decided he didn't want me to know where he went and that's his prerogative. For whatever reason, he wants to pretend I don't exist. If William asks about him when he's older, then I'll help him to take up the search, but for now, we don't need him. We've managed nearly a year without him already. I don't want him in my life now.'

'Good,' said Emily. 'I was hoping you would say something like that.'

So was I.

On Saturday morning, William went to the park with Emily while Tuesday and I went to our meeting. She made sure to give me a very good brushing before we left the house, so I didn't shed all over her potential new client's trousers.

As we walked to number twenty-four I caught the unexpected whiff of a familiar scent on the air. Zena. I knew her fragrance anywhere. But she was far away from her usual patch here. Had Andrew walked her down my street that morning, I wondered? How had I not noticed? The wind must have been blowing in the wrong direction as she passed by.

But it wasn't just a trace of Zena on the air. The smell of her was getting stronger and stronger as we drew close to our destination. She must be somewhere nearby. I looked up at Tuesday but of course I couldn't convey to her the reason for my excitement.

'Here we are then,' she said as we reached the door. 'Look smart. No jumping up.'

She rang the doorbell. Deep inside the house, a dog barked. I knew that bark anywhere.

'Zena!'

I'd been right. When the door was opened, Zena leaped out to greet me.

Andrew was smiling as he stood on the threshold but . . .

'Oh no,' murmured Tuesday, seeing who had answered the door.

'Tuesday King?' Andrew asked.

'That's me.'

Chapter Twenty-One

For a moment, Tuesday struggled to find anything to say, while Andrew leaned against his door frame with a quizzical expression on his face.

'Is there a problem?' he asked after what felt like a very long while.

'Well, sort of. Look, I didn't know . . . I'm sorry. I might as well come clean. We've met before. At the pedestrian crossing. And at the tills in SuperSave.'

'You're the woman who . . .'

'Called you an arse. Exactly. For which I am eternally sorry. I can't tell you how many times I've played that moment over in my mind and wished I could take it back. But since I can't take it back, I won't waste any more of your time. You can put that on Twitter. Have a great weekend, Mr Thomas. I'm sure I'll see you around since I live just down the street, but if I do, rest assured I'll do my very best to stay out of your way.'

She set off down the path at speed, pulling me along behind her.

'Wait!' Andrew called after us.

'What?'

'I accept your apology, Ms King.'

'Thanks,' Tuesday muttered, in a way that I knew was

not grateful at all. In dog language, it was the equivalent of a snarl.

Andrew continued, 'I need someone to sort out my garden as quickly as possible and, judging by your kerb-side manner, you probably need the work.'

Tuesday's mouth dropped open as she struggled to find a comeback.

'I think we can keep it civil, don't you? So are you coming in or what?' Andrew asked. He stood to one side so that we could pass by if we so decided. 'I don't have time to keep looking for a gardener. I need the work done right now.'

'Can I bring my dog?' Tuesday asked.

'I thought I heard unfamiliar paws on the path. I suppose so, though he'll have to stay on the lead. I can't have Zena getting into a fight.'

'Oh, I don't think they will. They know each other. From the park.'

'Do they?' Andrew seemed surprised.

'I've seen you there a few times. Your dog and mine get on very well.'

Zena and I shared a glance. We got on very well indeed.

It was Zena who led us through the house. Andrew didn't need to hold her harness while they were inside, he explained. He knew where everything was in his own home.

As she stepped out of the kitchen door into Andrew and Zena's back garden, Tuesday clapped her hands together.

'That sounds like a good sign,' Andrew said.

'It is. I always thought that the man who lived here before might have been a good gardener because of the plants he chose for the front but . . . well, you have the bones of something truly beautiful here. I can see . . .' Tuesday hesitated. 'I mean, I can imagine . . .'

'You can use the word "see" around me,' said Andrew.

'I'm sorry.'

'There's no need to be sorry about that choice of word,' he said. 'It's hard not to talk in visual terms.'

But it didn't stop Tuesday blushing.

'Anyway, what I envisage for this garden . . . envisage?'

'You can say envisage too. I'm not policing your language.'

'OK. It's just . . . I'm very nervous.'

Andrew just nodded at that.

'I haven't done a first meeting with a client for a while and so I think I let myself get a bit wound up thinking about it, and then of course it turned out to be you and . . .'

'. . . you've already insulted me. It can only get better from here on in, right?'

'I suppose. I prepared a file of pictures of plants that I thought might be good but . . .'

'Obviously, I can't see them,' Andrew said.

Tuesday flipped the file shut. I could tell she was in agony.

'Look,' Andrew continued. 'All I really need is to have someone tidy this place up so that Zena can go out into the garden without my having to worry about her being unsafe or finding a way out on to the road. I just want to be sure that there are no hazards that I obviously won't have noticed myself. I want the fences to be secure and I also need a smaller area of the lawn separated off from the rest that Zena can use for spending.'

'Spending?'

'As in, going to the toilet. It doesn't need to be fenced in but it does need to be marked off from the rest of the garden in some way so she knows where she can go and I know where she's been. None of it has to be fancy. I don't care what you do with the flower beds, etcetera, so long as the garden is secure and safe for Zena. In terms of weedkillers and all that, I need you to avoid using anything that might be dangerous for her too.'

'Of course. I only ever use products that are safe for animals,' Tuesday said. 'I would never use anything to get rid of weeds or other pests that might harm a dog or any other creature. I'm one hundred per cent organic and pet-friendly.'

'Zena's not a pet.'

That was the end of that spiel.

'I'd like the garden to be easy for you to maintain on an ongoing basis too. Assuming that's something you'd be interested in.'

'Yes,' said Tuesday. 'Yes. Absolutely. That's something I could definitely do.'

'For how much?'

'You want me to tell you?'

'Do you want me to guess?' Andrew asked.

Silently, I willed Tuesday to pull herself together and tell him what she'd come up with the previous night. At last she outlined the costs, both of getting the garden into shape in the first place and of keeping it that way, and Andrew agreed to the budget without quibbling.

'That sounds reasonable,' he said.

'I have a standard contract that I'd need you to sign,' Tuesday concluded.

'Send it to me by email.'

'But . . .'

'It's the 21st century. I have voice tech and a Braille reader for my laptop. When can you start?'

'Right now, if you like,' Tuesday said. 'I'll go back to mine and fetch my tools. Assuming you don't mind listening to a lawnmower on a Saturday afternoon.'

'I just want it done,' said Andrew. 'The sooner you can get going, the better.'

'Welcome to Bracken Avenue, by the way,' Tuesday said. 'It's a lovely street. Very quiet and—'

'That's why I chose it,' Andrew interrupted. 'Look, I've got work to do. The side gate is on the latch so you can go in and out. All I ask is that you remain alert to Zena's whereabouts at all times. She's a very valuable animal as I'm sure you can appreciate.'

Zena raised her eyebrows in my direction and reminded me of the cost of her training. 'You're looking at a six-figure dog here.'

Back at our house, Tuesday called Emily, who was still at the park with Elvis and William, to give her the news. She had not, until this moment, told Emily about the arse incident at the crossing or the subsequent altercation in the shop. Now, she had to. The story didn't make sense without *all* the gory details.

'Of course I apologised and he seems to be happy with that. But I still keep saying the wrong thing. I'm sure he thinks I'm an absolute moron.'

'I'm sure you're not the first person who's asked him a couple of stupid questions.'

'I only wish I *had* asked questions. I didn't even get that far. I just kept starting to say something stupid and he filled in the rest of the sentence for me. Oh, Emily. Do you think I should just tell him that I don't want the job? I don't think I can stand working for him already knowing that he thinks I'm an idiot. Or just a bitch.'

Emily was always practical about such things. 'How many other calls from potential customers have you had this week?' she asked.

'None,' Tuesday had to admit.

'Then no, I don't think you should tell him that you don't want the job. You're going to be in the garden. He's going to be in the house. You'll hardly have to interact with him at all. And if you do have to interact, I'm sure you can keep any further "arse-ing" outbursts in check. I have faith in you, Tuesday King. Just get on with it.'

So that is what we did. We got on with it. Tuesday loaded up the wheelbarrow with the tools she thought she would need first. We went back to Zena's house and let ourselves in through the side gate. Zena was shut inside, to keep her out of our way. We pressed our noses against opposite sides of the glass in the patio door.

'It's going well so far,' Zena suggested.

I told her how nervous Tuesday was.

'She thinks Andrew thinks she's an idiot.'

'Andrew thinks everyone is an idiot,' Zena said. 'Except me, of course. And it took a while for him to come to that conclusion.'

As he had told us, Andrew was spending his Saturday working. He had headphones on as he listened to emails. Tuesday need not have worried that he would hover over her while she worked as some of her clients did.

Luckily, Mr Harris, the previous owner, had left his lawn-mower in the shed. It wasn't a very fancy lawnmower, but it was serviceable (it wouldn't matter too much if it conked out in the seriously overgrown grass) and it wasn't long before Tuesday had filled a big garden-waste sack with grass cuttings. I loved the smell of freshly mown grass. It was the smell of green. The smell of summer.

That bright green smell brought several of the neigh-bourhood creatures to Zena's garden, eager to see what was going on. A trio of squirrels took up a vantage point in the holm oak that matched the one in our garden on the other side of the street. Merle the blackbird alighted on the right-hand-side fence. A robin took the fence on the left-hand side. They both watched with keen attention as Tuesday lifted a couple of old terracotta pots and moved them on to the path so that she could mow the grass around them. Where the pots had been standing, the grass was bleached white from lack of sun. All the better for the birds to see the earwigs and worms that had been hiding in the dark. As soon as Tuesday moved far enough away, the birds took their chances and dived towards the lawn like two fighter planes on opposite sides of an aerial dogfight. Fortunately, Merle and the robin didn't have to

fight over the bounty that had been revealed. They got a
worm apiece and both flew back to their nests in triumph.

By late afternoon – nearly William's teatime (and mine)
– the back garden at number twenty-four was already
looking very different. Cutting the grass had revealed a
path of flat stones and the broken remains of a sundial,
which Tuesday had carefully put to one side.

'I could fix that,' she announced to herself.

She loaded her tools back into the wheelbarrow and
tapped on the patio doors to attract Andrew's attention.
Zena ran from the doors to her master and nudged him
with her nose in case he hadn't heard the knock.

Andrew opened the doors, keeping Zena behind his
legs so that she couldn't run out.

'I've finished for today,' Tuesday told him. 'The grass
is cut and I've made a start on the borders. I've cleared
up everything I thought might be an immediate issue for
Zena. I'll secure the side gate as I go out and then she'll
be perfectly safe.'

'Good.'

'By the way, I found an old sundial. It's broken in two
but it should be pretty easy to fix. I can do that for you
if you like.'

'I don't think I'll need it unless you can invent a way
for me to feel shadows,' Andrew said.

'No.' Tuesday blushed crimson again. 'Of course not.
I'll just get rid of it then, shall I? I'll be back on Monday
morning, if that's OK with you?'

'That's OK with me. Come via the side gate again. I'll
leave it unlocked from eight so there's no need to disturb
me unless you absolutely have to.'

'I'll see you on Monday,' Tuesday said, before berating herself for her choice of words again. 'I mean, I'll . . .'

'Have a good evening.'

Andrew slid the door shut and we were dismissed.

'He didn't even say thank you,' Tuesday noted when she recounted the day's progress to Emily.

'Then perhaps you were justified in calling him an arse after all,' Emily said, laughing. 'But he's agreed to your fee estimate so I wouldn't get too bent out of shape about it. And an ongoing maintenance contract is great news. Plus he can't be that bad if he loves his dog. You may even come to be friends,' said Emily, ever optimistic.

'I very much doubt that,' said Tuesday.

Chapter Twenty-Two

Then

On Monday morning, Tuesday and I set off for work again. We let ourselves into Andrew and Zena's garden via the side gate and I sniffed around the fences while Tuesday made a plan for the day. Andrew stayed in the house all day long even though the sun was shining and it was wonderfully warm outside. Tuesday had brought a flask so that she wouldn't have to go indoors for so much as a glass of water. She'd also made a plan that if she needed the loo, she would dash all the way back to number thirteen rather than bother Andrew to use his. He was at the table in his dining room, using the Braille reader attached to his laptop. Zena and I could only press our noses to opposite sides of the glass on the patio doors. At four in the afternoon, Tuesday packed up her tools and we left without saying goodbye. Rather than knock on the back door to let Andrew know we were going, Tuesday texted Andrew to tell him that Zena could safely go outside, understanding now that his phone would read the text out to him.

The following morning began in the same way. We let ourselves in and started where we'd left off the day before. OK, perhaps it's more accurate to say that Tuesday picked up where she'd left off. I merely stretched out in a patch of sun on the lawn, occasionally offering my moral support in the form of a tail wag. Again, we didn't see Andrew all day.

Wednesday was the same, until elevenses time when Andrew opened the back door and asked if we minded if Zena joined us. Having confirmed that the side gate was shut, Tuesday said she was very happy for Zena to wander as she pleased. I, of course, was delighted.

Tuesday took the opportunity to give Andrew an update on her progress. She'd been digging over the flower beds, removing the tangle of weeds and getting the earth ready for new plants. Though Andrew had said that all he wanted from the garden was that it was a safe place for Zena, Tuesday had suggested it would be easier to replant the beds rather than put turf right up to the fences.

'And it will give the garden some interest,' Tuesday said. 'Should you ever have . . .' She must have been about to say, 'have people over,' but settled instead for, '. . . should you ever decide to sell. A nice garden is always a good selling point.'

Andrew agreed. 'Do whatever you like,' he said. 'Within the budget.'

It wasn't exactly the enthusiastic agreement Tuesday had hoped for but it would have to do.

There were some big stones in the flower beds. It looked as though at one point someone had sought to make a feature of them, but they didn't fit with Tuesday's plan. One by one, she moved them to a pile by the shed so she could decide what to do with them later.

While Tuesday worked, Zena and I played tug of war with one of her toys – a ratty old rope pull with rubber hoops on each end. It was, she explained, one of her favourites. It had come with her from the house where she'd been a puppy. Once we'd tired ourselves out, we lay down on the grass and Zena told me more about her life before Andrew. She was one of a litter of five. 'The Z litter. Every guide dog litter is given a letter of the alphabet. Hence all our names begin with Z.'

Two of her siblings, Zoe and Zeke, had also gone on to be guide dogs. Zach was in the police force. The smallest of the litter, Zane, had unfortunately failed all the early guide dog tests.

'Went berserk every time he heard a toilet flush. He's living on a farm now.'

Zena said she'd lived with a family during her puppy-walking days, the period between her being weaned and starting her training in earnest. The family had a little girl called Daisy, who was two when Zena arrived. The adoration between Zena and Daisy was mutual, just as it was for me and William.

'I miss her terribly,' Zena explained. 'But I see her at the guide dog tea parties and she always remembers me.'

'How old was she when she was first able to throw a ball?' I asked, wondering when William would be able to have a proper game with me.

'She could throw a ball when I arrived,' Zena said. 'Though not very far. She soon got better though. You'll have William trained up in no time.'

We were interrupted by a tremendous howl of pain.

Chapter Twenty-Three

Tuesday was on her hands and knees in a flower bed. Zena and I rushed straight to her side. As we got to her, she rolled on to her back clutching one of her feet between both hands. The expletives came thick and fast. And loud. Even the squirrels and Caligula came to see what the commotion was all about. As did Andrew.

He shouted from the back door, 'Is everything alright out there?'

Tuesday was rocking backwards and forwards, still holding her right foot tightly. Her eyes were squeezed shut and I could tell she was trying not to cry. Eventually, between gasps, she managed to say, 'I think I've broken my foot.'

'Where are you? Can you get up? Come into the kitchen,' Andrew said.

Tuesday did not risk putting any weight on her foot. Instead, she got on to all fours and crawled towards the house. Zena and I stayed close by. I tried to give Tuesday some help with my nose.

'Stupendo,' she said. 'Give over. I'm not playing.'

Neither was I. But I backed off a little and resorted to giving her moral support instead of a shove. Eventually, Tuesday made it to the back door and pulled herself up by the door frame, still making sure she did not put her injured foot on the floor.

'I need to go to A & E,' she told Andrew.

'Sit down first,' was his response. 'Tell me what happened.' Andrew had already taken a packet of peas out of the freezer. He'd wrapped them in a tea towel. 'Take your shoe off. Carefully. Hold these against the part of your foot that hurts. It'll slow down any swelling.'

'That won't be enough. I need to go to the hospital. My foot's swelling up. It's going to be the size of a balloon. I've broken something for sure.'

'That would be very unlucky,' Andrew said. 'Please just sit down, hold the ice in place and tell me exactly what happened.'

'What? I'm calling an ambulance. I don't think you're taking this seriously.'

Tuesday frantically searched her pockets for her phone, which had dropped out on to the grass when she fell.

'I assure you I am.' Andrew sat down opposite her. 'Put your injured foot in my lap.'

'No.'

'Give me your foot, please. I know what I'm doing.'

'What kind of weirdo are you?'

'Tuesday King, please give me your bloody foot.'

His exclamation shocked us all.

'I'd like a professional opinion, if that's alright with you,' Tuesday snapped.

Andrew responded calmly, 'And I will give you one. Before I lost my sight, I was a doctor.'

'What?'

'You've heard of doctors? It means I'm not entirely ignorant about first aid. Foot?'

'You were a doctor.'

'Surprising but true.'

Tuesday frowned as she placed her foot in Andrew's lap. When he took hold of her ankle to move her foot into the centre of his lap, Tuesday squealed. I barked.

'He's not hurting her deliberately,' Zena told me. 'He's trying to find out what's wrong.'

'You're OK,' Andrew said calmly. 'Just breathe. I'm going to press on a few spots and I want you to tell me how it feels.'

'It hurts. Obviously.'

'Of course your foot is generally painful right now, but I need you to be more specific.' With infinite care, Andrew took Tuesday's foot in both his hands. 'Does this hurt?' he asked as he pressed along Tuesday's bones.

'It all hurts. Why am I letting you do this?'

Andrew ignored her. 'Please answer me seriously. Does this hurt more than that did?'

'Ow!' was Tuesday's first reaction, then, 'No. It hurt more before. Really, what are you doing?'

'The Ottawa ankle rules. They're designed to help a physician decide whether or not you might need an X-ray. It's exactly what they'd do if you went to the hospital.'

Tuesday didn't look convinced.

'Tell me exactly how you fell.'

'I was moving rocks from the flower bed. I stood up to get my spade and tripped over a rock I'd already moved on to the grass. I landed on my knee. That hurts too.'

'Did your foot bend in any particular way?'

Tuesday muttered, 'I don't know. It all happened very quickly. One minute I was up and the next I was down.'

'OK.' Andrew patted the top of Tuesday's foot. 'I don't think you've broken or fractured anything. Which isn't to say it doesn't hurt. You've had a shock. You're probably going to get some bruising. But I don't think there's any need for you to go to A & E. You'll end up spending the whole day there just to get the advice I'm going to give you now. You need to ice it, keep it elevated and rest it for a while. Stay off it for as long as you can. At least for the rest of the day. You can take painkillers if you feel you need to.'

Andrew stood up and moved his chair a little closer to Tuesday's so that she could put her foot on it, then he went to the kitchen sink to wash his hands.

'But . . . you can't . . .'

'See? Right. But I've still got my hands, and most of my skill was in my ability to feel where things were going wrong anyway. I was a registrar in orthopaedics. I've seen more broken toes and fractured metatarsals than I've had hot dinners. Look, I don't think you need to go to A & E, but if you disagree or you want a second opinion from someone who can *see*, I'm not going to stop you. Or you could just sit there and see if you start to feel better with the ice and the elevation. I'm going to make myself a cup of tea now. Do you want one?'

'Should you be making tea?' Tuesday asked.

'I don't think there's any law against it.'

'But hot water . . . Should I do it for you?'

Andrew snorted. 'Tuesday King, you're the one who's hurt. Stay where you are. Sit still with your foot on that chair. I'll put the kettle on and I promise I won't scald myself, if that's what you're worried about. What do you think I do when there's no one here to make tea for me?'

'Stick to cold drinks?' Tuesday suggested.

Andrew laughed properly this time. 'Without tea and coffee, I cannot function. How do you take yours? And does your dog need a drink while I'm at it?'

Chapter Twenty-Four

Tuesday seemed to forget all about her accident for a moment as she watched, intrigued, as Andrew moved about his kitchen, getting together everything he needed to make tea. He put two mugs side by side on the draining board, threw a teabag into each and hung something over the lip of one. Tuesday held her breath as Andrew picked up the kettle and started pouring boiling water into the first mug.

'Uh!' she exclaimed, as it seemed certain that hot water would start pouring all over the floor. But right at that moment, the gadget on the side of the cup bleeped and Andrew stopped pouring. He switched the gadget to the other mug and did the same again.

'I'll let you add your own sugar and milk,' he said, as he held out the first mug to Tuesday. 'You might want some extra sugar for the shock . . . of seeing a blind man make a cuppa.'

Andrew smiled to himself as he took a bowl out of another cupboard and filled it with cold water for me. I could tell by her face that Tuesday felt embarrassed.

'I didn't mean to . . . I just . . .' Tuesday struggled. 'I suppose it's never really occurred to me to wonder how someone makes a hot drink when they can't see what they're doing.'

"There's only one really important rule. Never use your finger to measure the depth of the boiling water. Do you want a biscuit?'

'Yes, please.'

I gave a little whine to let Andrew know that I'd like a biscuit too. He must have heard it. Having offered Tuesday the biscuit tin, he opened a second tin and picked out two dog treats. One for Zena and one for me. They were gone before Andrew had time to put the tin's lid back on.

Andrew sat back down at the kitchen table.

'It's all about knowing where everything is. So long as everything is in its place, I can look after myself perfectly well. Now, tell me how the gardening is going,' he said. 'Or *was* going, before you tripped over.'

'The garden is looking much better. I mean . . .'

'The only way you can tell me how it's going is by telling me how it's looking, right?'

'It is hard to talk about the way things are without describing the way they look,' Tuesday admitted.

'I know. But I'd rather hear how they look than not have you tell me anything at all. One of the strangest things about being visually impaired is that people seem to lose the ability to talk when they're around me. Perhaps that's why they always talk to my dog.'

'Dogs do make it easier somehow,' Tuesday said, with a glance at Zena and me. I leaned my head against her thigh and she scratched my ear. 'I don't know what I'd do without Stupendo.'

'I don't know what I'd do without Zena,' Andrew agreed. He reached out a hand and Zena tucked her head beneath it. She and I shared a happy glance.

'How's that foot feeling?' Andrew asked Tuesday.

'OK,' she said tentatively. 'Better for the ice. I'm sorry about all the swearing,' Tuesday added then. 'When you were trying to help me.'

Andrew just laughed at that. 'Believe me, I understand only too well that there are moments when there's every need to swear. I turn the air blue on a regular basis. It's been scientifically proven to help us deal with pain. That's my excuse anyway.'

'I didn't know you were a doctor.'

'I didn't tell you. And you didn't ask. But feet were my speciality, as it happens. Don't worry,' he added quickly, 'I'm not some kind of foot fetishist. It's just that as soon as we started to study feet at medical school, I was fascinated. Feet are such a triumph of engineering. The way the bones and tendons and muscles act together to provide a foundation for the whole body is so beautiful. The pressures they can withstand are extraordinary. The mechanics of walking are amazing. Think what we put them through, day after day, year after year. Your feet will give you a lifetime of faithful service if you look after them. Have you never thought what a wonderful thing they are?'

'I'm not sure I ever really think about them at all.'

'Most people don't, until they start hurting.'

'I've never met a foot doctor before.'

'Well, I'm not one any more,' Andrew reminded her. Suddenly he frowned as if in slight pain. 'Look, do you

mind if I get back to my laptop and leave you here with
the dogs? I've got emails to respond to. I consult on
disability access now and I'm working on a couple of big
projects. End of the month deadline for both.'

'Don't let me hold you up.'

'Shout if you feel your foot starting to get worse. I can
drive you to the hospital if you tell me when to turn the
wheel.'

'But . . .' It took Tuesday a couple of seconds to realise
Andrew was making a joke. 'Thank you for taking care of
me. Thank you for the tea. And the biscuit. And the peas.'

'Hold them to your foot for a little while longer. Doctor's
orders.'

As Andrew left the room, I wondered whether he really
wanted to get back to work or whether it was more the
case that he wanted to end the conversation because
talking about his former life was difficult for him. Zena
thought it might be the latter.

'But that's the most I've heard him say to anyone outside
a work call in a very long time,' she said. 'When it comes
to Andrew, that was quite something.'

Zena wasn't the only one who had noticed a change
in Andrew that afternoon. He'd seemed very different to
me too, energised somehow, when he took control of the
situation with Tuesday's foot. It was as if, for a moment,
he had shrugged off a cloud.

Tuesday's nasty trip had brought that day's work to a
sudden end and once she'd finished drinking her tea, she
decided it was time for us to go. Andrew agreed that she
should finish for the day.

'Rest your foot as much as you can,' he reminded her. 'Keep it elevated.'

Using a broom as a makeshift crutch, Tuesday gathered up her phone and her tools to make sure that the garden was safe for Zena in our absence, then we went home to await William and Emily. Emily had offered to pick him up from the nursery on her way over for supper.

'How was Mr Grumpy?' Emily asked.

Tuesday told Emily the saga of her fall.

'What? He held your foot?'

'In a professional context!'

As Tuesday described the interaction in the kitchen, Emily nodded. 'Ottawa ankle rules.'

'So he wasn't making it up?'

'I'd have done the same. Best way to tell if someone needs an x-ray. It must be hard,' Emily concluded, when she heard about Andrew's previous profession. 'Not being able to do the work you love. Especially when you trained for so long to be able to do it.'

'Yeah,' Tuesday agreed. 'No wonder he always seems so hacked off.'

William climbed into Tuesday's lap. Once he was settled, she took hold of his chubby little feet. 'Look at these, William,' she said to him. 'These little feet are miraculous.'

'And tasty too,' I thought, as I gave them both a quick lick that made William giggle with delight.

Chapter Twenty-Five

Tuesday's accident in the garden changed things. Though her fall had been dramatic, Andrew was right in diagnosing the damage as much less serious than the initial shock and pain suggested. After an evening with her foot elevated and a good night's rest – Emily stayed to put William to bed, with my assistance – Tuesday felt much better. Her foot and her knee were both still sore the following morning but Tuesday could put weight through both her feet again. Andrew had told her that there was no need for her to hurry back to work, but Tuesday felt ready. The job was taking her slightly longer than she had planned and she hadn't even started on the front garden yet. She had to fit in her weekly work at Mrs Wilson's too.

As usual, we let ourselves in through the back gate but this time Andrew acknowledged our arrival and even offered Tuesday a coffee before she started work. He wanted to know how 'the patient' was getting on. He asked if Tuesday would like him to give her foot another quick examination but she insisted that it was fine, blushing furiously all the while.

'Good. But you must let me know at once if you have any concerns,' he said.

Having knocked back the coffee, Tuesday threw herself

into her work. She had ordered a variety of plants from the garden centre she liked and they were being delivered that morning. The friendly driver helped Tuesday carry the plants through to the back garden.

'You've got some lovely stuff here,' he said. 'Good choices. Lots of fragrance. This lavender is really special.'

Tuesday ran her hands through the plant's purple-tinged fronds, releasing the scent of French summer fields into the air.

'Perfect,' she said. 'This is exactly what I wanted.'

When it was time for elevenses, Tuesday, Zena and I sat down in the middle of the lawn and Tuesday opened her flask. She had the new plants arranged in a line in front of her, as she worked out exactly where each should go. She was quietly concentrating on drawing a plan of the flower beds when Andrew came outside.

'Hello,' he said.

'Hi,' Tuesday called back.

Having oriented himself by Tuesday's voice, Andrew walked straight towards her.

'I'm just having a break,' she explained.

'Me too. Can I join you?'

He started to sit down.

'Stupendo's right behind you,' Tuesday warned him.

'Don't want to sit on you,' Andrew told me. I stepped out of the way. 'What kind of dog is Stupendo anyway?' he asked.

'Half-Labrador, half-Staffie. He sort of looks like a sawn-off Labrador. Thicker-set with a shorter nose. He's still handsome though.'

I was glad she added that.

'He's got a Staffie's tenacity and a Labrador's appetite. Eats anything.'

'Except sprouts!' I wanted to say.

'Except sprouts,' Tuesday clarified, as though she could hear my protest.

'And how did he get his name?'

'Well, he was called Stuart Little when I brought him home, but that seemed a bit pedestrian. When he was a puppy, he was absolutely bonkers. He'd bounce off the furniture like a canine acrobat. The Great Stupendo seemed much more fitting for a dog with his energy and daring.'

Andrew reached a hand towards me and I moved closer so that he could give me a friendly scratch between the ears.

'How did you come to choose Zena?' Tuesday asked.

'You mean her name? Or Zena herself? I got no say in either. But I got lucky. Guide Dogs matched me to her on the basis of her size, her speed, her temperament and her ability to navigate the sort of world I live in. She had to be good at being in a busy urban environment as well as a backwater like this place.'

'This is my home town,' Tuesday pointed out.

'I didn't mean to suggest it's not a lovely place.'

'But definitely a bit of a backwater,' Tuesday agreed.

'Zena seems to like Stupendo very much,' Andrew observed.

'They've known each other for a long time,' Tuesday said. 'They've been playing together in the park since Stupendo was one. That's about three years now.'

'I didn't know.'

'You usually sit on the opposite side of the big lawn. But Stupendo sometimes chases Zena in my direction. It's probably why Zena said hello to me at the crossing that day.' Her voice trailed away.

She changed the subject to talk about the garden and what was left to do at the back of the house before she moved on to the front. She told him about the cherry tree and Mr Harris.

'He'd owned this place for as long as I could remember. When I was a little girl, he lived here with his wife and their teenage daughter, who seemed impossibly glamorous to me. I used to ride my bicycle up and down the street, hoping to see her. She never took any notice of me, of course. I still had stabilisers.'

'You've been on Bracken Avenue since you were a kid?'

'I was here from the age of four until I left school at eighteen.' Tuesday told him how she had moved away to the big city to make her fortune but ended up returning to the house where she grew up.

'I think it was the right decision,' she concluded.

It turned out that family had brought Andrew back to our little town too. Since qualifying as a doctor, he had been living in Manchester. 'After I lost my sight, I had to come back and live with my mother for a while, until I got used to navigating the world again and was matched with Zena. Now we're close enough for her to visit whenever she gets a "feeling" that I need her.'

'Mothers can't stop mothering,' Tuesday observed.

Andrew came out into the garden for a tea break that afternoon too. Zena and I could hardly believe it. He and Tuesday sat down together on the grass again. This time, Tuesday asked him more about Zena.

'I don't know anything about how you learn to work with a guide dog,' she said. 'I'd love to know. How do you trust her to take you where you need to go?'

'It's not easy,' Andrew admitted. 'But there's a long process of training before a guide dog and owner are allowed to go out alone. Before Zena came to live with me, we were sent on a residential course.'

'At a really fancy hotel,' Zena said to me.

'At a Holiday Inn near the Guide Dogs centre,' Andrew told Tuesday. 'With three other VIPs who'd been matched to their dogs at the same time.'

'Famous people?' Tuesday asked.

'Visually Impaired People,' Andrew explained. 'It was tough. Ten days of non-stop training in all sorts of conditions. Ten days of getting used to our new dogs.

'I'd been looking forward to it but about halfway through I began to wonder if I'd made a mistake. The trainers kept telling me that Zena only needed a light touch but it didn't feel that way. I seemed to be tripping over her all the time. The trainers said I was holding Zena back and that was confusing her. I started to worry that we wouldn't pass the course and I'd have to give Zena up and start again. It can take a long time to get matched. I'd been on the waiting list for two years already. But I just couldn't let go and relax. I just couldn't quite trust that a dog, no matter how well trained or intelligent, wouldn't get distracted and walk me out into the road.'

'I can understand that,' said Tuesday.

'On the second to last day of the course, Zena woke

me up really early. Like five o'clock early. I'd been looking forward to having a lie-in. We weren't supposed to be starting until ten. I tried to ignore her but she jumped up and pawed at my back. Then she licked the side of my face. She bounced on the mattress. She made it impossible for me to go back to sleep. She whined. She whimpered. Finally, she barked.

'That is when I knew something was really wrong. In the whole week we'd spent together up to that point, I'd never heard Zena bark. I'd heard the others. But not her. She pulled on the sleeve of my pyjama top to drag me out of bed. I got her into her harness and decided I'd take her to the trainer's room, in case she was hurt in some way I couldn't see. It was only as I opened the door to the corridor that I smelled the smoke, just as the hotel's alarm system picked it up too. Zena got me out into the car park just as the sprinklers came on.'

'I did,' Zena told me.

'Everyone came out of their rooms then, of course,' Andrew went on. 'The fire had started in a storeroom on the corridor where Zena and I were sleeping. I asked the trainers if it was really possible that Zena had smelled the smoke so much earlier than the detection system picked it up and they told me it was. We're nose-blind, compared to dogs.'

Zena and I agreed with that.

'What happened next?' Tuesday asked.

'Everyone was evacuated and the fire brigade arrived. The fire was localised and the damage wasn't extensive so we were eventually allowed back to our rooms. After that, I had a new-found respect for Zena. I didn't try to hold her back any more. It was a turning point. I knew I could trust her.'

'What an amazing dog she is,' said Tuesday.

As I listened to Andrew and Tuesday talking, sitting beside Zena on the grass, I was agog at my friend's determination and skill.

'Zena, you're incredible,' I said.

She touched her nose to mine.

'You know, I don't think I've ever heard you bark either,' I mused.

'When you do, then you'll know you're in trouble!'

Chapter Twenty-Six

After that, Tuesday and Andrew spent every break in their working days together. Tuesday had hundreds of questions about Zena. I loved to listen to Andrew's answers, though I was a little put out when Tuesday asked, 'Do you think it's too late for me to use some guide dogs' tricks to teach Stupendo to be better behaved?' I gave her the side-eye for that.

Eventually, of course, one question had to come up.

'Andrew, can I ask you . . .'

Tuesday didn't even need to finish the sentence before Andrew said, 'Can you ask me how I lost my sight? Of course you can.'

'You don't have to talk about it if you find it painful.'

'Not talking about it doesn't make it any *less* painful,' he replied.

He inhaled deeply and began. 'It happened seven years ago. I was in a traffic accident. I was on the back of a colleague's motorbike. He was giving me a lift home from the hospital, as he sometimes did. He was always trying to persuade me to buy a bike of my own. It was a cold night. On a dual carriageway, a lorry hit some black ice and turned over right in front of us. We couldn't stop in time. My friend didn't survive. I was luckier. I was just in a coma for a week. But when I came round, I couldn't see. The front of my helmet had hit the back of my friend's helmet with such force that the jolt caused permanent damage to my optic nerve.'

'And there's nothing they can do about it?'

'It would appear not. They tried everything they could think of – and believe me, I made them try everything I could think of too. There's no worse patient than a medic. In many cases, people who lose their sight in the way I did do get it back eventually – at least partially – but not me. Sod's Law.'

'It must have been very frightening,' said Tuesday.

'It was. I took being able to see for granted. Even though I'd spent all those years training in medicine and thought I knew the body inside out, I didn't really understand how intricately our sight is linked to everything else. It was amazing how quickly I lost track of time. Without those messages from my eyes, I couldn't tell if it was night or day. My sleep cycles were all over the place. And I was in pain all the time. Nothing the doctors gave me seemed to touch it, and of course I knew exactly what to ask for.'

Andrew took a contemplative sip of his coffee.

'It's quite something, going from being the one who makes people better to being the one who needs help. But that's life, I suppose.' He seemed to physically pull himself together as he said that. 'Everything can change in an instant and suddenly all the plans you made are as nothing. You just have to make a decision to get on with it and make different plans, right? Embrace the new, however much you think you don't want to. There's always a silver lining.'

'I'm not sure I would be so brave. So stoical.'

'Of course you would.'

Andrew suddenly stood up.

'I should let you get on,' he said. 'I've got things to do.'

Once again, Zena was of the opinion that Andrew had called the conversation to a close because he felt he'd given just a little too much away.

Humans. Zena followed Andrew inside. Looking through the window, I saw her lean her head against his thigh and I knew it was her way of reminding him he was loved. As Tuesday stood to look at the work she'd done that day, I stood close by and pressed my head against her hand, trying to tell her the same thing.

Chapter Twenty-Seven

On Fridays, Tuesday took the day off so that she could take William to the local library for baby music club. That Friday was no different. After the club, which I couldn't attend despite my natural musical abilities – 'You mean your howling,' as Tuesday would say – Tuesday spent the rest of the morning doing her chores while William and I amused ourselves on the floor. As far as William was concerned, my toys were his toys. He was having a wonderful time loading my squeaky plastic Minions and pigs and sprouts into his push-along trolley before Tuesday spotted what he was doing and put the lot out of his reach.

'They're dirty,' she said. 'Dirty toys.'

I was a little insulted. If Tuesday had a nose even half as well-tuned as mine, she would have known that William's own toys weren't exactly pristine.

After lunch – William had baked beans and toast fingers; he fed me two – Tuesday announced that we were going to the park. I let her put on my harness and waited patiently while she tried to strap William into his pushchair. He'd recently worked out that as long as he kept moving, Tuesday could not get the buckles closed. She would have found it easier to wrestle an octopus. Eventually, however, we were all ready to go. And as it happened, the delay caused by William's insistence that he would not be strapped down turned out to be a lucky one, because we reached the top of our driveway just as Andrew and Zena were walking by.

I was relieved that Tuesday didn't try to ignore Andrew this time. Instead, she called out a shy sort of greeting.

'I'm taking Zena for some exercise,' Andrew explained.

'We're going to the swings,' said Tuesday.

'Want to go together?'

Zena and I were very pleased when Tuesday accepted the invitation, and the five of us set out as a pack in the direction of the park. It took a little practice to get used to walking side by side with Andrew and Zena. And also to get used to the fact that Zena stopped at every single kerb, whereas if I didn't see any traffic coming, I'd just keep going.

'How does she know when it's safe to cross?' Tuesday asked.

'She doesn't,' Andrew explained. 'I have to make that judgement call. She's just trained to look for a crossing and stop at the kerb and wait until I tell her to walk on.'

'I think her good influence is rubbing off on Stupendo,' Tuesday said. 'Normally he'd have dragged me to the park in half the time.'

Because I'd be racing to see if Zena was there. Now that I was walking beside her, there was no particular hurry.

We got to the main road, with SuperSave and the post office.

'Isn't this the pedestrian crossing where we first met?' Andrew teased as we paused for the lights.

'You're making me blush,' said Tuesday. 'I don't know how to convince you how sorry I am about . . .'

'. . . calling me an arse? Tuesday, the more I've thought about it, the more I realise that I owe *you* an apology for that afternoon. The truth is I *was* a bit of an arse. I don't usually get quite so bent out of shape when people say hello to Zena. Usually, I can tell them why they shouldn't distract her without getting into lecture mode, but I'd had a bad day, if that's any kind of excuse. I know it really isn't. Anyway, I'm sorry. But I think we've moved past it now, haven't we? I hope we have.'

'Let's say we have,' said Tuesday. 'And there's the green man!'

'And you were right,' said Andrew as we crossed the road en masse. 'I was an arse before I lost my sight. Being blind hasn't changed my personality at all.'

Tuesday laughed at that and afterwards it seemed as though something had shifted again. The bad energy of that first meeting at the crossing – and the SuperSave till altercation too – was finally gone.

As soon as Zena and I were free to run, we headed for the centre of the grass for a debrief.

Zena told me that she didn't think she had ever seen Andrew so relaxed around someone else. I told her that I'd never seen Tuesday so happily nervous (not since that first meeting of the cancer carers' group at the pub on the river, when the dreadful Kenton crashed into our lives – the less said about that, the better).

Having played a game of tag or two, Zena and I returned to our humans at the children's playground. Tuesday was pushing William on a swing. Andrew leaned against one of the swing's uprights, safely out of the way of William's flying feet. Zena and I arranged ourselves behind him.

Tuesday and Andrew were talking about the accident that had led to Andrew's sight loss. Something about the fact that she was occupied with keeping William happily swinging seemed to have given Tuesday the courage to be nosier than she had so far. To ask more personal questions.

'Were you living on your own when it happened?' she asked as Zena and I listened. 'I mean, were you single?'

'No. As a matter of fact, I wasn't.'

Andrew took a deep breath, preparing himself to say more than he had expected to. 'I was engaged. Her name was Joanna. We'd been together since our first year at university. She was studying French. She went on to be a translator. We were planning to get married. After the accident happened, Joanna was right there with me. During the weeks when we didn't know what was going on, she took time off work and came with me to all my hospital appointments. When I didn't have the strength to fight for myself, she fought for me.

'She was amazing and I thought we were unbreakable. Turned out that wasn't the case. When Joanna realised I really wasn't going to get my sight back ever, the idea of being my Florence Nightingale started to pall. I'll admit I can't have been easy to live with – in fact, I *know* I wasn't easy to live with – and perhaps there was a part of me that was determined to push her away too. I thought she deserved better.'

'Are you still in touch?' Tuesday asked.

'No,' said Andrew, with a sad smile. 'But that's probably for the best. She married one of my best friends.'

'That's terrible.'

'For me, perhaps. At the time. But I've thought about it a lot and it was the right thing for her. And if I'm honest, it would have been the right thing for her even if I hadn't lost my sight. Fate would have brought them together someday somehow.

'And if Jo hadn't left me when she did, then I might not be where I am today. With her around, I had no incentive to break out of my funk and work out how I was going to live the rest of my life without my sight. Though she'd nagged me about it endlessly, it wasn't until the week after she left and I had to move back in with my mother that I decided to start white-cane training. There was no way I was going to live with Mum for the rest of my life and I had to master white-cane training before I could be put on the waiting list for a guide dog. And that really changed my life. Isn't that right, Zena?'

Zena thumped her tail against the grass at the sound of her name.

'But so many changes in such a short space of time,' Tuesday mused. 'I don't think I could have coped.'

'You'd be surprised. I remember reading about some happiness researchers who looked into the difference big life events make to our base happiness level. They discovered that when people won the lottery, of course that made them happy, and when people were disabled in an accident, of course that made them sad. But that wasn't the whole picture. The change in underlying mood wasn't permanent. After a couple of years, the lottery winners were back to being as miserable as they had been before their lucky windfall, while the people who'd had life-changing accidents had regained the level of happiness they'd had before the unthinkable happened. Human beings are infinitely adaptable and yet, at the same time, it takes an awful lot to change us deep inside. As I told you, I was an arse all along.'

Tuesday laughed. 'I don't believe it.'

'Well, I was definitely a miserable, arrogant sod who always saw the glass as half-empty. Still do, really.'

Tuesday laughed again.

'Just as I bet you've always been sunny and kind,' Andrew said.

'When I'm not being rude to complete strangers at pedestrian crossings, I suppose that's true,' said Tuesday.

'You know what? It's nice to have company on a walk,' Andrew said then.

Zena and I rolled our eyes at one another. Wasn't that what we'd been saying all along?

Chapter Twenty-Eight

Now

On my sixth day of being dead, I thought about that long-ago afternoon in the park. How happy I had been that day. It was always great to be in the park with William and Tuesday, but to be there with Zena too, and see Andrew and Tuesday's friendship really start to blossom had made it very special indeed.

Of course I could go to the park as a ghost but it wasn't the same now that Tuesday and William didn't even know I was there with them. On day six, Zephyr and Buster weren't around to talk to. Zena wasn't there. When Tuesday and William turned for home, I slunk along behind them. It didn't even cheer me up that I could follow them right into SuperSave and see for myself all the marvellous things that Zena used to tell me about. What was the point of being able to stick my head in a chiller cabinet full of sausages if I couldn't run out of the shop with a packet clenched between my teeth and scoff the lot in one go?

As night fell, I went in search of Caligula, hoping that he would be able to pull me out of my funk. It took me a little while to find him. It was a wet night and he wasn't hanging out on top of the fence watching the comings and goings of the night-time animals as he usually did. Instead he was dozing on top of a pile of freshly washed and dried towels in Mary Brown's kitchen.

It did look very comfy. Caligula rolled on to his back and stretched himself in an extravagant yawn that drew Mary's attention. She was at the kitchen sink, washing up a single cup and plate.

'Oh Mr Boots,' she said. 'You do pick the most irritating places for a nap! Why do you always make a beeline for my clean laundry? Shoo! Shoo! Get off there, Bootsie. Shoo!'

Mary waved the tea towel towards him but Caligula didn't move an inch. Instead, he started kneading the top towel with his claws to plump it up, pulling dozens of tiny threads. As he did so, he noticed that I was watching him through the window and winked. I let myself into Mary's house.

'Caligula!' I was astonished at how brazen he was about it. He just didn't seem to care.

'Mr Boots!' Mary sighed theatrically. 'What am I going to do with you?'

'Give me another piece of salmon,' Caligula suggested sotto voce.

'I can't believe you come round here making a mess of her laundry then expect her to feed you as well,' I said.

'She loves it,' said Caligula. 'One of the things she misses most since her husband died is having someone to be frustrated with on a daily basis. I'm simply fulfilling a need.'

Indeed, Mary didn't seem to mind Caligula's bad behaviour that much. Once she'd finished the washing up, she ambled over to the laundry pile and gave Caligula a scratch between the shoulder blades. 'Look at all those threads you've pulled. Good job these towels aren't my best ones, eh? Bad cat.'

Caligula seemed happy to settle in for a long session of being adored but Mary had other things to do. She went back to the kitchen and built an elaborate tower in the middle of the table using placemats, a couple of well-thumbed cookery books and the fruit bowl. The fruit bowl had a couple of oranges and a banana inside it. I watched with interest, wondering whether her plan was to lift the fruit out of Caligula's reach. It wouldn't have worked since he could easily jump on to the table. Neither would there have been much point anyway. Caligula didn't eat fruit. I used to, I remembered. I was always partial to a bit of banana and liked a satsuma too, so long as it was carefully peeled and Tuesday washed the sharp scent of the rind off her fingers before she fed me a segment.

Then Mary's plan became clear. She had made a sort of tripod with the oranges and banana and rested her mobile phone upon it. She fussed about with it for a while, getting it into the perfect position. Then she sat back and stared at the phone screen, checking her watch every couple of minutes to see what time it was now. Every so often, she picked the phone up and shook it to see if it was still working. As she was putting it back in place for the fifth time, it suddenly rang and Mary quickly jabbed at the screen to answer the call. Unfortunately, she pressed a little too hard and fast, sending her makeshift phone stand – fruit bowl, books and all – tumbling off the table.

'Oh dear! Oh dear!' Mary got to her knees to find the phone on the floor. She had to get right underneath the table to find it and, as she finally answered the call, she sat up, forgetting quite where she was, and banged her head.

'Mum?' a voice came from the phone. 'Mum? What on earth are you doing?'

'I'm OK, dear,' Mary said cheerfully. 'Mr Boots just knocked my phone off the table, that's all.'

Caligula looked affronted. 'What is she talking about? I have not moved from this pile of towels,' he said to me. I understood at once that Mary didn't want her caller to know about her clumsiness.

Mary crawled out from beneath the table. Somehow, she'd managed to put her daughter on speakerphone, but she still had her ear pressed to the screen.

'Mum? You need to take the phone away from your head, Mum. We're on video call but all I can see is your ear.'

Mary pulled herself up on to a chair and held the phone at arm's length. 'Oh!' she exclaimed. 'Kathy! I can see you!'

'I know, Mum. That's the whole idea. Toby, say hello to Grandma.'

I put my paws up on to the kitchen table so I could see what Mary was looking at. On the screen of her phone were the faces of the little boy from in the photograph on her mantelpiece and his mother, Mary's daughter. They were the ones Caligula said lived in Australia. They waved at Mary across the miles.

As I stared, the little boy pointed at me. Or at least, at where I would be if anyone could see me.

'What are you pointing at, Toby?' Mary asked.

'Dog!' he said.

'There's no dog here,' said Mary. 'Do you mean the cat? Look, Mr Boots is sleeping on the laundry again. Isn't he a naughty puss?'

Caligula lazily opened one yellow eye as Mary tried to get him in the picture.

'Mum? Mum? You need to turn the camera round so we can see you,' Kathy said. 'All we can see is the back door now. What have you pressed?'

'I don't know. I don't think I've pressed anything.'

'Mum? Are you still there? We can't hear you either now. Have you put your phone on mute or something? There should be a button. It looks like a microphone with a cross through it. Did you press that, Mum?'

'I don't know,' said Mary. 'Tell me again.'

But of course, Mary's daughter couldn't hear her asking.

'Mum,' Kathy said. 'I'm going to end this call then call you back and see if that helps. Don't touch any more buttons!'

It didn't seem to make a difference. When Kathy called back, she still couldn't hear Mary talking or see her.

'Mum,' said Kathy. 'I'm going to call you on your landline.'

The landline duly rang.

'I don't know what I pressed,' said Mary.

'Me neither.'

'This new phone is too complicated for me. I'm not clever enough to use it.'

'Mum, you are! Just look at all the idiots on the street who are using their phones just fine. Maybe the best thing is if you ask someone to help you sort your mobile out tomorrow. One of your neighbours, perhaps?'

That was an excellent idea. Derren or Zoe would both know what to do. So would Tuesday. But Mary said, 'I don't think I can go round knocking on doors to get help with my phone, Kathy. I don't know half the people who live on this street these days and in any case, I'm sure they've got better things to do than help some silly old woman who doesn't know how to use her mobile.'

Kathy protested.

'No,' said Mary. 'I'll have to take it back to the shop when I go into town next week. Oh, I'm so disappointed. I was so looking forward to having a Face Chat thingy with you and Toby.'

'So were we. Look, we'll have that call next week, Mum. If you can get to the shop this week, by this time next Sunday, you'll be an expert.'

'I think it might be beyond me.'

'It absolutely isn't, Mum! My next-door neighbour here can do it and she's eighty-three next week. Look, I'd better go. Toby has wandered off into the garden and I don't know what he's up to.'

'Of course,' said Mary. 'I'm sorry I'm such a silly old woman.'

'Mum!' Kathy sighed. 'Please don't talk like that. Look, we've got to go. We love you.'

'I love you too,' said Mary.

After Kathy ended the landline call, Mary just stared at the blank screen of her mobile phone. I knew what she was feeling. Over the past few days, I had come to know, all too clearly, the sense that thousands of miles stood between me and the people I loved.

Caligula, too, could tell that Mary was feeling very low. That messy call with her daughter and grandson had left her feeling worse than having no call at all. A glimpse of their faces had left her with a stronger longing than ever to have them near. Silently, Caligula jumped down from the clean towels and resettled himself on Mary's lap. He retracted his claws and gently kneaded her legs with his soft paws to let her know that he was there for her.

'Oh, Mr Boots,' she said. 'I miss them both so much.'

I rested my head on the edge of Mary's chair. Of course she didn't know I was there but I hoped that on some level she could feel my supportive presence too.

Caligula let himself be stroked for a few minutes before Mary announced that she was going to bed.

'It will all look better in the morning,' she said, ostensibly to Caligula but mostly to herself. 'Yes. It will all look much better. I'll get that silly phone sorted out and maybe I'll even go to the travel agent and ask how much a flight to Australia would cost over Christmas. I can't let being scared of flying keep me from seeing Toby grow up, can I? Though who would look after you if I went to Australia, Mr Boots?'

'Don't worry about me,' Caligula said in words that only I could hear. 'But yes, you must book that flight, Mary. You must be brave.'

Mary nodded to herself, then she made sure the back door was locked for a third time. Caligula had his own cat flap. Mary dabbed at her eyes with a handkerchief as she climbed the stairs to bed. I felt a painful squeeze in my heart, dead though it may have been.

'Mary won't book that flight to Australia,' said Caligula, when we were outside again. 'She's been psyching herself up to go since her husband died. They went together when Kathy got married there six years ago. But Mary can't convince herself to go alone. She's much more scared of everything since she lost him. I almost wish I could go with her but I had a cousin who went on a flight once and she told me it was horrendous. Couldn't look out of the windows. She had to sit in her cat carrier under the seat the whole way. What's more, she said the person whose seat she was tucked beneath farted all the way across the Atlantic.'

Something else was on my mind. 'Caligula, do you think it's possible that Mary's grandson could see me? He said "dog". And he pointed at the screen. Do you think he could see me standing behind her when he said that?'

Caligula shrugged. 'Kids say words because they can. Doesn't necessarily mean he knew what he was saying. Not really. He didn't see you.'

It was not what I wanted to hear. I'd wanted Caligula to tell me that perhaps human children could see animal spirits if they were still young enough to be tuned in to the magic of the universe. Because that meant there was still a chance that William could see me, and I could let him know I wasn't going anywhere until I knew for certain that he and his mother were happy and safe. That had to be why I still hadn't crossed over to the Rainbow Kingdom.

Chapter Twenty-Nine

After we left Mary's house, we went to Caligula's official home. It was late and Derren had gone to bed. He had the duvet – which didn't have a cover on it, I noticed – pulled up over his head but we could still hear him snoring.

'Have you ever heard anything like it?' Caligula asked me.

I had to admit I hadn't. Derren's snoring was almost as loud as the sound of the aeroplanes that had flown low over our street the previous summer to celebrate the end of a long-ago war. Tuesday had kept me inside that day, explaining to me that there was going to be a fly-past and there was no need to worry. To me, it was worse than the late autumn, when some of Tuesday's neighbours let off fireworks without a thought as to how they sounded when you weren't expecting them. And I was never expecting them.

'So,' Caligula said, stepping lightly around the buttons on his soundboard, until he found a yellow one. 'I've been experimenting with improving my human communication skills. I decided I was being too *literal* with Derren. Human communication is all about context.

Particularly when talking what they call "English". Watch this.'

He pressed the button with his right front paw. It said, in that voice that didn't sound human at all, 'sad'.

'Sad?'

'Yep. Sad.' Caligula nodded and pressed the button again. He pressed it five times in quick succession. At the same time, he pulled that big-eyed face that made even me feel quite sorry for him.

'Caligula, are you really sad?' I asked. 'Has something happened?'

'Of course I'm not sad, Stupido. But when I say I'm hungry, Derren tells me I'm not, then he reminds me I was fed a couple of hours ago and ignores me. When I say I'm sad, however, he gives me a treat to make me happy again. Works. Every. Single. Time.'

Caligula pressed the button another five times. 'Sad, sad, sad, sad, sad!'

'Caligula,' I gasped. 'Derren's asleep.'

'Not any more, he's not.'

Indeed, Derren was scrambling to get out of bed and searching for his glasses in a panic. They were on the bedside table but in his hurry to find out what Caligula was saying, he knocked them on to the floor and had to pat his way across the carpet to find them. Once he had his glasses on, Derren raced to see what was going on. With pointed slowness, Caligula pressed the button saying 'sad' one more time and added a deeply pathetic 'miaow' for good measure.

'That yowl means, "Feed me, human idiot,"' Caligula told me in an aside.

Though he had been woken from his slumber, Derren did not seem unduly upset. Instead, he fell to his knees next to the soundboard and tried to scoop Caligula into his arms for a cuddle. Caligula deftly slipped away. But Derren reached out to pet him again and this time managed to get hold of him. Caligula gawped in alarm as Derren stood up, cradling him in his arms like a human baby. That didn't last long. Caligula executed an extraordinary twisting move that released him from Derren's grip, whereupon he dropped straight to the floor, landing perfectly on all four feet. I was impressed.

Derren got down on his knees so that he was level with Caligula's eyeline again.

'Oh, Caligula. You were trying to talk to me, weren't you? But I was asleep. I'm so sorry. What is it you wanted to tell me? Can you tell me again?'

Caligula sighed and said to me, 'I only said "sad" sixteen times. Once more for the hard of understanding, eh?' He pressed the button again. And did the eyes.

Derren did likewise. 'Sad, yes. You're sad, Caligula. Not happy.'

Caligula widened his eyes still further, feigning gratitude at being understood.

'We can't have you being sad. Why are you sad? What would make you happy, Caligula? Tell me. I'll do whatever I can.'

Almost as if by accident, Caligula brushed against the button that said 'food'.

'Food. Right. Wait there. I'll see what I can do.'

As though he were Caligula's butler rather than his owner, Derren went straight for the cupboard where he kept Caligula's food. He pulled out a packet of Dreamies.

'Not my favourites,' Caligula complained to me. 'But I suppose they will have to do.'

Caligula stared intently at his bowl as Derren shook out one, then two, then three treats, before standing up again. Caligula stepped forward delicately and chomped them down. Then he tried the eyes again.

'Didn't that work?' Derren asked. 'Are you still sad?'

Caligula padded back to the soundboard and confirmed that he was. 'Yes. Sad.'

'Caligula!' Derren was delighted. 'That's a whole sentence.'

'No, it's not,' I said. 'It doesn't have a verb.'

'But the verb was implied and it's working,' Caligula told me.

'Damn,' said Derren. 'I didn't get it on film. Caligula, I'll give you more Dreamies if you say all of that one more time so I can record it?'

Derren left the packet of Dreamies on the floor while he went to look for his phone. By the time he came back, Caligula had finished off the rest of the Dreamies and was ready to get out of there.

'Happy,' Caligula confirmed with a swipe at the board. 'Come on, Stupido,' he said to me then. 'Let's scoot.'

'It's not Stupido,' I reminded him.

'I just made a whole sentence in human language. I think that entitles me to make the call.'

We left via the cat flap. Caligula threw Derren a miaow again as we went.

'What did you say just then?' I asked.

'I said, "Next time you're at the shop, get HiLife." None of that Dreamies rubbish.'

'And what did Derren say?' He had offered Caligula a corresponding miaow.

'He said, "I hear it will be wet again tomorrow." With the accent of a common tabby.'

Who knew speaking cat was so fraught with difficulty? Speaking dog seemed so simple by comparison. Not that Tuesday always got it right. But she never caused me any offence. Just then, Derren opened the door and tried one more plaintive mew. Caligula turned to answer it with an affronted hiss.

'What did he say then?' I had to know.

'He said, "Your mother was born in a wheelie bin." If he had any idea . . .'

We continued on our way. The street was sleeping. At least the human residents were.

Because it was a warm night, Zoe had left her bedroom window ajar to let in the breeze. The gap was just big enough for Caligula to squeeze through. I hesitated, thinking I would be too big to do the same, before I remembered that no space was too small for me now.

Zoe had not made it into bed that night. Not properly in any case. She must have fallen asleep while scrolling through Instagram. She was still fully dressed in a pink sequinned mini-skirt and a top embellished with feathers and wearing the make-up she had taken hours to apply. One of her false eyelashes had come adrift and was stuck to her cheek. Caligula gently moved it from her face so that it fell on to the floor, where he batted it around as though it were a big dead spider.

'Little things,' he said, when he saw I was watching him play.

'I get it. Sometimes I play with my own tail.'

'I thought that was because you had worms.'

'That too . . . Zoe must have had a very good night out,' I suggested. 'To fall asleep without even getting under the duvet.'

'Oh, she didn't go out,' said Caligula, drawing my attention to the wine bottle on the desk. The empty wine bottle. 'She's been in all evening on her own again.' He sniffed at the top of the bottle with great delicacy. 'Ugh. That wine was corked. She's going to have the most appalling headache in the morning.'

'You know about wine?'

'Like I've told you, I know a lot about a lot of things. Though even a dog would be able to tell that this bottle wasn't worth drinking.'

I took a sniff myself.

'I see what you mean. Why does Zoe never go out?' I asked. 'She's so pretty – in that human way – and she seems to be very nice.'

'I don't know. I guess she just doesn't have any real-life friends. It seems to me that humans are losing their ability to connect. They're strange creatures. There are probably a hundred of them living in this street alone but how many of them know each other's names? They could all be having a wonderful time with each other. Instead, they rely on animals, like you and me, to fill the gaps in their emotional lives. They don't need us, they need each other.'

'Caligula,' I dared to ask. 'You seem to understand so much. Were you a human in another life?'

'You've uncovered my secret. I was Cleopatra.'

'I knew it!'

Caligula snorted. 'Of course I wasn't Cleopatra. Though I did meet her. Assuming you mean Cleopatra the Seventh.'

'Is there any other?'

'The clue is in the name. Interesting woman. Great line in wigs but terrible teeth. I met her when I was a cat at the Temple of Ra. I've always been a cat and I always will be. You don't get to *become* a cat, no matter how great a human being you are. Cats are entirely outside this planet's reincarnation system. We come from elsewhere.'

He adopted an expression which I guessed was supposed to be mysterious. I did not take the bait and ask where this 'elsewhere' was.

'But does that mean people can become dogs and dogs become people?' I asked instead. 'I mean, if I did go over the Rainbow Bridge now, could I come back as a person and look after Tuesday that way?'

'You'd have to come back as a baby – like William – and it would be years, hundreds of dog years, before you were mature enough to speak to Tuesday on a level. And there's no guarantee that if you did come back as a human and not a flea, you'd come back in the right place. You could be born in another country far, far away, like Mary's grandson. You could even grow up speaking a different language. But what am I talking about anyway? The answer is, I don't really know. All I know is that I wouldn't want to come back as a human being for all the fish in the sea. A cat's life is a good one. We get to go wherever we like. We don't have to work. We don't have to take instructions. Look at Mary, Zoe and Derren. Would you want to swap places with any one of them?'

I admitted that I wouldn't. 'Except that it would mean I could just walk over the road, knock on Tuesday's door and talk to her and ask her what happened. I could ask to give William a cuddle.'

'But would you? Mary, Zoe and Derren could do that any day of the week, but they don't, do they? They all three of them stay stuck in their own little worlds, communicating with other humans only virtually. They go for weeks on end without getting so much as a nuzzle from anyone but me. What kind of life is that?'

'Not much of a life,' I agreed. 'I can't imagine anything worse than being nuzzled by you.'

'The feeling is mutual.'

We laughed, but all the same, the sadness of the human beings Caligula had shown me that night was almost unbearable.

Caligula decided that he would end his wanderings at Zoe's house that evening. He told me he wanted to be there with her when she woke up.

'I know she has a packet of chicken HiLife hidden somewhere. Seek me out if you find that rat again, won't you?'

I promised I would. Then I went by myself to Zena's house. She was still awake. I crept into the kitchen and joined her under the table where Tuesday and Andrew had shared their first cup of tea over Tuesday's injured foot. The garden was looking uncared for, I observed.

'Tuesday hasn't been here since you died,' Zena confirmed. 'But I think it's because of what happened three weeks ago. Before your accident.'

'What happened?' I asked.

And as Zena started to tell the story, it began to come back to me.

Chapter Thirty

Then

After the day when Tuesday and Andrew decided to go to the park together for the first time, the development of their friendship really seemed to gather pace. Now, before she started the day's tasks, Tuesday always accepted the coffee Andrew offered and they sat in the kitchen together while she drank it, talking about anything and everything.

Andrew told Tuesday more about his life as a VIP. The frustrations and the strange consolations too.

'I think that in many ways I was on auto-pilot before the accident. I had life planned out but hadn't really considered whether it was what I wanted or what was expected of me. And I was lazy.'

'You were a doctor!' Tuesday protested.

'But it came easily to me. I had a terrible bedside manner. Especially when I was a junior doctor, working in a hospital. I thought badly of many of my patients. I thought that bad luck and illness happened to people who had somehow asked for it by being stupid in some way. I thought that when they didn't get better or couldn't stick to an exercise regime I'd prescribed, it was because they were being pathetic. I soon learned the truth about that. Having to start again from scratch in so many areas of my life was humbling, to say the least.'

'So, it did make you less of an arse,' Tuesday dared to suggest.

Andrew laughed and slapped his hands on his knees. 'I guess it did.'

Zena told me that Andrew laughed much more when Tuesday was around.

In turn, Tuesday told Andrew more about her life as a single mum. Eventually, she even told him about Kenton.

'I think I was so desperate to have a man in my life that I overlooked some very obvious red flags. He was judgemental. He thought he was better than most of the people he met. He was always ranting about what incompetents other people were. He made me start to doubt myself. And he didn't like Stupendo.'

'How could anyone not like Stupendo,' Andrew said, reaching out his hand to invite me over for an ear scratch. I was only too happy to oblige. Andrew was very good at scratches. I liked him more and more.

'So,' Andrew asked, 'how is your relationship with Kenton now? How often does he have William?'

Tuesday gazed into her coffee as though the answer might be there.

'You don't have to tell me,' Andrew said when she didn't answer at once.

'It's OK. The fact is, he doesn't see William at all. He doesn't even know he exists. You see, after Kenton left, he ghosted me. I tried to track him down in every way I could think of, but short of filing a missing person report . . . Kenton doesn't want to be found. I won't stop William from trying to find him when he's older though. I do worry that he doesn't have a good male role model in his life.'

Andrew tapped his own coffee cup thoughtfully. 'You know, there are ways to make sure he does without having to stay in a bad relationship,' he suggested. 'There will be all sorts of male influences in his life. There will be people on television, teachers at school, the men he sees working in the community – and your friends, of course. They'll be around him.'

'I suppose you're right.'

'But maybe your son doesn't need a "male role model" in the way you think he does. Maybe he needs dozens of role models – of every gender, colour, class, creed and ability – to show him all the possibilities for a happy, helpful life. And then there's you: being all the parent he needs and showing him what it takes to run a home and a business and generally conquer the world. All while staying true to your dreams, of course.'

'When you put it like that . . .' Tuesday smiled.

'Plus he's also got an excellent dog in his life,' Andrew added. 'Can't underestimate the civilising power of having a good dog.'

'Well, exactly,' said Zena.

I agreed with that.

The following Friday, Andrew suggested we all take another walk in the park. Since it was going to be such a beautiful day, he said, we should go over lunchtime and have a picnic. He would bring the sandwiches.

'I can do that,' Tuesday said.

'No,' Andrew insisted, 'you just bring crisps.'

And when we got to the park and he opened up the Tupperware box to reveal the feast inside, he joked, 'One of them may have half a finger in it.'

But Tuesday was coming to understand that Andrew was actually an excellent cook. 'I went on a cordon bleu course before I lost my sight. Picked up some excellent knife skills. Still got them. You should let me cook for you properly one night.'

Tuesday began what might have turned into a protest. Then she stopped herself and simply said, 'That would be lovely.'

'I do a mean chilli.'

'Chilli is my favourite.'

I hoped there would be some for me.

It was the kind of afternoon that you wish could last forever. Zena and I amused William with our most outrageous zoomies, then lazed on the rug beside him while he flipped our ears inside out and back again. I let Zena have some of the sandwich crusts William discarded. Andrew and Tuesday were too deep in conversation to notice that Zena was eating things she shouldn't be.

'I don't normally do this,' she said, as she delicately picked another crust from the bottom of William's plastic bib.

'Live a little,' I said.

'I'm not supposed to eat anything that Andrew hasn't approved. You're getting me into bad habits,' Zena complained, but I could tell she was enjoying being a rebel for once.

When it was time to go home and William baulked at the idea of going back into his pushchair, Andrew said, 'Perhaps I could carry him?' He did, with Zena guiding the way. William was more than happy to be on Andrew's hip for a while. He gazed up at his new friend with something approaching awe.

'You're a natural,' Tuesday said.

'I've got two nephews. They're both in their teens but when they were little, I loved to carry them like this. I miss those days. Though it's still fun to spend time with them, even if they think I'm a dinosaur rather than a hero now.'

'You've got siblings?'

'A sister. Susie. Two years my senior.'

'I've got a half-brother. He grew up with Dad in Spain. I envied him having Dad around all the time. I felt as though when he came along, Dad forgot all about me. It's like he had a chance to start again and get it right and didn't want to be reminded of everything that had gone wrong before.'

'That must have hurt. And it explains why you're so keen for William to have a male role model.'

'I don't ever want William to feel like I did. Like I didn't matter.'

'I don't think he'll ever feel like that. I get the feeling that you love him enough for two.'

'I do,' said Tuesday, gently smoothing down William's hair where it was always sticking up.

With every conversation, another piece of the jigsaw slotted into place, and Zena and I could tell that Tuesday and Andrew were growing to like each other more and more. When we got to number thirteen after that picnic in the park, they lingered at the top of the drive, indulging in an excruciatingly long goodbye.

'Why doesn't she just invite him in for tea?' I complained to Zena after what felt like an hour.

'It's a delicate dance,' said Zena. 'This human mating game.'

Chapter Thirty-One

Just a few days after that, Tuesday's work on getting Andrew's gardens into shape was done. The lawn in the back garden was pristine. She'd built Zena a special 'spending area', marking the border with a small white fence. The broken sundial was mended and back on the wall. Though Andrew wouldn't be able to see it, I knew it gave Tuesday great pleasure to think that the sundial was back in the place where it had hung for so many years.

Meanwhile, the front garden was looking very smart. The cherry tree was much happier now that Tuesday had cleared the tangle of plants that had grown up around its trunk. The path to the front door was less of a trip hazard. It was time to let Andrew know the work was finished.

'Great,' he said. 'I'm really glad you were persuaded to take the job on.'

But he didn't step out of the kitchen.

'You've got to come outside,' Tuesday insisted. 'I want you to know exactly what I've done here. Please. Let me tell you.'

Andrew quickly let himself be persuaded. Tuesday told him to follow her along the path, describing the terrain as she went.

'It occurred to me that a garden is more than something to look at,' Tuesday said. 'You can experience a garden with all of your senses. So that's what I've thought of here. There are things to touch. There are things to smell. I want you to enjoy this garden as much as Zena and your guests do.'

She guided him to a flower bed where she ran her hand over the lavender to send its scent up into the air.

'Lavender. Reminds me of France,' Andrew said.

'Yes. And here's Italy.' She walked him around to the jasmine and encouraged him to get close to the small white flowers with their fragrance of summer nights in Mediterranean cities.

'And here's England.'

She took him to a rose that had just one, highly scented flower.

'When I cut back all the weeds in the flower beds, I found lots of mature roses, left by the previous owner. Most of them still had their garden-centre labels. This is a Gertrude Jekyll,' she said. 'Named after one of my heroines. She was a famous garden designer and author. The rose is bright pink. It's a double, which means the petals are very tightly packed. It will flower the whole summer long.'

'Hello, Gertrude,' Andrew said.

'And next to Gertrude is a Boscobel. When this rose blossoms, you'll be able to smell elderflower, almond and pear. The flowers are salmon pink with a sort of orangey tinge. And here's Lady Emma Hamilton. Her red buds open to orange flowers. She's the most fragrant of all.'

'Delighted to meet you, Lady Emma,' Andrew said.

Tuesday walked Andrew back to the centre of the lawn. 'There are things to hear too. You can hear the bees in the lavender. If you stand very still, you can hear the breeze in the leaves of the holm oak. And the squirrels complaining.'

'That weird chattering sound?'

'Exactly. It's the noise they make when there's a cat nearby. Right now, they're probably telling each other about us.'

The squirrels were in fact being lairy, teasing me and Zena about our humans and their obvious attraction to one another. It was fortunate that Tuesday didn't speak squirrel or she would have blushed. She continued, 'The different trees and plants make different noises according to the time of year and then, of course, there are the birds.'

As if he was in on the plan, Merle appeared. He looked to me to let him know what was going on.

'Give them one of your fancy whistles?' I suggested.

'Whistles?' Merle pretended to be insulted but obliged with a snatch of song all the same.

'Is that a blackbird?' Andrew asked.

'It is. He's been watching the whole process, waiting for me to turn up a worm or two whenever I'm digging. There's a robin too. He's been getting closer and closer every day. Yesterday, he actually sat on the handle of my spade. He didn't even care that the dogs were out.'

'Why would he,' I thought. We were all friends, the birds and the squirrels and the dogs. Ethelred knew us and he knew we'd never hurt him.

'And that "peep, peep, peep" sound you can hear?'

said Tuesday. 'Two sparrow fledglings. They left their nest in the ivy by the fence for the first time this morning.'

'There's a whole world out here,' said Andrew.

'Yes. It feels like there's a whole other universe that we don't usually notice.'

If only Tuesday knew.

She and Andrew stood in silence while Merle sang another song. It was one of Merle's favourites; an old, old tune passed down through the avian generations. Something about the sun being at its highest and all the world in love. I'd heard it many times before and it only grew more beautiful with every hearing.

When Merle finished singing and flew away, Tuesday broke the human silence. 'Andrew, I've been thinking. I've told you about the garden but . . . would you like to know what *I* look like? I mean, I could just describe myself to you – and I suppose it doesn't really matter – but I wondered if perhaps . . . if perhaps you would like to touch my face?'

There was a tense moment before Andrew rocked back on his heels with mirth.

'What's funny?' Tuesday asked. 'I thought if you touched my face then you would know, you know . . . How big my nose is? What shape my eyebrows are? That sort of thing.'

'Is that how you think it works?'

'Have I said something really stupid? I thought that was how VIPs "saw". With their hands?'

'You're thinking of the Lionel Richie video from the eighties. Where the drama student makes a sculpture of Lionel and then feels his face to see if it matches. The

thing people always seem to miss is that the student makes
her sculpture of Richie before she gets her hands on his
moustache. She had an idea of him in her head first. It
wasn't the other way round, though I can understand why
people got confused.'

'I'm sorry. I shouldn't have asked. It was an idiotic
thing to say.'

'No. It wasn't,' Andrew responded. 'It was a perfectly
reasonable assumption to make. And it was a generous
offer.'

'You're just being kind.'

'Maybe.'

Tuesday shoved her hands deep into the pockets of her
dungarees. She looked miserable. But then Andrew
continued, 'The thing is, Tuesday, the shape of your nose
doesn't matter to me. I don't care about your eyebrows
either. Or what your teeth are like. Or whether your hair
goes frizzy in the rain.'

I pricked up my ears. Both Zena and I now listened
intently. We could both sense the sudden change in the
tone of the conversation though it was quite possible that
neither Andrew nor Tuesday had noticed it yet themselves.
Humans put so much importance on words. Zena and I
tuned into the cadence and the silences, which said so
much more. She put her paw upon mine and we shared
a worried glance. What would Andrew say next and how
would Tuesday respond?

'Don't blow it,' both Zena and I prayed.

Andrew exhaled with some purpose before he carried
on. 'I already have a very good idea of what you look like,
Tuesday King. I can guess how tall you are from the

sound your footsteps make as you walk into a room. I can tell how gracefully you move from the way you pull out a kitchen chair and sit down. I can imagine your capable hands when I hear you working in the garden. I know you have bitten fingernails too, because sometimes you talk to me while you still have a finger in your mouth.'

It was true! Tuesday did bite her fingernails. In fact, she was worrying at a hangnail right then. She quickly took her hand from her mouth. Andrew smiled at the knowledge he'd been on the money. Then he picked up his thread.

'I know that your mouth is wide and generous from smiling. I know that your eyes are soft and kind and they're crinkled at the edges from a lifetime of laughter. But at the same time, you have the faintest lines on your forehead from the way you knit your brows together when you're concentrating hard on what your friends say. You're a good friend, I know. You're a wonderful mother. The very best. I can hear that you are beautiful, Tuesday. I can sense it. I don't need to see or feel your face to believe it.'

Silence hung between them but there was so much being said in that quiet moment.

'Which isn't to say that I wouldn't love to touch you to confirm what I've just told you I know. To confirm what my heart sees . . .'

Slowly, Andrew lifted his hands towards Tuesday's face and she fitted her pointy chin into them. He drew her closer. Their lips hovered millimetres apart.

And then Tuesday's mobile rang.

Chapter Thirty-Two

William's nursery was calling.

'I've got to get this,' Tuesday said.

It was bad news. William had been sick and Tuesday had to fetch him home at once. She told Andrew that she would be back to tidy up the last of her garden tools then she and I left at a clip. We ran to the nursery. Of course, by the time we got there, William was already feeling much better. He had a dog's ability to chuck up his lunch then carry on regardless. He greeted me with an excited squeal. I licked his nose.

'You have no idea what bad timing you have,' I told him. He didn't have a clue what I was saying, of course. He merely giggled.

Back at number thirteen, Tuesday unclipped William from the pushchair and he immediately toddled towards the back door into the garden. Tuesday followed him there. She sat on the step while William busied himself with digging in the flower bed with a little plastic spade. He chucked plenty of dirt over me as he did so. I was happy to be part of the game but I had one eye on Tuesday. She did not seem quite herself. She rested her chin on her knees.

She murmured to herself, 'Did that really happen? Was he going to kiss me?'

I couldn't wait to see Zena again and ask her if Andrew had been having the same reaction. This muttering wasn't a bad thing, I knew. Tuesday was secretly thrilled with everything that had happened in Andrew's garden that day.

Later, while William was busy throwing most of his dinner in my direction – I got a whole fish finger – Tuesday composed a text.

'I've invited Andrew and Zena to William's birthday party,' Tuesday told me, in the absence of anyone else to tell. 'Will that be nice?'

I wagged my tail. It would be better than nice! Andrew responded within seconds. I could tell he'd said yes by the way his text made Tuesday smile.

Sunday – the day of William's first birthday party – seemed to take forever to come. It was another beautiful day. The party wasn't going to be a very big affair – just a few close friends – but Emily and Elvis arrived early to help set everything up. Like me, they took the business of godparenting seriously. They carried chairs out into the garden and cleaned off the garden table, which was cluttered with William's toys and some of mine, so they could lay out a buffet upon it. As Emily and Tuesday chatted and set out cling-film-covered plates of sandwiches, and Elvis and William played with a ball, I guarded the table to make sure that none of the garden animals or birds tried to sneak a snack.

Caligula was observing all from the top of the fence but he knew he wouldn't get near the smoked salmon on my watch. Of course, I didn't know back then that Caligula was already being fed by three different households on Bracken Avenue and had probably stuffed himself with salmon just that morning. The last thing he needed was an extra meal.

The human guests started to arrive at around one o'clock in the afternoon. William was delighted to be the centre of attention as he greeted each familiar face with a squeal of happiness. He was a natural clown and loved nothing more than to make people laugh. I liked to think that he and I made a good double act as we played in the garden while everyone had their first drink.

I heard Tuesday tell the story of how I had helped William learn to walk to a couple of people.

'There's nothing like the relationship between a child and his dog,' someone agreed.

'Perhaps you ought to get Stupendo a saddle,' Elvis suggested. 'So that William can ride him to the park.'

I'd have been up for that. Anything to make my little buddy happy.

As they prepared drinks for the other guests, Emily took Tuesday to one side. I listened in on their conversation.

'Is he coming?' Emily asked. 'Your friend with the guide dog.'

'He's been invited,' Tuesday said. 'And he said yes, but he's got to have Sunday lunch with his mum and his sister first.'

'I bet he's been telling them all about you!'

Tuesday flushed from nose to toes again. 'Why would he do that?'

'Come on. Admit it, Tuesday. You like him, don't you?

And he likes you. I have not seen you get so nervous about anyone in a long while.'

She was right. Not even Kenton had made Tuesday so thoughtful. Anxious, yes, but not nervous in a good way like this. An excited way. A very, very happy way. I approved.

'I do like him,' Tuesday blurted out. 'I hope you like him too.'

'He couldn't be any worse than . . .'

'Don't say his name,' said Tuesday, waving her hand in front of Emily's face.

'Quite,' I thought. The last thing we wanted to do was accidentally conjure up that particular demon. This was a special day!

It was a hectic afternoon. At around four, tired from playing with William and Elvis in the sprinkler, I took myself off for a doze in a patch of sun by the bird table. It was one of my favourite spots and with so many friends around to keep an eye on William, I should have been able to relax. But something kept me from entirely surrendering to my dreams.

I smelled him long before I saw him. My nose twitched at the familiar whiff on the air and a sense of danger woke me. Following my instincts, I got up and went into the house, moving quickly to the front door as someone approached from the other side. All the time, I was hoping against hope that I was imagining things. I had to be wrong.

Alas, I was not.

A dog's nose never lies.

The man on the doorstep was Kenton Harding.

Chapter Thirty-Three

I barked and, believe me, it was not a bark of welcome. It was a bark of warning. A bark to say, 'Go away while you still can. Before I rip your head off.' When he'd lived with us, I'd done my best not to bark every time Kenton put his key in the door – it wasn't easy – but now he didn't have the privileges of a member of our household. He had the status of a stranger again and I would treat him as such. A hostile stranger.

But I couldn't scare Kenton off.

He pressed on the doorbell just as Tuesday and Emily came into the hallway together. They were laughing about something. Emily was carrying William, who had birthday cake smeared all around his mouth and down the front of his special birthday outfit.

'I'll take him upstairs and get him cleaned up,' Emily said.

Ordinarily, I would have done my best to help, and hoovered the crumbs off William's trousers, but right then I had more important things to do.

'I'll get the door,' said Tuesday.

She noticed that I was growling then, so took hold of my collar to keep me from flying at our visitor the minute she opened the door.

'What the matter with you?' she asked me but she didn't wait for an answer and of course I didn't have the words to tell her.

'Please don't let him in. Don't let him in. He's going to ruin our lives,' was what I wanted to say.

Kenton Harding stood on the doorstep with one arm behind his back. As Tuesday looked up at him with her mouth open in a mixture of surprise and horror (she was still bending low to hang on to my collar so that I couldn't rip his throat out), he flourished a bouquet of flowers and a heart-shaped balloon full of helium at her. How I hated those big balloons.

'Ta-da!' he said.

I lunged for his knees, pulling Tuesday with me.

'Stupendo!' she gasped, tugging me back again.

'Calm down, boy!' said Kenton. 'It's me, your old friend.'

'You were never my friend,' my bared teeth told him.

Tuesday shuffled me into the house behind her and closed the door so there was just a narrow gap for her to see out and Kenton to see in. I shoved hard against her legs. She shoved me back.

'Kenton, what are you doing here?' she asked our unwelcome visitor.

'*Well, hello, Kenton, how lovely to see you,*' he mocked. 'Is that the kind of welcome I get after all this time?'

'After all this time. Exactly,' I said with my growl.

He thrust the flowers and balloon towards Tuesday again. She took them.

'Thanks. I think.'

'You *think*?' Kenton echoed. 'Don't make me wish I

hadn't bothered. What happened to the sweet and lovely Tuesday I used to know? Aren't you going to let me in?'

'It's not a great time. I've got some people here,' said Tuesday.

'Anyone I know?'

Tuesday shook her head. She was trying to play it cool but I could smell that she was upset by Kenton's sudden appearance and worried too.

'A new boyfriend?' he probed.

'No,' said Tuesday flatly. 'Look, this isn't really a good time,' she tried again. But Kenton was looking over the top of Tuesday's head and he'd spotted Elvis, who was heading upstairs to the bathroom.

'Who's that?' Kenton asked.

'That's Emily's boyfriend, Elvis.'

'Elvis?' Kenton didn't disguise his disdain.

Elvis froze on the stairs upon hearing his name. He was wearing one of the party hats Tuesday had bought for all the guests. He put his hand up to it and took it off, as though embarrassed to be caught wearing it.

'Hi?' he said warily, picking up on the strange atmosphere. Elvis at least could read my body language.

'Are you having a *party*?' Kenton asked. 'Don't tell me I forgot your birthday. No, of course I didn't. You're a Pisces. Overemotional. This isn't Pisces season.'

Tuesday looked down at her shoes and frowned. I growled from behind her legs.

'This is a bad time,' she tried for a third time. 'It's best if you just go and text me with some other dates to meet up. I'm still on the same number. Unlike you.'

'Look, I know I should have called, but I was sure that

if I did call ahead and ask if I could see you, you would only say no, and why should I be surprised about that? So I decided it would be better if I just showed up and made my case in person. You have every right to tell me to get lost, but all I'm asking for is the chance to explain myself. If you don't like what you hear, I'll leave and you'll never have to see me again. Just give me ten minutes of your time, Tuesday. Your guests will understand.'

I growled again.

'Please, Tuesday,' Kenton whined.

Don't soften, don't soften, I tried to tell her with my eyes. Don't let him get round you. He's not our friend!

'Please . . .'

In another vain attempt to get at Kenton's jugular, I managed to push the front door open a little wider, accidentally allowing him to see further in. As I did so, Emily appeared at the top of the stairs. She was holding William, who was just in his nappy now.

'Tuesday,' she called. 'Where do you keep the nappies?'

Kenton looked from William to Tuesday and back again. A strange, slow smile spread across his face and we all knew the computations he must be making.

'Shit,' said Emily. 'It's him.'

'Yes, it's me,' said Kenton.

Tuesday finally stepped aside so that Kenton could step into the house.

'Come into the dining room,' she said. 'And I'll tell you everything.'

Of course, in deference to Kenton's dislike of dog hair – and possibly because I had not stopped growling since he walked down the garden path and I smelled him on the air – I was shut out of the dining-room summit that afternoon. However, I stayed close by the door, ready to spring into action should Tuesday need any assistance. Emily and Elvis stayed close by too, whispering to one another, as they eavesdropped from the hall. Emily bounced a freshly-changed William on her knee, trying to keep him from crying.

'What on earth is he doing here?' Emily hissed to Elvis. 'He just turns up after eighteen months without a word and expects to walk right in? He's got a bloody cheek.'

Elvis agreed. He didn't know Kenton but he'd heard a lot about him and none of it was good.

With my ears pricked in the right direction, I could hear Tuesday quite clearly as she explained what had happened since Kenton last darkened our door.

'You were pregnant and you didn't tell me?' Kenton's voice was full of disbelief.

'I tried to,' Tuesday told him. 'But you blocked my calls. You blocked my emails. You didn't leave a forwarding address. I didn't know where to find you. I'd never met any of your friends or your family so I couldn't even ask them where you'd gone. You made sure I couldn't find you.'

'You could have . . . I don't know, you could have called the police or something. They would have been able to track me down.'

'And if I had, would you have wanted to speak to me then? Would it have made a difference? Would you have come back?'

'Of course it would have made a difference,' Kenton

hissed. 'We're talking about my child here. What kind of man do you think I am?'

Emily, still listening at the dining room door, had her own answer. 'The kind of man who disappears for a year and a half then rocks up and expects to be welcomed home like the prodigal son.'

'I'm hurt,' said Kenton in the dining room. 'I'm hurt and I'm disgusted. I can't believe you would be so thoughtless and unkind. You of all people . . .'

'You were the one who left!' Tuesday reminded him.

'I may have left *you*, Tuesday, but I would never have left my child.'

The conversation continued like that for quite a while. Kenton's indignation was loud and only got louder as time went on but it didn't quite sound right to me. Listening to the way he said the words, rather than the words themselves, I could tell that his anger was not genuine. I guessed instead that he was using this unexpected situation to his advantage. The wrongs of his having disappeared without a trace were suddenly as nothing set against Tuesday having kept him from his child. Even if that hadn't been her choice or her intention. Her protestations got quieter and quieter and I could hear that Tuesday was letting Kenton win. From arriving with his tail between his legs, he had somehow managed to take the moral high ground.

After fifteen long minutes, Tuesday and Kenton emerged from the dining room. Hearing that the two of them were finishing their conversation, Emily and Elvis had already moved to the bottom of the stairs with William so that it wouldn't look as though they had been listening in. I had no such niceties to worry about so I remained by the dining room door until it opened and started growling the minute Kenton stepped out. Tuesday grabbed my collar right away. I could tell she had been crying. She seemed anxious still but Kenton was beaming like it was the best day ever.

'Come on then,' he said. 'It's time I met my son.'

Emily was still holding William. When Kenton held out his arms so that he could take him, Emily held William tighter, but a brief nod from Tuesday told her what she needed to know. Reluctantly, Emily went to pass William to Kenton but William wasn't having any of it. He was always a little shy around strangers but, seeing Kenton, he actually reared away from him. Tuesday stepped in, taking William from her best friend.

'He's a bit tired,' she told Kenton by way of an excuse.

'He'll get used to me,' Kenton said.

'Assuming he ever sees you again after today,' Emily muttered.

'What's that?' Kenton challenged her.

'You heard me. I'm not taken in by you, Kenton Harding. Becoming a father is easy. It only takes one lucky shag. Being a dad requires effort. It requires presence. It requires love. You don't just get to turn up when it suits you, for the big-ticket events.'

'I know that, thank you, Emily. I know that very well. But how could I have been here for William when I didn't even know he'd been born? Rest assured, now that I know he *exists*, I will never, ever neglect him. Good to know what kind of father you think I'll be, though,' he added with a sneer. 'I look forward to proving you wrong. Tuesday's already heard me apologise for disappearing like I did a year and a half ago. I had my reasons, though I know Tuesday must have thought I was a dick.'

'You can say that again,' said Emily.

'You don't need to speak for her,' Kenton said, rounding on Emily. 'She's got a voice of her own.'

Emily looked at Tuesday, hoping, as I did, that Tuesday would say what we were both thinking: 'Get lost, Kenton. We all still hate you.'

Instead, Tuesday said, with an embarrassed look on her face, 'He *is* William's father.'

'So you're saying he can stay?' Emily was incredulous. As was I.

'It is his son's first birthday.'

'And everyone who has actually been around for the whole of William's first year is here celebrating with him.'

Tuesday looked from Kenton to Emily and back again. I could tell she was torn between the pair of them. Emily was speaking to Tuesday's head but Kenton was playing Tuesday's heart like a violin.

'He is William's dad,' Tuesday said again. 'And if I'd tried harder to get hold of him as soon as I knew I was pregnant, then he would have been here all along. I believe that.'

Emily gawped. 'Tuesday, you could not have tried harder. The only thing you didn't do was put in a missing person's report. Since it was quite obvious that Kenton was not missing by mistake . . .'

Kenton didn't wait for any further debate. He walked past Emily into the kitchen. The extravagant balloon, which he was carrying again, bumped against Emily's face, forcing her to take a step back. Kenton was in the heart of the house. Tuesday was arguing his case. He knew he'd won.

As Kenton helped himself to some of the leftover sandwiches curling on the kitchen table, Emily grabbed her jacket and bag from the rack in the hall. Tuesday asked, 'What are you doing?'

'I'm leaving. Come on, Elvis. If Kenton's staying, then we are not.'

'Please yourself,' said Kenton.

Emily went to the kitchen door to tell him, 'If you hurt my best friend or my godson, you will have me to answer to.'

'Ooooh. Scary,' Kenton mocked.

'Tuesday?' Elvis pleaded. But Tuesday had been shocked into silence. I could see that she had no idea what to do for the best.

I couldn't believe it. Tuesday was letting Emily and Elvis leave while Kenton got to stay. The wrong people were going. Had Emily not slammed the front door behind her, leaving me stuck in the hall, I would have run out to let her know that I wanted her with me and Tuesday and William until the danger had passed. Until Kenton had gone back to wherever he'd come from. Crawled back under his rock (though that's an insult to those creatures that do actually live under rocks, some of whom are perfectly lovely).

Kenton tipped his head on one side as he took Tuesday's chin in his hand. It was a gesture that was at once both tender and threatening. A dog can read these things. Unfortunately, I guessed that Tuesday was only seeing 'tender'.

'You always did let Emily talk for you, didn't you?' Kenton said. 'Your friendship was always so unbalanced.'

'Tuesday!' I wanted to say. 'Emily has been there for us all the way along and now this jerk turns up with flowers and a funny-smelling helium balloon and suddenly her opinion means nothing. What are you thinking?'

But Tuesday wasn't even looking in my direction.

'Can I hold him? Can I hold my son?' Kenton asked her.

Kenton let go of the heart-shaped balloon so that it floated up to bounce against the ceiling. He placed the big, gaudily wrapped bouquet on the kitchen table. Then he held out his arms towards William once more. William, quite rightly, buried his face in Tuesday's chest and again resisted being handed over.

'He's going through a phase,' said Tuesday. 'He doesn't like to go to people he doesn't know.'

And he should know his father, I harrumphed.

'He'll get used to me,' said Kenton. 'Come on.'

He gestured to Tuesday to hand William over. Impatiently, I thought. I stepped between them. I let out a small growl. Kenton nudged me with his foot. It would have been all the provocation a good dog needed but by this point, William was hovering above my head as Tuesday handed him over, and as much as I wanted to bite Kenton in the crotch, I dared not risk any harm coming to that baby boy. My boy. I had to stand down.

'Here he is,' Kenton cooed. 'My son. I'm your daddy. That's right. I'm Daddy. Da da da.'

William looked at me and said, 'Do-do-do.'

'Clever boy!' said Kenton. 'You nearly got it. Da da da . . .'

'He's saying "dog",' I wanted to yell. William was even pointing in my direction.

Tuesday watched anxiously. 'You need to support William's bottom,' she said.

'I knew that,' said Kenton, tucking one arm underneath William so that he was better supported. 'Come on. Let's go out into the garden and get someone to take a photograph of our happy little family.'

Chapter Thirty-Four

With the arrival of Kenton, William's first birthday party was ruined. I couldn't relax in Kenton's presence. Every time he picked William up, I could sense my favourite boy's distress at being handled by a stranger — for that's what Kenton was to him. I could tell by the way William stiffened his back and clenched his little fists while he was in Kenton's arms that he was scared and unhappy but Tuesday didn't seem to notice. She just beamed when Kenton bounced William up and down on his knee. Much too roughly in my opinion.

I followed Kenton around the garden and the house, sticking close by him in case William's distress became too much to bear and I had to take action. At the same time, I kept an ear out in the direction of the street, longing for Zena to arrive with Andrew and make everything better again. They said they would be at the party by late afternoon. They should have been here by now. I needed back-up. Allies. When Andrew arrived, Tuesday would stop making googly eyes at Kenton and be reminded that we'd all been doing perfectly well in his absence. Better than well. When Andrew arrived, he would kiss Tuesday in such a way that Kenton would know he had no chance of getting back into her heart.

He'd given up any right to her affections and his spot had been taken.

But Zena and Andrew did not come to the party that afternoon.

Soon all the guests were gone except for Kenton – the one person who hadn't been invited. He sat at the table in the kitchen, with his feet propped up on another chair, and drank a cold beer while Tuesday loaded the first of three loads of dirty plates, glasses and cutlery into the dishwasher. William was asleep in his pushchair by now. I sat beside him in the manner of an elite guard dog, ready to attack as soon as I needed to.

'Well, hasn't today turned out to be full of surprises,' Kenton said.

'Too bloody right,' I growled.

Kenton launched into a monologue about how busy he'd been at work and how he was on the verge of signing a huge property deal that would make him a million. All he needed was to raise some capital against a guarantee. Tuesday nodded along but I could tell that she wasn't really listening. She was waiting for the moment to ask an important question.

'Kenton, what made you decide to come back today?'

Kenton put his beer bottle down and took his feet off the chair. He arranged his features to look faintly sincere.

'I've been thinking about it for weeks – months even – but every time I made my mind up to come to you, I had an actual panic attack thinking about you telling me to go away. And you would have every right to. I know I've hurt you badly,' Kenton continued. 'I was a coward.

The thought of being in a properly committed relationship scared me. After Helen died, I didn't want to make myself vulnerable again. I didn't want to let anyone rely on me because I didn't think I could step up to the challenge. I felt sure I would fail them. So when I realised how deeply involved we were getting, I panicked, Tuesday. I admit it. It all felt like too much. But I missed you every single day and now, if you'll let me, I want to be part of your life again. Of William's life.'

Tuesday was facing away from Kenton when he said it. Now she turned around.

'Do you mean that?'

'You know I do. And I know how important it is that a boy has his father around. I know how important that is for any child. I remember everything you told me when we were together about how much it hurt that your dad wasn't around when you were growing up. And to think I was on track to be the same kind of deadbeat. Though not deliberately, of course,' he couldn't resist adding. 'Had I known you were pregnant – if you'd just tried to contact me that little bit harder . . . But that's water under the bridge now. I suppose it's not your fault. Not really.'

'The bloody cheek,' I thought.

'And it's definitely not William's fault. He deserves a father who is a proper presence in his life and you . . . you deserve a man who'll look after you too. Properly. Like you need.'

This time I groaned loud enough for both Tuesday and Kenton to hear. That was exactly what Tuesday deserved, hence my disappointment that Kenton had come back just when things were going so well. She deserved a man

like Andrew. One who was as interested in her as she was
in him. Who could make her laugh and yet listen carefully
when she needed a thoughtful ear. She needed a man
who was, first and foremost, her most steadfast friend
and supporter. Kenton cared only for himself. I did not
buy a word he was saying.

Suddenly, Kenton grabbed Tuesday's hand and pulled
her down on to his lap. He tried to kiss her.

'It's too soon,' she said, leaning away from him.

'I understand.'

But he didn't let her get back up again. Instead he
looped his arms around her waist and kept her close. He
buried his face in her shoulder.

'I'd forgotten how wonderful you smell.'

I couldn't help myself. I growled from my place by
William's pushchair. Kenton raised his face from Tuesday's
shoulder to look at me. He narrowed his eyes. 'That dog,'
he said.

'What?' Tuesday asked.

I could tell that it had been on the tip of his tongue to
say something terrible about me but he managed to rein
himself in and say only, 'That dog really cares for William,
doesn't he?'

'Yes. He does. They're best buddies. They're insepa-
rable.'

'Right. As long as you make sure they're never left
alone together. Tuesday, you know that even the best
trained dogs can be unpredictable and, let's face it, your
dog was never that well trained.'

I had to growl at that too.

Tuesday got up from Kenton's lap. 'There's so much

cleaning up to do,' she said brightly. 'I'd better get on with it.' I knew she wanted to change the subject. As she walked by me, she nudged me back a little with her foot, realising I'd been creeping ever closer to Kenton. I'd got well within 'attack' range.

'Why did you call him William Stuart?' Kenton asked then.

'William was my granddad's name,' Tuesday said.

'I know that; you already told me. But why Stuart? Where did that come from?'

She glanced down at me and I waited for her to tell him that William Stuart was also named after me – the one male who had been there for Tuesday when she needed him most – and that his full name was actually William Stupendo. Instead she said, 'I just liked the sound of it.'

'Tuesday!' I was astonished at the casual betrayal.

'So you could still change it to something else, right?' Kenton said, adding insult to injury.

Kenton left shortly afterwards. He kissed both Tuesday and William on the foreheads but acted as though I wasn't there.

'I want to be around as much as you'll let me,' he said as Tuesday saw him to the door. 'Starting tomorrow. I'll take the day off work and come by at lunchtime. You're not working tomorrow, are you?'

She wasn't. Not now that Andrew and Zena's garden was finished. She had nothing to do until she went to mow Mrs Wilson's lawn on Wednesday.

'Great. We can have lunch together and then we can

take William out in the pushchair. Go to the park and put him on the slide, something like that.'

'He's still a bit young to go on a slide,' Tuesday said.

'Well, whatever he can do, we'll do. I'll push him on the swings. Whatever he wants.'

'OK.'

He took Tuesday's hands in his and kissed them in turn. 'Thank you, Tuesday, for giving me this chance. I promise you won't regret it.'

I wished I could believe that. I gave him one last barely audible growl and saved my tail wag until the door was safely closed behind him and I felt like I could relax again.

Tuesday sat down on the bottom of the stairs so that she and I were almost nose to nose for a heart-to-heart.

'Well, what do you think about that, Stupendo?'

Oh, if only I could have formed the words, I would have told Tuesday exactly what I thought! I was furious that I couldn't even rely on Emily to put those words into human talk for me because Kenton had chased her off and Tuesday had let him do it.

Tuesday put William to bed, then came back downstairs to sit on the sofa with me. She poured herself a glass of leftover champagne and fed me a sausage roll. I tried to show my anger at the way the day had evolved by turning my nose up at the tasty titbit but my Labrador nature overcame my Staffie stubbornness so in the end I just did my best not to make too many crumbs and swiftly hoovered up the ones that did fall.

I was glad when Tuesday's phone started ringing and I saw Emily's face light up the screen. But Tuesday didn't answer the call. When Emily called again, I jumped off the sofa and pushed the phone across the coffee table towards Tuesday with my nose, though I was pretty sure it wasn't that she hadn't noticed Emily was calling. The horrible fact was that Tuesday didn't want to talk to her best friend.

However, upon my prompting, Tuesday picked the phone up and tapped the screen, putting Emily on speaker-phone.

'Hi,' she said, with a coolness to her voice that I didn't recognise.

'Hi,' said Emily. 'Is he still there?'

'You mean Kenton? No, he left about an hour ago.'

'Good. Look, I'm sorry for storming out earlier. I know that kind of behaviour never wins the argument. It was childish of me. It's just that it made me so angry, the way he turned up thinking we should all be pleased to see him.'

'It's OK. I understand. I know you don't like him. And I can't pretend I haven't given you reason for that.'

'You mean, *he* hasn't given me reason. You didn't have to tell me what he did to you. I could see he was an arsehole for myself. What did he say to you? After we'd gone.'

'He told me he wants to be part of William's life. Of *my* life,' she added.

'After being AWOL for more than eighteen months?' Emily snorted. 'Tuesday, did you ask him why he's had this sudden change of mind?'

'He said he didn't come back sooner because he needed to pluck up the courage. He said he had a panic attack at the thought I might reject him. But he also said that if he'd known about William, then of course he would have come back sooner. He told me he wants to be a proper father.'

'Right.'

'Why do I feel like you're being cynical?'

'Because I am. I can't believe you're not. Here are some more questions for you to ask: where has he been living since he left you? More importantly, *who* has he been living with? Has she kicked him out? What is he doing for money?'

'He's finalising a property deal. He just needs to find a way to guarantee the loan.'

'Such as against your house? Like last time?'

Emily always knew to ask all the right questions. I was very glad she'd got them out there. But Tuesday didn't even want to contemplate the answers.

'Emily, this isn't helping at all. I'm sure I'll find out everything in due course. But for now, Kenton wants a second chance and everyone deserves one of those. I want William to grow up with a proper male role model in his life. He needs to have a proper relationship with his father. I don't want him to have to grow up like I did, not having a dad around.'

'Tuesday, I get what you're saying, but you can't put right the things that went wrong in your childhood by giving Kenton unfettered access to William all of a sudden. Your dad was your dad. Kenton is different. He's a waste of space. A narcissist. You were doing perfectly well without him and so was William. You were happy.'

'I wasn't. Not really. I was lonely.'

'But even that was changing! What about Andrew?'

'We're just friends. That nearly kiss in the garden was just a heat-of-the-moment thing. We never could have been anything more. We're too – too different, Andrew and I. But Kenton . . . well, Kenton is my soulmate.'

'He doesn't have a soul!' I thought.

'Tuesday, there's something behind Kenton's reappearance and I'm afraid to say it isn't simply that he's been missing you. I would put money on him needing a place to stay because he's screwed up another relationship somewhere else. He must think it's Christmas, finding out about William. You can't refuse him anything now he's got that over you. He's looking for a place to stay or access to free money, not another chance with you.'

'Why can't you just give him the benefit of the doubt for once? You never really gave him a chance. Right from the beginning, you were determined to dislike him. From the very first time I told you about him, you wanted him to be too good to be true.'

'Which is exactly what turned out to be the case. And after all the time you spent getting over him, you're going to throw yourself back into a relationship with him again? I can't listen to this any more,' Emily said.

'You don't have to,' Tuesday replied. 'Maybe Kenton's right. You don't want me to make my own mind up about this, do you? You want me to always be your sidekick. It makes you feel better about your own life to see me struggling. You don't want me to be happy.'

'What? That is not true. You know that's not true. Tuesday, I've always had your happiness at heart. We've been friends since we were six.'

'Then perhaps it's time we admitted we've outgrown each other.'

I heard the shock in Emily's sharp inhale before she said, 'Fine. If that's what you really think, then fine. I'm done. Perhaps you and Kenton deserve each other after all.'

I heard a click as Emily's face disappeared and the screen went back to its usual picture, which was a photograph of William and me sitting on a rug in the garden.

Pushing her phone away, Tuesday curled up in a ball in a corner of the sofa. I suspected she was thinking of crying. I pressed my nose to her face and then climbed back on to the sofa alongside her, ready to lick away her tears.

'Oh, Stupendo. Am I doing the right thing?'

'Of course you're not doing the right thing!' I wanted to shout. 'Emily is our friend. She loves us and we love her. She's not telling you to be careful for the hell of it. She doesn't trust Kenton, I don't trust Kenton and you shouldn't trust him either.' But even if I had been able to talk, Tuesday didn't really want to hear what I wanted to say. I knew Tuesday was going to make the decision that felt right for her even if it was all wrong for the rest of us. All I could do was continue to be there. Silent but faithful. It was the code of the good dog.

As he'd promised, Kenton was back the next day. This time he came bearing more flowers: big smelly ones that made me sneeze.

'I think they're your favourites, aren't they?'

'They are,' she said. 'Peonies are the best.'

'I'll put them in a vase for you.'

I tried not to bristle as Kenton moved around the kitchen as though he'd just been to the shop instead of disappeared for eighteen months. I didn't like how relaxed he seemed to be now that he was back in our space. Had I not been brought up properly, I would have peed right next to his feet just to remind him what was what and whose territory he was invading.

Instead, I sat on the mat by the back door and watched him with a growl in my heart. When he'd finished arranging the flowers, Kenton looked in my direction. I gave him some serious side-eye. Tuesday followed Kenton's gaze.

'Oh!' she said. 'I should have put him outside. I'm sorry.'

'No, it's OK,' Kenton interrupted, surprising both Tuesday and me. 'You don't have to shut him out.'

I was glad to hear it but of course I was suspicious too. What, if anything, had really changed? And how long would that change last for?

'I know how much that dog means to you,' Kenton said.

That definitely rang alarm bells.

I found out a couple of days later, in the park, why Andrew and Zena had not come to William's birthday party. Zena told me that they had been on their way. They were almost at our front gate when Emily and Elvis came rushing out on to the street. Emily had asked Andrew if he was Tuesday's friend then told him that it was probably better if he didn't go to number thirteen right then.

'Her ex has just turned up,' Emily said. 'And it's complicated. You really don't want to get involved.'

Andrew thanked Emily for the warning and told Zena
to turn for home.

'He acted like it didn't matter,' said Zena. 'But I could
tell he was upset. So was I! He spent the rest of the
afternoon composing a text on his phone. I knew it was
meant for Tuesday. He didn't send it. He told me, "Best
forget all about that afternoon in the garden, eh, Zena?"
I know he'd been hoping for more.'

'I'm sure Tuesday was too, until Kenton turned up.
What can we do?' I asked Zena.

Zena admitted that she didn't know. 'Maybe we
shouldn't do anything. We can't know what really goes on
in a human heart. Perhaps Tuesday sees goodness in
Kenton that you don't.'

Zena and I both knew she was being overly optimistic.
There is no better judge of a man's character than a dog.
If Kenton had hidden goodness that I hadn't already
spotted, then I was a hedgehog.

Chapter Thirty-Five

Now

I was looking at my grave and thinking back to William's first birthday party and the days that followed when Caligula jumped out at me from behind the rosemary bush.

'Aha!' He laughed at having caught me out for once.

'You nearly scared me to death,' I said, before remembering that I was already dead.

'You look miserable,' Caligula observed.

'Of course I do. My favourite humans can't see me. They can't hear me bark. I can't even eat the sandwich crust William dropped on the lawn earlier on. There isn't a lot to be happy about.'

'What kind of sandwich?' Caligula asked.

He had his priorities straight.

'Marmite,' I said.

'Ugh. What's wrong with a nice bit of fish?'

'I like Marmite.'

'Yes. But you're a dog. You like rolling in fox poo. Not that I'm judging you for that, Stupendo. I understand it's an evolutionary thing for you canine weirdos. Each to their own.'

I noticed then that Caligula was wearing a new outfit. Well, a new collar at least. It was made of thick black rubber and was studded with red flashing lights. Caligula saw me looking at it.

'It's a tracker,' he confirmed. 'Fourth one this year. I foolishly let my guard down. Derren distracted me with a handful of HiLife. I need to get it dealt with. I'm a cat, for heaven's sake, not a teenage human on an ASBO. This thing is an invasion of my privacy and a violation of my sacred feline right to roam. Not to mention, it'll alert Mary and Zoe to the fact that someone else is feeding me.'

'How are you going to get it off?'

'The squirrels. Want to come with me?'

Over the years, I'd come to know the squirrels who lived in the holm oak at the back of number thirteen well. Napoleon was still a young squirrel when I moved into Bracken Avenue. Pipsqueak was born a year later. When he was very small, Pipsqueak fell out of the nest – or dray – where he lived with his parents and three brothers and sat there dazed on the lawn, not knowing quite what to do with himself. A big tomcat – not Caligula – was sitting on the fence when it happened. I saw everything from the dining room windows and decided I had to get out there fast, before the cat got to the little grey ball of fluff.

I scratched at the door and whined until Tuesday let me out, then I legged it down the garden, barking all the way. Pipsqueak's mother Primula had returned to the nest with some food and noticed that Pipsqueak was missing. She was at the other end of the fence to the tom, flicking her tail and making a loud clicking sound designed to warn him that he had better not think about jumping down while her son was on the grass. It was a scary sound that brought all the garden's residents rushing to see what was happening. I backed Primula up with my deepest bark. I was fourteen in dog years at the time and it wasn't quite the bark I hoped for. It ended in a sort of squeak, but it was effective. The tomcat raised an eyebrow at me and left the garden.

'Stupendo! No! No! Don't eat the squirrel! No!'

Rushing out, Tuesday had grabbed me by the collar and dragged me inside, totally misunderstanding what had been going on. There was little point trying to explain to her what had really happened and how I had actually been doing my best to protect the little creature. I was just happy he had come to no harm.

Tuesday had told Kenton about the baby squirrel when he got home that evening.

'Vermin,' was all that Kenton had said, which rather took the fun out of the story.

Anyway, after that day, the squirrels treated me with more respect. Though they continued to raid the bird table, never again did any of them try to get me on the back of a head with a peanut shell when I was dozing underneath the holm oak. Primula had invited me into the dray so that the squirrel family could thank me properly with a peanut supper but obviously I couldn't take her up on the invitation. Not while I couldn't actually climb trees and weighed as much as all the squirrels put together.

Things were different now that I was dead.

Caligula climbed the holm oak in the usual way while I simply floated up until I was level with the dray's entrance. When Caligula poked his head between the branches, his sudden appearance set off a cacophony of sounds similar to the ones Primula had made when Pipsqueak fell out of the nest. Napoleon punched Caligula on the nose.

'Ow,' said Caligula. 'That's not friendly.'

'Sorry, sir,' said Napoleon. 'I thought you were that tom from down the road. He's been hanging around all day.'

'Perhaps it's because I'm not alive to scare him off any more,' I suggested.

'Stupendo!' Primula exclaimed from further inside the dray. 'Come in.'

Napoleon moved aside so that Caligula and I could squeeze in. It was tight. It was a good job I didn't have a real body since it meant I could be half in and half out without breaking the walls.

'What can we do for you?' Napoleon asked.

Caligula lifted his chin so that the squirrels could see the new collar with its twinkling lights. Napoleon made a clucking sound when he saw it.

'Again?' he muttered.

'What can I say? Derren distracted me with treats. I did my best to resist but he wrestled me to the ground. He didn't get away entirely unscathed, though.'

Caligula flashed a claw.

The smaller squirrels giggled nervously.

'Let me at it,' said Napoleon, hopping closer. He parted Caligula's thick fur so that he could see the collar's buckle. 'Oh dear, this is a serious one.'

'Can you sort it out?'

'I think so. Might have to use my teeth though.' Fortunately, it didn't come to that. Using his dextrous paws, Napoleon soon had the collar undone. As he was released, Caligula shook his ears in relief.

'Thank you, Napoleon. I can't tell you how grateful I am.'

'Do you want us to do what we did last time?' Pipsqueak asked.

Caligula blinked with pleasure.

'Would you? That would be wonderful. And in return, I will make sure that no stinking tom comes anywhere near this tree.'

'Thank you,' Napoleon said, nodding.

Pipsqueak and two of the others picked up Caligula's collar between them.

'They'll take it for a walk,' Caligula explained to me. 'Though not too far, remember! That way Derren will assume I'm staying in my usual patch, leaving me free to roam further afield without him sending out a search party. Remember not to be too erratic!' Caligula called after the youngsters. 'I don't skitter like you lot do. Try to be cat-like.'

With the youngsters gone, Napoleon passed around the nuts. Caligula refused. 'I'm on a restricted diet,' he said. 'Restricted to stuff that's actually edible,' he added in an aside to me.

'I can't,' I said, when Napoleon offered me one, ready cracked.

'Oh, yeah. How's the "being dead" thing working out?'

'It's not as bad as it could be,' I assured him.

The squirrels were actually in mourning for one of

their own that day. An uncle of Napoleon's called Nutjob had been killed in a house fire not far away.

'How did it happen?' I asked.

'He chewed through one electrical wire too many. God rest his soul.'

'What a terrible way to go,' I said.

'He went with a smile on his face,' said Primula.

'Because he was gripping a wire between his teeth?' Caligula suggested.

The squirrels ignored Caligula. 'Thank goodness no one else was hurt,' said Napoleon. 'The humans were woken up by their smoke alarm. They got out. There were no other squirrels in the loft.'

'Did your cousin come back?' I asked. 'As a ghost? Like me?'

'No. He went straight over to the other side. He had no purpose when he was alive, so there wasn't much point him hanging around dead. Not like you. And Emmaline.'

'Who's Emmaline?' I wanted to know.

'She was a rat.'

'Your rat,' said Caligula.

'She lived in your shed,' said Primula.

'*Died* in that shed,' said Napoleon. 'Rat poison. I was disappointed to hear that. Always thought your Tuesday understood about these things. How unkind they are. Poor Emmaline had a nasty death.'

'But Tuesday would never use rat poison,' I protested. 'She wouldn't even put down a slug pellet. Especially not now she's got William. I've heard her explain to her gardening clients a hundred times why she won't use poisons and pesticides.'

'Then Emmaline must have picked the poison up somewhere else,' said Napoleon. 'Whatever happened, it's bad news if there's a human round here using that sort of stuff. It's dangerous for all of us. Rats, squirrels, cats and dogs.'

The other squirrels murmured their agreement.

'It's worrying to me, all these unexpected deaths in the last few weeks. Yours included, Stupendo. We must all be careful out there,' Napoleon concluded. 'Even you,' he said to Caligula.

As Caligula and I gathered ourselves to leave, the squirrels all dropped their heads as Napoleon recited their traditional blessing of farewell. 'May the mighty oak shelter you, the god of the forest remain your steadfast friend, and the hazelnut and walnut be ever generous with their bounty.'

'Amen,' said Caligula. It sounded almost as though he meant it.

Outside the dray, I asked Caligula, 'Do you really think Emmaline was poisoned?'

'Looks like it.'

'But by Tuesday? I don't believe it. She would never have put down poison. In any case, I don't think she knew there were rats in the shed. She never mentioned it. Why would she buy rat poison if she didn't even know rats were living here?'

'Beats me.' Caligula shrugged. 'I guess the only way you'll know is if you ask Emmaline.'

But Emmaline was nowhere to be seen in the garden of number thirteen, so instead I joined Caligula on his nightly tour. We were too late to catch Mary – she'd already gone to bed – so we went straight to Zoe's house.

Zoe was alone. The two other young women with whom she shared her home were out again. Zoe was in her room, sitting on her bed with her laptop on her knees, scrolling through photos on Instagram. Her window was open because it was a warm night, so Caligula slipped inside easily.

'Hey, Gorgeous George!' She seemed happy to see him. Caligula jumped up on to the bed and settled himself on top of the huge pile of cushions that Zoe had pushed to one side. I joined him there to look at the Instagram feed over Zoe's shoulder. Though of course she didn't know I was watching, she played a short video of a puppy trying and failing to climb some stairs. I chuckled to myself as I remembered the days when I too found stairs tricky.

'Did you find it difficult to climb the stairs when you were a kitten, Caligula?' I asked.

'What kind of stupid question is that?' he responded. 'I am a cat. Climbing is our raison d'être.'

I had no idea what climbing had to do with raisins.

Then Zoe's phone rang. She picked it up and sank back into her pillows to talk to the caller. I joined Caligula on the cushions to listen in.

'Hi, Mum. Of course it's not too late. What time is it where you are?'

Caligula explained. 'Zoe is from New Zealand. It's the other end of the day there because they're on the other side of the planet.'

'Is that far?'

'About as far as you can get from here. It's even beyond where Mary's family lives.'

Zoe continued to talk. 'Yes, Mum. I've been having a really good week. You know that temp job I had at the council offices? The one in the refuse department? They asked if I wanted to make it permanent. I said yes, so I'm part of the fly-tipping emergency response team now. It doesn't sound very glamorous, dealing with reports of fly-tipping and stuff, but it makes me feel like I'm making a difference. And the people there are all really nice and friendly. I went out with them for a drink after work tonight.'

'News to me,' said Caligula.

'What am I doing this weekend coming? Oh, you know. I'll go shopping with my housemates tomorrow morning. We'll get lunch somewhere nice then come back here and spend the afternoon getting all dolled up for a big night out. Yes, it is a good job you called me tonight. I just decided I would have a quiet one. I was the first to leave the work drinks. I'm saving myself for tomorrow.'

Zoe's mum said something that I couldn't quite hear but it got a big response.

'Mum!' Zoe exclaimed. 'You can't keep asking me about boyfriends. I'm having a great time being single. I'm not going to throw myself at the first guy I meet just so you've got an excuse to buy a hat. But, yes, since you're asking, I have been on a few dates. They were all very nice but no one special. I'm holding out for the perfect guy.'

'She has not been on any dates,' Caligula said, frowning.

Zoe put her mum on speakerphone while she started to take off her make-up.

'I'm sorry, love,' Zoe's mum said. 'I just want you to be happy, that's all. And I know you don't need a man to be happy. I'm glad you've got good friends. The girls you share your place with sound nice.'

'They are,' said Zoe.

'No, they're not,' Caligula told me.

'Well, it's breakfast time here,' said Zoe's mum. 'And your father is on the hunt for something to eat as usual.'

'Hello, Zoe sweetheart,' came a male voice over the phone. 'We didn't think you'd pick up the phone. We'd thought you'd be out at a nightclub.'

'Not tonight, Dad.'

'Well, I'm glad we caught you on a rare night in.'

'We miss you, pumpkin,' said Zoe's mum.

'I miss you too.'

'When you're not out partying!' her father joked.

'Yeah. When I'm not out partying.'

'Tell your dad about the new job, Zoe,' said her mum.

'I've been given a permanent job in the refuse department. I have to watch videos of people fly-tipping and get as much info as I can – make of car and registration and all that – so the council can pursue a prosecution.'

'Sounds important,' said Zoe's dad. 'You get big criminal gangs involved in fly-tipping. I saw a programme about it on the telly the other day. They charge people to take away their rubbish then just dump it in the countryside. So you be careful, Zoe. You don't know what kind of people you're dealing with.'

'Oh, I won't be getting involved personally, Dad. I'm just in the office. But I've already seen things you wouldn't believe on the CCTV tapes. It's not just old sink units. People chuck some really dangerous stuff: asbestos, barrels full of dangerous chemicals. One guy even dumped a dog.'

Caligula and I looked at each other open-mouthed.

'It certainly hasn't raised my opinion of the human race,' Zoe concluded. 'What kind of monster dumps a dog at a fly-tip rather than try to find it a new home?'

'Let's hope you nail that bastard,' her father said.

'Oh, we will. He was driving a very distinctive van. Fly-tippers aren't the most intelligent people, it seems.'

'I'm glad to hear it. Keep up the good work. We're proud of you, girl, we really are.'

Zoe beamed. But by the time the call ended and Zoe sat down on the bed again, she was crying. It wasn't long before her cheeks were slick with tears that carved little rivulets through her thick make-up.

'I miss home so much,' she blubbed.

She made a grab for Caligula and I watched him struggle with the urge to flee. But he let Zoe cuddle him for as long as he could stand, which was much longer than I expected, until he slipped from her grasp and made a dash for the window.

I caught up with him outside Derren's house.

'Too. Much. Emotion,' he said.

Before I could think of anything to say in response, he had sprinted away into the darkness. I knew I was not supposed to follow.

Chapter Thirty-Six

Then

On the Saturday after William's first birthday party, Kenton arrived in the early evening for supper. He'd timed his arrival so that William was already in bed, I noticed. He didn't even ask about him, just settled himself at the kitchen table and said, 'What's cooking?'

I think he thought it sounded charmingly cheeky. Tuesday pretended that she did too. She took a beer out of the fridge and popped the top off it before handing it to him.

'This is what I like,' Kenton said. 'So have you thought any more about what we've been talking about? About me moving back in?'

'Of course I've been thinking about it.'

'It seems like the most sensible thing to do. Then I can be properly involved with childcare.'

'I can't cope with the uncertainty,' Tuesday blurted out. 'If you're moving back in then it's got to be a proper commitment. I can't go through another break-up six months down the line. It was hell, Kenton. The Christmas after you left I was a wreck. I kept wondering what I'd done wrong.'

'You didn't do anything wrong,' he said, in an emollient tone. 'I just had to work some things out. This time will be different. I promise. This time I'm back for keeps. We can be a little family. Maybe we could even . . .' He paused, significantly. 'Maybe we could even get married. You know. To give William stability. Not right away, but at some point.'

Tuesday regarded him warily.

'Like I keep saying, it's important for William to have a father figure around. All the stats show that boys who grow up without a male role model in the house have a much bigger chance of dropping out of school, committing crime, taking drugs. Having a father in the home makes all the difference. It'd be borderline negligent to deny him that chance when here I am, waiting to step into the breach.'

I could not believe that he was leaning on Tuesday like this, by making it about doing the right thing for her son. Tuesday had always done the right thing for William. He had never wanted for anything. He had all the love he could possibly need.

'I need to think about it,' Tuesday said.

'Don't think too long,' said Kenton. There was an undertone to his words that I really didn't like.

Upstairs, William had woken and started crying. Tuesday's eyes flicked towards the door. Kenton continued to sip his beer as the crying grew louder. I knew that Tuesday was subconsciously setting him a test here and I willed him to fail it. Alas, after a moment or two, Kenton put down his glass and said, 'Why don't I get that? What do you think he needs? Something to eat or a new nappy?'

'You'll know as soon as you get up there,' Tuesday said. 'It's usually quite obvious. Especially if he needs a new nappy.'

I knew from the sound of William's cry that he didn't need food or a new nappy. He just wanted a cuddle. He'd woken up, perhaps from a bad dream, perhaps because he'd heard Kenton's voice, and he wanted to be picked up and soothed.

Kenton took his time getting up from his chair, as though he was hoping that his kind offer would be turned down. Tuesday held her nerve. She kept her eyes on the carrots she was chopping. I went ahead of Kenton, ignoring his tutting to Tuesday that I was obviously still being allowed upstairs.

When I slipped into his room through the narrow gap in the door, I found William standing up in his cot, holding on to the rail. His eyes glittered with tears but the moment I walked into the room, he stopped mid-wail.

'Hello, baby boy,' I said with my tail. 'What seems to be the matter?'

Holding on to the bars of his cot, William bounced in reply.

Kenton was still taking his time coming up the stairs.

Eventually, I heard him step on to the landing. There was a creaky floorboard. He paused outside the bedroom door with his hand on the handle, pushing it further open it ever so slowly as though he didn't want to wake William up. Though he knew William was already awake because he'd heard him crying. William looked towards the door in anticipation, as did I, but Kenton didn't come in. Instead, he called back downstairs to Tuesday, 'He seems to have stopped crying now. Perhaps I shouldn't disturb him after all. He's probably gone back to sleep.'

'Have a look,' Tuesday suggested.

Kenton leaned into the room briefly. He glanced at me. He must have seen that William was still standing in his cot, but he called to Tuesday in a whisper, 'He's asleep.'

And then he went back downstairs, leaving me and William alone again.

So it was me who stayed with William until he went back to sleep that night. It was me who kept watch while Kenton started another bottle of beer and continued to set out the case that Tuesday and William would be much better off if he moved back in and completed the family unit.

He said he'd had to leave his flat because his landlady decided that she wanted her daughter to be able to stay there instead. 'It was very sudden.'

'Where are you staying now?' Tuesday asked.

'I'm with my friend Ted,' he said. 'You don't know him. We used to work together. I'm on a sofa bed in his spare room. It's not ideal – especially with my bad back, which seems to be getting worse every night – but it's OK. I can stay there for as long as you need to make your mind up. I understand you need to feel one hundred per cent sure of me. I've only got myself to blame that you don't. I can only pray that you'll give me a real second chance.'

He picked up Tuesday's left hand and kissed each of her fingers in turn.

'How could I ever have let someone as wonderful as you go? I was mad, I tell you. Crazy.'

A smile flickered on Tuesday's lips.

As midnight chimed, Kenton was still in our house.

'Seems like a waste of time going back to Ted's tonight,' he said, 'if I'm going to be here for lunch tomorrow. Can I stay?'

I sighed audibly as Tuesday nodded yes. That was me stuck out in the hall again.

While Kenton cleaned his teeth with the toothbrush he had presumptuously packed for the evening, I joined Tuesday in William's room. As she rearranged the blankets to cover his shoulders, she thought out loud, 'I owe it to you, don't I, William, to see if I can make things with your dad work out? I know that what Andrew said about male role models is probably true, and many people grow up in single-parent families and with same-sex parents now, but . . . well, I can't help thinking of my own experience and how different my life might have been if Dad had made more effort to be around for me. I feel like there was so much I missed out on.'

I wished I could tell her that the trade-off was not worth it and the only influence Kenton could possibly have on William would be bad. I wished I could tell her how Kenton had stood at the bedroom door, seen William standing in his cot with a tear-streaked face and yet resisted the urge to pick him up. If I'd been able to pick William up, I'd never have put him down. What kind of father was Kenton really going to be?

Alas, Tuesday had already decided that he would be

good enough. While I listened with incredulity, she told Kenton that she had made up her mind. She wanted him to come back to live with her and William. They could be the little family she'd always dreamed of.

'You've made the right decision,' Kenton told Tuesday.

I could not believe it. As far as I was concerned, Tuesday had just made the most foolish decision of her life and I had no way of telling her. Perhaps she wouldn't have listened if I had.

Chapter Thirty-Seven

On Sunday morning, William was the first to wake, of course. I'd spent the night downstairs so that Kenton wouldn't be upset with Tuesday, but as soon as I heard William begin to cry, I decided to break the unspoken rules. I crept up the stairs and into his bedroom. He put his fat little hands through the bars of the cot to grab my ears. I licked his fingers and he quietened down again. I stayed with him for as long as I could, but when I heard voices from Tuesday's bedroom, I skittered straight back down to the hall, not wanting to meet Kenton on the landing. So far Kenton had not been explicit in saying that I should not be allowed on the first floor but I didn't want him to end our truce early.

I expected that it would be Tuesday who came out of the bedroom first, but it was Kenton who appeared at the top of the stairs. He padded across to William's room and called back to Tuesday, 'He seems OK. Shall I leave him in his cot for a bit longer?'

That was the wrong question. He should be asking if he could get William out of his cot for a good morning cuddle and a nappy change, but I heard Tuesday tell him not to worry. She would be getting up soon.

Kenton passed me on his way to the kitchen. He didn't

exactly give me a fond 'good morning' but he didn't try to nudge me out of his way with his foot either, which was an improvement on how things used to be. I was grateful when he remembered to open the back door to let me out into the garden.

It was another half an hour before Tuesday came downstairs with William in her arms. As I wagged a morning greeting, I noticed that she did not look very well. She was pink in the cheeks – hot pink – and yet she had her dressing gown pulled tightly around her and was complaining that she felt really cold.

'I think I'm coming down with something,' she said.

Kenton was solicitous. He took William from her arms and bid her to sit down. He made her a Lemsip. It was all a little unexpected. From what I remembered of him, Kenton was no Florence Nightingale. When he'd lived at number thirteen before, whenever Tuesday felt under the weather, Kenton was abrupt and impatient. I'd heard Tuesday tell Emily about it.

'He doesn't mean to be unkind. It's because he had to spend so much time acting the nurse when his fiancée was unwell,' Tuesday had decided. Emily was unimpressed.

However, on this occasion Kenton was the perfect nurse. He insisted that Tuesday get straight back into bed, telling her that he would take care of everything else. He gave William his breakfast. He brought the kitchen television upstairs so that Tuesday could watch it in bed. He looked after William for the rest of the morning. If you can call putting William in his playpen while sitting on the sofa fiddling with a phone 'looking after'.

Mid-afternoon, Tuesday came downstairs, saying she

was feeling better. Once again, Kenton was suspiciously considerate. He told her to make herself comfortable in the living room. He offered to make William's afternoon tea and fed him too. He made a round of sandwiches for Tuesday, even cutting the crusts off. Unfortunately, he didn't drop the unwanted crusts on the floor for me, as Elvis might have done, but Tuesday seemed happy enough.

'I feel like a princess,' Tuesday said, as she sat on the sofa and Kenton buzzed around her.

'You deserve it,' said Kenton, dripping charm.

'But I can't sit here all day. I've got to take Stupendo for a walk.'

'No, you haven't. Not today.'

'He needs to go out.'

'I can do that. You just stay where you are.'

'Are you sure?'

'Of course I am. If I can borrow your van, I'll take him up to the country park. He can have a proper run off the lead then. If I walk him to the park you usually go to, he'll have pulled my back out before we even get there.'

Tuesday didn't argue with that. Neither would I. I very rarely got to go to the country park and it would be nice to see what was going on up there. But with Kenton taking me? It did not compute.

'OK,' Tuesday said. 'Make sure you take some snacks for when you want him to come back to you. No matter how much fun Stupendo's having, he can always be persuaded to do what you ask with food.'

Kenton gave Tuesday a little salute. 'I've got snacks,' he said.

* * *

So we were going for a walk, Kenton and I. Tuesday still had to get me into my harness – Kenton didn't have the first clue – but he seemed happy enough to be taking me out. I watched with interest as he reached into his rucksack and pulled out a box that rattled like it might contain treats. He decanted a few into a small plastic bag and put them into the pocket of his jacket. I looked forward to getting a better look at them while we were on our adventure.

We were outside the house and about to get into the van when Andrew and Zena arrived. Kenton intercepted them at the top of the drive.

'Tuesday's not well,' he told Andrew before he even said hello.

Andrew was holding a parcel wrapped in bright birthday paper.

'I just wanted to drop this off. It's William's birthday present. I meant to bring it on Sunday but . . .'

Kenton had my lead looped around one wrist and his hands in his pockets. As he took them out to accept the gift, one of the treats he was bringing on our walk came out at the same time. It dropped on to the floor and bounced into the gutter. Zena and I both followed its trajectory. She sighed. She couldn't eat it. Andrew would know. He had bat-like hearing for the sound of Zena munching something she shouldn't. Out of solidarity, I didn't make any attempt to get to the loose snack either.

Kenton took the parcel from Andrew. 'I'll make sure he gets this,' he said.

'I'm Andrew, by the way. Andrew Thomas.'

'Oh yeah,' said Kenton. 'You're Tuesday's favourite client.'

Andrew started to smile before Kenton added, 'I suppose it isn't every day you meet a blind person.'

'I suppose it isn't,' Andrew said.

His smile faded a little with the implication that Tuesday had only talked about Andrew because he was a novelty.

'I'm Kenton,' Kenton said then. 'Tuesday's boyfriend. William's dad. You'll be seeing a lot of me. Well, you won't be seeing anything, I suppose. But I'm going to be around because I've moved back in.'

Now Andrew's smile disappeared altogether.

'I'll give Tuesday that present and then Stupendo and I had better be on our way. We're going for a walk, aren't we, dog?'

Zena gave me a quizzical look.

'You're not the only one who's surprised,' I whispered.

'Well, it's nice to meet you, Kenny,' Andrew said.

'Kenton.'

Kenton hated it when anyone shortened his name. Zena and I both knew Andrew had done it deliberately. It was a little thing but I was pleased.

With Andrew and Zena gone, Kenton loaded me into the van. When Tuesday was driving, I would usually sit in the front – I had my own special seat belt harness to keep me safe – but Kenton didn't know how to use that and he didn't seem to want to go back into the house and ask Tuesday for instructions. So I slid around in the back of the van, trying to steady myself against Tuesday's favourite gardening bucket. It was difficult not to be sick. But I reminded myself that Kenton was doing Tuesday a favour and that perhaps his offering to take me for a walk was also an olive branch to me. It was an opportunity for us to bond and negotiate how we might live together going forward. If we were really going to have to. I would do anything for William's sake.

The journey to the country park seemed longer than usual. Perhaps because Tuesday and I didn't go there often, I'd forgotten how far away it was. But when Kenton stopped the van and let me jump out of the back, I found myself standing in a place where I had never been before.

Chapter Thirty-Eight

Now

In the fortnight immediately after my death, Kenton had been away 'on business' but now he had properly moved back in again.

Tuesday was doing her best to make him feel welcome at number thirteen. She'd given over half her wardrobe space for his fancy suits (and was persuaded to give up even more when he told her he didn't think some of the clothes she'd bought in his absence really suited her). She turned one of the bedrooms upstairs into a little office for him, though he didn't use it. Every meal was made with Kenton's preferences in mind. Every evening, the television was tuned to the shows he wanted to watch. There were many evenings, however, when Kenton didn't come home in time for dinner, claiming that the best way for him to make contacts and hear about new deals was by joining his business acquaintances in the pub.

Neither – despite what he'd said when Tuesday was making up her mind to let him stay – did he throw himself into helping with the childcare. In the last round of negotiating with Tuesday, he had promised that he would share the work, taking sole charge of William for two days a fortnight so that Tuesday could save on the cost of nursery fees while she continued to build up her gardening business. But there was always a reason why it didn't work. If anything, from where I was sitting, it looked as though Kenton's return meant Tuesday was working harder than ever to juggle her responsibilities.

It was especially hard on Tuesday that she and Emily had still not made up. I'd heard her ask Kenton whether she ought to reach out. He, of course, was of the opinion that she should not.

'Emily is the one who stormed off, so she's the one who needs to reach out to you. Though why you would ever bother with her again is beyond me. You don't need her any more. You have your little family now. You, me and William.'

I wondered if Emily and Elvis even knew that I had died. I decided that they couldn't possibly know. Emily would not have let Tuesday grieve my loss without reaching out a friendly hand or sending a kind word.

Another Friday morning rolled around. I was in my usual place on the landing, snoozing lightly, when the postman arrived. I barked, but of course he couldn't hear me, and the letters I'd tried to repel still fell on to the doormat. I went downstairs to give them a good sniffing. There were three envelopes. Two white and one pink. The white envelopes were pretty boring. Probably bills. The pink one had a sticker with a picture of a flower on it sealing it shut. I may not have been able to read but I knew that the pink envelope had come from Emily. I could smell her perfume all over it.

Kenton was the next to get up. At the bottom of the

stairs, he paused to pick up the post. He flipped through the envelopes and left the two white ones balancing on the flat end of the bannister. Emily's letter, he tucked in the pocket of his jeans. He called up the stairs.

'Tuesday, I'm going to SuperSave to get some milk.'

He did not mention the letter from Emily, which was still in his pocket when he left. When he came back, he no longer had the letter with him. I sniffed all his pockets to be sure. He took the milk he'd brought into the kitchen along with the two white envelopes which he placed on a shelf. Tuesday came downstairs with William shortly afterwards. The letters remained unopened while she gave William his breakfast and put on the first of three washes she would do that day. While she buzzed around the kitchen, Kenton sat at the table, scrolling through emails. He looked up at William in his high chair only once, when William dropped his spoon on to the tiled floor with a loud clang. Kenton did not pick the spoon up. Instead, he pointedly picked up his laptop and went into the living room to work.

Tuesday seemed very tired. I wished that she had the letter from Emily to lift her spirits. I felt sure that it would have been a cheering, friendly letter. Beneath the flower sticker on the back of the envelope, Emily had drawn a smiley face. I was sure it would have been an olive branch, with the intention of restarting their friendship. I think Kenton must have known that too, hence his decision to dispose of it.

All day long Tuesday ploughed through her chores, saw to William's needs and returned calls generated by the additional flyers she had placed in local shop windows.

Mid-afternoon, she negotiated a new job. When Kenton came into the kitchen to get himself a glass of water, Tuesday told him the good news.

'It'd be great if I could go over there tomorrow morning. If you were able to watch William . . .'

'I can't,' he said flatly. 'I was just coming in here to tell you that I need to go to London right away, for a meeting of my own. It's first thing tomorrow so I'm going to have to stay there overnight. I won't be able to get an early enough train otherwise.'

'You're leaving now?'

'In about half an hour, yes. So you'll have to do your meeting another time. I'm sure mine has the potential to generate more money, in any case.'

'Sure,' Tuesday agreed. 'I'll – I'll rearrange . . .'

Half an hour later, Kenton was gone. Tuesday finished her busy day alone. At seven she put William to bed and came downstairs to eat supper. It wasn't until she was getting ready to go to bed herself that she spotted the letters on the kitchen shelf. She sat down at the kitchen table to open the two white envelopes. The first was covered in figures. A statement of some sort. The second was an official-looking letter with a photograph of a van that looked like Tuesday's at the top. Tuesday's forehead crinkled into a frown as she read it and read it again.

'This can't be right,' she said to herself.

She got up and looked around the kitchen. I knew she was looking for her phone, which she had left on the windowsill in William's room, where she'd put it while trying to persuade him to go to sleep.

In something of a hurry, she climbed the stairs two by two. As she came back down again, she had the phone in her hand and was leaving a message for Kenton.

'I need you to call me right away. Now.'

She was obviously angry and distracted and thus she didn't see the pile of William's clothes that she had managed to step over on the way up. Kenton was supposed to have carried them to William's bedroom earlier that day. Just another small task that he couldn't be bothered to do. This time, Tuesday didn't miss them. Catching one heel on the precarious pile, she fell down the rest of the stairs, landing head first on the tiled floor in the hall, her phone skittering out of reach.

Chapter Thirty-Nine

I raced to Tuesday's side and barked for help. But there was no one there who could hear me and nothing I could do. Tuesday lay awkwardly, with one of her arms at a strange angle. I tried to move her but of course could make no impact on her body though I put all my energy into my efforts. Neither did my licking her face make any difference. Her eyes were closed and she did not open them. I barked and barked again. The sound of my voice echoed only in my ears.

I knew I had to alert someone who could make themselves heard in the human world, so after checking that William was safe in his bed, I headed out into the garden. Caligula was the friend I was looking for. Caligula would know what to do. But he wasn't in the garden of number thirteen or with the neighbours. I didn't find him at Mary Brown's or Derren's and I had a momentary blank on what number Zoe lived at. Frustrated and worried, I stood in the middle of the road and howled Caligula's name.

He appeared from the front garden of number thirty-seven. I wasn't aware he knew anyone at number thirty-seven.

'New family,' he said. 'Just moved in. Thought I'd better investigate.'

I didn't have time to hear about Caligula's hope that he might have found yet another set of humans willing to feed him. I blurted out the issue.

'Tuesday, stairs, landed on her head . . .'

Caligula immediately started working on a solution.

'This is serious. The most obvious thing is to let Zena know. She can wake Andrew and take him across the road to your house.'

It seemed like a sensible idea to me. When we got to Zena's house, Andrew was already in bed. Zena was in her basket downstairs, also asleep. And snoring. Under different circumstances, I would have felt bad about waking her but this was an emergency. I barked.

'Zena! Zena! Get up. It's urgent.'

She woke with a start. Her big brown eyes blinked wide.

'It's you. I was just dreaming about you, Stupendo. We were in the supermarket and there had just been a delivery of . . .'

'Tell me later,' I said. 'We need your help.'

I told her what had happened. As we reached the part where I told her that I needed Andrew to raise the alarm, she was already on her way up the stairs.

'I'm trained to get him out of the house in an emergency,' she said. 'And obviously this is an emergency.'

I watched as she put both paws on the bed and licked Andrew's face until he woke up, gently pushing her away so he could sit up.

'What are you doing?' he asked.

Zena whined.

'Are you feeling OK?' Andrew asked. 'Do you need to go outside?'

Zena whined again.

'Come on then,' Andrew said. He swung his legs out of the bed and stood up. Zena was back at the top of the stairs.

'It's working,' she said to me. 'Let's go.'

She hurried downstairs ahead of Andrew and went straight to her harness. But he didn't follow her. He went instead to the back door, which he opened and stood beside, waiting for Zena to go out into the garden.

She whined again.

'I've opened the door,' Andrew said. 'What more do you want?'

Zena ran down the hall and pawed the front door.

Andrew joined her there instead.

'You want to go out the front? It's the middle of the night.'

Zena scratched the door harder. Andrew opened it and Zena ran out.

Caligula was at the top of Andrew's garden path.

'Bring him here then,' he said to Zena.

'I'm trying.'

But after turning his head so that he could hear what was going on in both directions – which was nothing, as far as he was concerned – Andrew called Zena back indoors. The street was silent – to human ears – apart from the sound of the rain. Zena tried to stand her ground but eventually Andrew took hold of her collar and pulled her in. He closed the door again, shutting himself and Zena inside. I stood with him and Zena in the hallway. I looked from one to the other in disbelief.

'Tell him,' I said.

'I'm trying!'

'There's nothing happening out there,' Andrew insisted. 'Is there something wrong with you, Zena? Are you feeling unwell? In pain? Sit down.'

He gently felt her back, her head and her limbs, to see if she had somehow injured herself. Then he felt her stomach to see if it was distended. Perhaps she'd eaten something she shouldn't have again.

'You're OK, Zena. And everything is calm out there. Let's get back to bed.'

Zena could only whimper. And all the time, Tuesday was still in danger.

'Forget it,' said Caligula when I joined him outside. 'Andrew isn't going to help us. I'll tell Derren.'

I followed Caligula to Derren's house. Derren was at his computer, wearing headphones as he listened to a podcast. He didn't look up when Caligula walked in so Caligula went straight to the soundboard and pressed a red button.

'Play,' it said.

'Damn,' said Caligula. 'I didn't mean to say that.'

He found the button that said 'outside' and then the one for 'help'. He pressed both in quick succession. Derren didn't even look up. Caligula marched over and put his paw – claws extended – on Derren's thigh.

'Ow!'

That got his attention. Caligula returned to the board. 'Outside,' he tried again. 'Help. Outside. Help. Outside. Help.'

'What's that you're saying?' Derren asked.

'Outside,' Caligula said. 'Outside, outside, help.'

'For goodness' sake,' Caligula said to me. 'He's the one who set up this bloody board. Why does he never listen?'

'You want me to go outside? But it's chucking it down,' Derren said. 'No chance.'

'Outside. Help,' Caligula tried again. 'Help, help, help.'

'Help what? Help food, I suppose?' Derren chuckled. 'You know you're on a diet.'

'Help,' Caligula tried one more time, pressing the button extra slowly and making deliberate eye contact.

Derren shook his head. 'Nope. No more food for you today.'

'Sod it,' Caligula said to me. 'This is a waste of time.'

Caligula threw an angry miaow over his shoulder as he headed for the cat flap again. Like Derren, I was far from fluent in cat, but I knew without needing a translation that it was a swear word and a bad one at that.

We needed a new plan. We went back to number thirteen. Caligula ran straight into the back garden while I checked the house. Tuesday was still at the bottom of the stairs, on her back on the tiled floor with her eyes shut. She was still breathing but she did not respond to my barking.

I dashed upstairs. William, thank goodness, wasn't awake. He was still sleeping peacefully. I knew he was OK so long as he remained safely in his cot. Of all the nights when Kenton wasn't there . . .

I joined Caligula in the garden. In the brief time I'd been indoors, he had gathered all the animals and birds he could find beneath the holm oak tree. The squirrels were there, as was Merle the blackbird, looking nervous to be out in the dark. There were two young foxes from the litter that had been born behind the shed at number twenty-two. There were a couple of other cats that I didn't know by name, though I knew them by sight. One was the tom who sometimes upset the squirrels (they were sitting well away from him). The other was a sleek Burmese who lived right at the other end of the street and rarely ventured this far. I knew how much it must have cost Caligula to get them here into the garden. Inviting those cats into his territory like this was no small thing. I knew that he'd tangled with the tom in the past.

'What's going on?' the old tom asked. 'What are we doing here?'

Caligula called for silence. The animals gathered in a semicircle and he began.

'Everybody. We have a situation. Stupendo's human Tuesday has fallen down the stairs of her house and is currently lying in the hall, unconscious. The only other human in the house is a baby, William, who is too small to sound the alarm. Obviously, Stupendo has tried barking, but none of the humans can hear him. We need to get somebody human out on the street and lead them to Tuesday's house. I've tried with Derren, but unfortunately he's a moron who couldn't understand the message I tried to give him in his own language on the very soundboard he built for me.'

The beautiful Burmese rolled her eyes in sympathy. 'Humans.'

'Zena tried to persuade Andrew to come outside but he's not getting the message either. She's going to keep trying and I'm sure she'll succeed at some point, but time is of the essence. We cannot hang around. We need to make all the humans on this street understand that there is an emergency unfolding at number thirteen.'

'But how?' Merle asked.

Chapter Forty

How indeed? Merle asked the question for all of us. I had no idea what we were going to do. Thankfully, Caligula did.

'It so happens that something Napoleon told me the other day has given me an idea. Napoleon's uncle set fire to a house by chewing through the electrical wires in the loft.'

'It was pretty spectacular,' Napoleon told his audience.

'It certainly brought the humans out,' said Primula.

'You want us to do that at Stupendo's house?' Pipsqueak asked. 'Chew through the wires until we start a fire?' He looked thrilled at the prospect.

'No!' Caligula and I said at once. 'But it would be a good idea to attract the attention of the emergency services. Squirrels, there may be some chewing involved.'

Pipsqueak punched the air.

Caligula pointed to each of the squirrels in turn as he assigned them to various addresses up and down the street.

'Napoleon, number seventeen. Pipsqueak, number nineteen. Primula, number twenty-one. There are boxes at the front of all those houses,' he said. 'They are burglar alarms. Your mission is to chew through the wires going into them, causing a short circuit that should make the alarm go off. The humans always react to a burglar alarm. Particularly if it's their own. Some of the boxes may be decoys that don't contain an alarm at all. If the house I have assigned to you does not have a working alarm, move straight to the nearest house that does and help the squirrel in that placement and so on and so on. You need to work fast.'

The squirrels nodded seriously, as though they understood any more than the fact that they needed to get chewing and quickly. Napoleon gave Caligula a curt salute then gathered his troops and led them out on to the road.

'Meanwhile,' Caligula continued, 'you cats and foxes need to get to work on the cars. Get out there on the street and jump on the bonnets until their alarms go off too. If you can't seem to get one to work, then move on to the next car, quickly as you can. Keep going until you reach the end of the road then come back again, keeping those car alarms going until the humans come out. Some of the alarms are specially calibrated not to react to a cat walking over the bonnet so you may have to do it several times or in pairs.'

The foxes, the old tom and the beautiful Burmese confirmed they had understood their instructions before they too disappeared into the street.

That left just me, Caligula and Merle. Merle was too small and light to set off any alarms, but he said that he would provide aerial surveillance and report back on the whereabouts of any useful humans he could see.

'What can I do, Caligula?' I asked.

Caligula briefly touched his paw to mine before withdrawing as if he'd had a shock. 'Just go back into your house and stay with Tuesday until help arrives. Keep talking to her, Stupendo.'

'But she can't hear me.'

'Just keep talking,' he said again. 'Some part of her will hear you, I know it. Somewhere in her heart. You've got to keep her spirit in this world until human help arrives. You can do it, Stupendo. Go.'

I didn't wait for more instructions. I went straight back to Tuesday's side.

Tuesday had not moved since I left the house to get help. I dashed upstairs quickly to check on William. He was still asleep. Then I went back to the hall and crouched down low so that my face was level with Tuesday's.

I felt the soft whistle of her breath against the fur on my snout. Just like old times when we'd fall asleep on the sofa together, nose to nose.

'Help is coming,' I promised her. 'You wouldn't believe how Caligula has got everyone together to work on this. The cats, the foxes, the squirrels . . . Everybody is going to raise the alarm.'

As I spoke, I heard the first of the car alarms go off.

'You hear that? That'll be one of the cats. It's going to be OK, Tuesday. Help really is coming.'

I wished I felt as confident as I sounded.

Later, the other animals would fill me in on how events unfolded.

After Zena tried to wake him and persuade him to

leave the house, Andrew had gone straight back to bed and was soon fast asleep again. When she heard the first car alarm go off, Zena went back into Andrew's bedroom and jumped up to draw his attention to the noise.

'It's just a car alarm, Zena,' he said, batting her away. 'Nothing to worry about. Why are you so jumpy tonight? Go back to sleep, sweetheart.'

Then the second alarm went off. Zena jumped on the mattress again. Andrew rolled on to his side and wrapped the pillow around his head.

And a third.

'What the—' Andrew complained but he still didn't see the need to get up. After all, he didn't have a car. None of the alarms had anything to do with him.

Those people whose cars were affected did, however, come out into the street. Within minutes of Caligula's strategy meeting in the garden, seven car alarms were wailing. And then the first of the burglar alarms went off.

Napoleon waved in triumph from the roof of number seventeen. He'd made a bet with his nephews that he would be the first to get a burglar alarm to sound and now the youngsters owed him six nuts apiece. Pipsqueak came a close second. He complained, 'I had to do an alarm with a much thicker wire. Otherwise I would have been first.'

'Pay up, Pipsqueak,' was all Napoleon had to say to that.

Up and down the street, people came rushing out of their houses still in their nightclothes to see what on earth was going on. Those who didn't come out leaned out of their windows. There was a great deal of swearing. Vandalism was suspected. The emergency services were called.

But while all this was going on, I still did not know that the plan was working. I could hear the noise but I couldn't see that it was encouraging the humans on to the street. No one had come near our house yet. All I knew was that I had to keep talking to Tuesday.

It was hard to know what to say, so I decided I would talk about the early days, when I was a puppy, before Kenton came into our lives.

'Do you remember the day we first met?' I asked her. 'When you came to Mandy's house to see me and my brothers? I loved you right from the moment you walked into the kitchen. When you were so kind about me widdling on your jeans, I knew for sure you were the one for me.

'I'm sorry I was so difficult to train,' I continued. 'But didn't we have a good time at puppy class? I did, anyway. I want you to know that I caught on to everything you tried to teach me right away. I was just playing with you when I pretended I didn't know "sit" or "stay". I'm sorry if I embarrassed you in front of the other humans because of that. I wanted to make you laugh. There's nothing lovelier to me than your laugh, Tuesday.'

I was sure that Tuesday's breath was growing more shallow with every intake. Her face was pale and growing colder. Suddenly, it struck me like a hammer blow. Was this the reason why I hadn't yet crossed over the Rainbow Bridge? Was my purpose to be here to walk Tuesday over to the other side when her time came? Was that what was happening? It couldn't be true. I couldn't bear it!

Tuesday was not ready to leave the earth. She was still so young and she had so much to do. And William – who would look after William if Tuesday and I weren't there for him? Kenton wasn't good enough. He showed so little interest in his son. William might as well have been a dog like me for all the attention Kenton paid him. I could not stand for William to grow up with so little love. The thought that if Tuesday crossed over we might be reunited was of little comfort to me when so much else was at stake. I had to keep talking. I told her, 'The best moment of my life was when you asked me to be William's dog-father. I know that you and Emily probably thought it was just a good joke, but when I stood next to the font, I took my vows seriously. I will stay in this limbo forever if that's what it takes to make sure that William is properly looked after. I'm sure he can feel my presence, Tuesday. He knows I'm still here. So long as he needs me, I'll be there for him.'

I thought I saw a smile twitch at the corner of Tuesday's mouth as I said that. Helplessly, I tried to nudge her into wakefulness. But of course, I couldn't influence the physical world. I could not so much as move a hair on her head. All I could do was be there and hope for a miracle that would set the world right again. But I was running out of hope.

'Tuesday, stay,' I said, reverting to the words she first taught me. 'Stay. Stay here. Good girl, Tuesday. Stay here. Stay.'

Then, like a sound straight from heaven, I heard Zena bark.

Chapter Forty-One

I knew that Zena never barked except when she really had to. As it became clear that Andrew was simply not grasping the gravity of the moment, Zena had to use the nuclear option. While Andrew tried to block out the sound of the car alarms by holding a pillow over his ears, Zena pawed his hands out of the way and barked right next to his head.

Having kept her powder dry – Zena hadn't barked at Andrew since the morning in the training hotel when she smelled an electrical fire – Zena was confident that he would have to take her seriously now. And he did.

'For heaven's sake. I'm getting up.'

At last Andrew put Zena into her harness and agreed to be led out on to the street.

I heard Andrew yelling as they drew near to my house.

'Zena! Slow down. Zena! Stop! Stop!'

I knew she would take no notice of him this time and indeed she didn't. She did not stop or slow down until she had dragged Andrew all the way to my front door and then she started scratching at the door and barking so loud, she out-barked the alarms and the sirens.

'Zena? What the hell is going on? Are we at Tuesday's?'

Andrew pressed the doorbell. But of course Tuesday didn't answer. He rang her mobile and heard it ringing out in the hall. He called through the letter box.

'Tuesday? Are you in there?'

No response. Andrew walked back to the top of the drive.

'Help,' Andrew called to the street. 'Can somebody please come and help me. I'm at number thirteen. I think something's happened in here.'

By this time, most of Bracken Avenue's residents were out in the road, puzzling over the cacophony (the animals were watching from bushes and trees). It was Mary Brown who first came to Andrew's assistance. She was wrapped in her dressing gown and wearing her slippers. At Andrew's request, she stood on tiptoes to look through the frosted glass panel in the front door.

'I think there's someone on the floor,' she said. 'At the bottom of the stairs.'

'It must be Tuesday.' I heard the anguish in Andrew's voice.

'It's Friday,' said Mary.

'No, Tuesday is her name. The woman who lives here. Tuesday King. Can someone call an ambulance, please?'

Derren and Zoe were already both at the top of the path, doing exactly that.

'We need to get inside,' Andrew said. 'Perhaps the back door's open.'

'The side gate's locked,' said Mary, rattling it to no avail.

'Erm, perhaps . . . If someone could give me a leg up,

I could probably get over the gate. It's not so high.' Zoe was all dressed up with nowhere to go. She was wearing her usual immaculate make-up and her hair was piled on top of her head in an especially extravagant style.

'Are you sure?' Derren asked, observing Zoe's outfit.

'There isn't any other way, is there? There's a woman in trouble in that house.'

Zoe kicked off her impractical shoes and rolled the waistband of her skirt to make it shorter and easier to climb in. She said, 'Don't look,' as Derren made a step from his interlinked hands.

'I wouldn't dream of it,' Derren assured her. 'Ready? And up?'

Derren put his back out but Zoe was over the top of the fence. Fortunately, she was able to use the top of the wheelie bin as a step on the other side.

She tried the back door. It was open. Thank goodness Tuesday hadn't finished closing up the house for the night. I ran to Zoe, as if to lead her from the kitchen to where Tuesday lay. Though she couldn't see me, she followed me down the hall. Tuesday was exactly where I'd left her. Zoe crouched down beside her, swearing loudly as she heard the seam of her tight skirt rip. But Zoe didn't let that stop her. She put her ear to Tuesday's face. Then she jumped up and opened the front door, letting Derren, Andrew and Mary in.

'She's definitely breathing.'

Andrew had dropped Zena's harness by now. Zena ran straight to Tuesday and licked her face. Tuesday did not react.

'How does she look?' Andrew asked. 'Is she pale? How

is she positioned? Is anything twisted? Is there blood?' His voice trembled.

Zena and I stood back as the humans set to work. Derren helped Andrew get down to the floor next to Tuesday so that he could take her vital signs. Then Andrew asked a series of questions of the others to work out what might have happened and what that might mean in terms of the right thing to do next.

'Her arm looks odd,' said Zoe. 'Like she might have broken it.'

'OK. Then we need to be careful not to dislocate it any further.' Andrew gave detailed instructions that would keep Tuesday safe until the ambulance arrived. Meanwhile Mary went upstairs and brought William, who had finally woken because of the commotion, down to be with us.

'William!' I wagged my tail at him and gave him my play face. 'Nothing to worry about!' I yipped.

William's eyes sought me out. He was definitely looking for me because he'd heard me. Could he see me too?

'William! William!' I jumped up and down. 'William!'

He could see me! He reached his arms towards me. I could comfort him at last!

But of course Mary didn't know who William was reaching out for and she kept him tight in her arms. Indignant, William let out a full-throated wail.

Tuesday's eyes flickered open as she heard William cry. She tried to get up but she squealed with pain as she put weight through her arm. It was broken, as Zoe suspected.

Derren and Andrew guided Tuesday into a more comfortable position.

'It's OK,' Andrew assured her. 'An ambulance is coming.'

'And I'm here,' I told her silently. 'I'll keep an eye on William.'

'Thank you, Stupendo,' she said.

I'm sure she said my name.

Chapter Forty-Two

The ambulance arrived in short order. Tuesday was sitting up and talking when they loaded her into the back of it. She agreed that William should stay with Andrew and the others until Kenton could be located. That proved harder than it might have been. Kenton was not picking up his phone or responding to any text messages and the later it got, the less likely it was that he would be able to get back from London that night anyway. I was secretly glad.

After the ambulance left, the rest of us decided to decamp to Mary's house. It seemed more sensible to go there than to stay at Tuesday's, where no one knew how anything worked except me and I couldn't tell them. While Mary gathered together the things William would need for a night at her house, I kept him calm. The adult humans saw William comforting himself by sucking his thumb. They didn't know I was sitting right in front of him, pulling my funniest faces.

I trotted alongside William's pushchair as we moved to number seventeen, where Mary plied her unexpected guests with tea and biscuits.

'How long have you lived on Bracken Avenue?' Mary asked each of her neighbours in turn. I could sense a little embarrassment as they each told how many years had passed since they'd moved on to the street – Zoe had been there for six months, Derren for twelve years – and yet none of them had known each other's names until that night.

While Mary, Derren, Zoe and Andrew discussed the evening, William slept in his carrycot in the corner of the sitting room, just in Mary's line of sight. When I wasn't checking that he was still safe and happy, Zena and I sat beneath the table, almost touching paws.

'Thank you for everything,' I told her.

She gazed at me with her pretty brown eyes. 'It was the least I could do. I'm just so relieved Tuesday's safe. As is Andrew,' she added.

We both knew that.

While I was at Mary's, making sure that William was being well cared for, Caligula had been in the garden at number thirteen, celebrating the success of his plan with the squirrels, the other cats and the foxes. Zena nudged me when Caligula stepped through the cat flap at Mary's, which had been, as usual, left unfastened so that he could come and go as he pleased. He obviously hadn't expected to find anyone but Mary there and his face was a picture as he realised that all three of his 'owners' were in the same room. He hesitated for a second, half in and half out, then turned to leave, but it was already too late.

'Mr Boots!' Mary cried in delight. 'Where have you been all evening?'

Mary drew everyone's attention to Caligula's efforts to make an exit unseen.

'That's not Mr Boots,' said Zoe. 'That's Gorgeous George.'

'His name is Caligula,' said Derren. 'He's my cat.'

'Your cat? But I've been feeding him for years,' said Mary.

'Eight years?' Derren suggested.

'That's about right.'

'Since I brought him home from the shelter. Figures.'

'I thought he came with my house,' said Zoe. 'He was in the garden the day I moved in. He walked in through the back door like he owned the place.'

'Of course he did. Have you been feeding him too?'

'He always seems so hungry.'

While they worked out how long Caligula had been hitting all three of them up for food, Zena and I watched him slink away into the darkness again.

We stayed up until the early hours, the rescue party. At around three o'clock in the morning, Andrew got a call from the hospital and was told that Tuesday was doing well. She was resting. She would be kept in for observation overnight, since she had hit her head and there was a risk of concussion, but she would almost certainly be discharged as soon as the doctor had seen her in the morning. Mary took the phone to tell the nurse who called that Tuesday could be reassured that William was happy and safe, asleep in her spare room.

I walked Zena and Andrew back to their house (not that Andrew knew I was with them) then I headed out to find Caligula again. I found him in the garden at number thirty-one, where he was engaged in a conversation with a hedgehog who had sworn at us a few nights before. The hedgehog gave me a small salute when he saw me.

'That was one impressive plan you guys pulled together,' he told me.

'Thanks.'

'I've never seen anything so funny in my life as all the humans coming out in their pyjamas.'

'It was pretty funny,' Caligula agreed.

'It was epic. Best laugh I've had in years.' The hedgehog carried on his way. He didn't swear once this time.

'Thank you,' I said to Caligula, when we were alone again. 'You saved Tuesday's life.'

'*We* saved Tuesday's life. It was a joint effort by all the animals.'

'But it was you who came up with our strategy.'

'I suppose. But no good deed goes unpunished. Now that Mary, Zoe and Derren all know that I'm getting fed by all three of them, there are bound to be consequences and they won't be good for me.'

He rolled on to his back and played dead for a moment. 'You know, I've only had two meals today. I am starving.'

'You could always try to catch something,' I suggested.

Caligula batted away the suggestion with his paw. 'You know what I think about that.'

'Aren't you a fearsome predator?'

'Let me tell you a secret, Stupendo. I have never caught another living creature in my life. Not a bird, not a rat, not even a teeny-weeny mouse. Not so much as a beetle! I just couldn't do it.'

'As I always said!' I laughed.

'It's not because I *couldn't* catch something if I wanted

to, thank you very much. But because I don't want to cause any harm. I'm not here on this earth to bring fear or pain. I like to think of myself as a secret guardian.'

'The animals round here have got a lot of respect for you,' I said. 'That's why it was so easy for you to pull them together when we needed them.'

'No. It was because they have a lot of *love* for you,' he corrected me. 'That's what really made them turn out like they did. That and the chance to chew some cables.'

'Those squirrels are nuts.'

'You are what you eat,' Caligula quipped.

'You never did tell me how you came to belong to three people.'

'I don't belong to them, dog. As I told you, we cats make beneficial alliances.'

'Whatever. When did you come to this street, Caligula? How did you end with Derren as your, um, principal human?' I asked.

'I don't want to talk about it.'

'Oh, go on. Meeting Tuesday was the happiest day of my life. Until the day I met William, of course. And then every day after that was happier and happier and happier until I got squashed by that taxi.'

'Well, maybe I don't have such happy memories of when Derren came into my life.'

'Why not?'

'The truth is, Derren picked me up at the cats home.'

'When you were a kitten?'

'I wasn't a kitten.'

'Were you a stray?'

'I was not a stray!' Caligula said emphatically. 'I have

lineage. Pedigree. I was already two. I lived with a family. Well, a couple to begin with. They got me when I was a kitten and they couldn't seem to get enough of me. Then she got pregnant and they decided I had to go. Couldn't risk me sitting on the baby's face and suffocating it or something like that. As if I would . . . Anyway, that's how I ended up in the cats home.'

'That's awful.'

'It was hell. All of a sudden I was living in a cage, in a room full of other cats in cages, and let me tell you, none of them were what you could call friendly. I spent my days with my head buried under a scratchy, smelly old towel, hiding from the noise and the chaos outside. I didn't think I would survive. I'd been raised in a beautiful house. I had an electronic cat flap. I had safe streets to roam, good food and a warm clean bed to return to when I was tired.'

'And you ended up in a cage.'

'It's hard to shake off, that feeling of being utterly helpless and at the mercy of anyone who wants you. It made me determined that I would never be so vulnerable again. After my first family gave me up, I vowed I'd never let myself love like that a second time. That's why, as soon as Derren took me home and let me outside, I straightaway looked into my options and found Mary. And then Zoe last year. When it comes to love, Stupendo, it pays to be hedged. Happy?' he asked.

'Are you?'

He batted my question away.

'You are loved, Caligula,' I said. 'More than you know. Your humans love you like crazy. I love you.'

'Don't be so soft.'

I tried to insist but he turned away and shook his head. Even after that night's adventures, still he kept me at a paw's length.

'See you tomorrow, dog.'

Chapter Forty-Three

Since Caligula obviously didn't want to spend the rest of the night hanging out with me, I headed back to number thirteen alone to check the place over. I was about to go into the house when I caught a flash of something pale grey heading towards the garden shed.

'Emmaline?'

It was her. It was the ghost rat.

I followed her tail, not even bothering to close my eyes and brace myself as she disappeared through the wooden wall of the shed and I did the same in pursuit of her. Inside in the musty darkness, she stopped and sat down, whiskers twitching. Her tiny black eyes searched my face. Her expression was wary but kind. She looked a little paler than before. As if she were somehow fading away.

'I need to talk to you,' I told her. 'It's urgent. The other animals are saying that you're dead.'

'Alas, I am,' she said, waving a paw through the spokes of Tuesday's front bicycle wheel. Her whiskers wilted as she watched her paw pass right through the metal struts. 'Yes. Still a ghost.'

'And that you died eating rat poison.'

Emmaline nodded. 'I don't know how I got caught out.'

'Do you remember it?'

'Dying? Thankfully not. Do you?'

'I don't,' I said. 'I suppose that's a good thing. But I don't even remember the days leading up to it. I just came round like this – a ghost – a day later. Here but not here.'

'Me too. It's strange, isn't it? Though not without its upsides. Now no humans can see me, I can run right through the kitchen of a house without anybody screaming or jumping on to a chair or trying to whack me with a broom. Yesterday, I sat in the fruit bowl at number nineteen all afternoon. I had a look in the fridge too but it's really dark in there when the door's shut.'

I nodded in agreement. I too had stuck my head through a couple of fridge doors since discovering I was able. What dog wouldn't?

'Emmaline, the squirrels were saying that you might have been poisoned here. At number thirteen. At my house. But I know that Tuesday would never put poison down. I know it. Will you tell them it isn't true?'

Emmaline closed her eyes for a couple of seconds. When she reopened them, she reached her front paws towards me, as if to take mine in the way Tuesday sometimes did before dancing me round the kitchen.

'I need to show you something,' she said. 'Something I don't think you'll like very much.'

I followed her to the very back of the shed, to the dark corner behind the bicycle and the empty pots and compost bags. Beneath a scrap of old hessian sack was a small cardboard box with a picture of a rat on it. The rat was in a circle with a cross through it, like a 'no entry' sign.

I couldn't read the writing on the side but, like Emmaline, I didn't need to. She knew only too well what it contained and so did I.

'It's rat bait,' she said. 'Grain mixed with poison. Smells quite good, doesn't it?'

I took a sniff of the box. It did smell strangely good. Actually, it smelled familiar. Like someone's hands? Like Tuesday's? No. I shook my head at the very notion. No. I knew what Tuesday smelled of and she had never smelled like this. I still couldn't believe she would ever have bought this stuff, let alone used it.

I looked into the bait box at Emmaline's insistence. Inside were neat blue cubes of something that wouldn't have looked out of place in a dog bowl.

'It's meant to smell delicious. It certainly had me fooled,' said Emmaline. 'I only ate a couple and that was the end of me. Oh, there were so many things I was going to do. Places to see . . .' Her lament reminded me of my own. 'I've lost so much.'

I didn't know what to say to her. I could empathise, of course I could, but here was the evidence that Tuesday – my Tuesday – had indeed used rat poison when she said she never would. Tuesday had killed Emmaline. And in such a terrible way. And it was so foolish. So dangerous. If William found these tasty blue blocks, he would put one straight in his mouth. I knew I would have.

Eventually, I plucked up the courage to offer Emmaline an apology on Tuesday's behalf. She probably wouldn't want to hear it, but . . .

'I can't say sorry enough times.'

'Oh no,' Emmaline said, stopping me as I began my heartfelt speech. 'It wasn't Tuesday who put this box here. It was a man.'

As she said that, I had a sudden, very clear memory of a man's hand offering me a blue-coloured treat.

Chapter Forty-Four

Then

Now I remembered quite clearly getting out of the back of Tuesday's van and sniffing around a pile of assorted human rubbish – garden cuttings, old mattresses, chopped-up furniture and broken bricks. Kenton didn't rush to attach the lead to my harness as Tuesday would have done while she checked to be sure our surroundings were safe. Instead I remembered Kenton dipping into his pockets for the dog treats. He tipped them out on to the floor then threw the empty bag on to the rubbish tip. I was confused. Why was he handing out the treats now? We hadn't even started our walk. It was odd behaviour but I wasn't complaining.

'Come on, Stupendo,' he said, picking a treat up and waving it at me. 'Try one of these.'

I crept forward to investigate. The treats didn't smell like my usual ones. I took the one Kenton held in his fingers. As I crunched it experimentally, Kenton jumped back into the van and restarted the engine. He began to drive off.

'Hey!' I barked. 'Don't forget me!'

But it wasn't that he had forgotten me, I quickly began

to realise. He had *intended* to leave me there by that pile of junk in a dark country lane. I watched in disbelief as Tuesday's van disappeared from view. I forgot all about the treats then.

For the longest time, I just stood there, hoping that Kenton was playing some kind of trick on me. Eventually, I sat down, confused. He wasn't coming back for me. How was I supposed to get back to Bracken Avenue without him? It had started to rain. It was not the sort of day when hundreds of people might be driving this way to start a country walk, so I couldn't just stand there and wait to be rescued. Then I remembered the treats. I should at least eat them to give me the strength to walk home.

'Do not touch that stuff, dog!' came a voice from the darkness, just as I was about to tuck in. I backed away warily. It was the voice of an older animal, possibly bigger than me. I wasn't about to fight him for a snack.

'It's not good,' said an old dog fox, as he emerged from behind the rubbish tip. He gave the treats a confirmatory sniff. 'I could smell it from over there. It's rat bait. Poison.'

'Poison?'

'Don't you recognise the smell, dog?'

Unfortunately, I didn't. And I'm ashamed to say that I wondered for a moment whether the old dog fox was only telling me that the treats were poisoned so he could keep them for himself. I suggested as much.

The fox gave me a look. 'You can believe me or not,' he told me. 'But I would strongly advise you to listen to what I say if you don't want to die on this tip.'

I decided I would believe him. Even if he was trying to con me out of a meal, the risk – never seeing Tuesday and William again – was too great to weigh against it.

'Thank you for warning me,' I said.

'That human has it in for you,' the fox said then. 'He wants you out of the way. You were meant to die here. When you get home, you'll need to keep your wits about you. In my experience, if a human wants you dead, they won't stop at one attempt.'

My mouth dropped open with shock.

'Kenton wants me dead?'

The fox nodded.

'Look after yourself, dog.'

And with that he disappeared.

All I wanted then was to get home, to get back to Tuesday, and try to tell her what was going on. Though it was grey, I got my bearings by looking up in the direction of the sun. I knew that the birds used the sun as a compass. I found that I too had a basic idea of where it came up and where it went down. And I had my nose. My formidable nose. I may not have recognised rat poison – I'd been lucky enough never to encounter it before – but I could recognise pretty much anything else. If I headed in the direction of the setting sun, then it would be a matter of time before I picked up a scent that meant something to me. I put my best paw forward and set off.

It was not a pleasant walk. Out in the country, the roads were quiet, but when cars did come, they came much faster than I expected, causing me to jump into the ditch to avoid being squashed. Being in the van had distorted my sense of distance and I was much further from home than I thought. It was at least two hours before I caught the distant hint of a scent I truly recognised. It was the yeasty warm smell of the brewery on the edge of town. When the wind was in the right direction, you could sometimes smell that brewery from the back garden in Bracken Avenue.

After that, it wasn't long before I saw landmarks that I recognised. The park. The post office. The supermarket. I passed the big house where Buster the gangsta dog lived in genteel luxury. And then Zephyr's house. She was out in her garden, sniffing around the flower beds for hedgehogs. She smelled me as I approached and ran to the front gate to see me.

'Stupendo, what are you doing out here?' she asked.

I told her that I would tell her the whole story next time I saw her in the park. 'But I've got to get home now.'

If only I had paused for just a moment then and told Zephyr about Kenton and the rat bait. The whole mystery might have been solved sooner. I might even have missed my rendezvous with the speeding taxi altogether. But I didn't stop to tell Zephyr what was happening. I had only one thing on my mind. Two people. Tuesday and William, Tuesday and William. I had to get back home.

It was growing dark by the time I turned into Walnut Road, the street that led into Bracken Avenue. My heart was beating fast. I imagined how things would unfold when I got to number thirteen. I prayed that Tuesday would be the one to open the door. I couldn't tell her in words what Kenton had tried to do but I would do my best to let her know with my eyes and by growling. Perhaps I would even give Kenton the bite he deserved. He'd tried to kill me. As I drew closer to Bracken Avenue, I felt myself growing more and more angry. All bets were off now.

'Let me at him,' I growled as I arrived at the junction of Walnut Road and Bracken Avenue. I snarled at an imaginary Kenton and saw myself ripping the bottom out of his fancy-pants trousers.

I stepped up the pace for the final part of my long walk home. From the top of Bracken Avenue, I could see all the way to number thirteen. I saw Tuesday's shadow through the living room window. She was holding William in her arms. It was past his bedtime. Was he refusing to go to bed because I wasn't there? I could not wait to see their faces and let them know how much I had missed them. I'd made it. It was the longest walk I had ever taken but I would have walked a thousand miles for Tuesday and William. I was born to love and protect them. My heart swelled with relief now that they were in sight. I stepped out into the road.

Bright lights.

A screech of brakes.

Then nothing.

So that was how it happened. Kenton had tried to poison me in a place far from home where no one would find me until it was too late. Thanks to the fox, I'd not taken his bait but, as I would later discover, Zena had eaten the small piece that fell out of Kenton's pocket as we all stood on the driveway – her guide dog discipline broken by the bait's tempting smell – and that was enough to set in motion the chain of events that ultimately did Kenton's dirty work for him. And there was, as far as I could see, still no way Tuesday would ever know.

Chapter Forty-Five

Now

After my conversation with Emmaline, I went back to Mary Brown's house. I lay down next to William's travel cot and stayed there all night. When Merle began the dawn chorus, I briefly went to number thirteen to check that the house was secure. When I returned to Mary's again, William was already up. He was at the kitchen table with Mary, who was still in her dressing gown. She was feeding him and chatting away as she did so. William seemed very happy to listen. He was enchanted, in fact. He didn't even glance in my direction. I wasn't put out, though. It was good that he was safe and happy. It meant that I could go to the hospital to check on Tuesday.

I didn't know the way to the hospital, but fortunately I knew a dog who did. Like William, Zena was up and eating her breakfast early. Andrew was already on the phone to the ward where Tuesday had been kept overnight.

'So I can come in to see her at what time?'

The person at the other end of the phone told him the visiting hours.

'And I can bring my guide dog?'

Andrew's nod said that the person he was talking to had agreed that he could, and an hour later, after Andrew had checked in with Mary and William, we were on our way to Tuesday's ward.

Zena caused a stir, of course. Just as she always did. It seemed that everybody loved to see a guide dog.

'If only I could turn all that love into biscuits,' she sighed.

I quickly located Tuesday's bed by sniffing the air. I ran straight up to her and jumped up so that my paws were on the mattress, even if she didn't know it.

I was hugely relieved to see that she looked much better than she had done the night before. Her cheeks were pink again. Her eyes were their usual bright blue. Her arm was in a cast, though.

Andrew stood at the end of the bed.

'Sit down, sit down,' Tuesday said. 'I'm so glad you're here.'

Tuesday explained the accident.

'I'd had some strange news. I was on my way down the stairs after fetching my phone. My foot slipped and I took a tumble. It was just one of those things.'

But far more interesting to her was how on earth it had come about that Zena dragged Andrew to her doorstep.

'I don't know. It's like she has a sixth sense sometimes. Perhaps she could hear you.'

'Above all the alarms? Does anyone know why they all went off at once?'

'No,' said Andrew. 'Though I've heard some pretty crazy theories.'

Andrew told Tuesday how everyone had been drawn out on to the street and how Zoe, Derren and Mary had come to his aid.

When he finished, Tuesday said, 'I don't know how long I was at the bottom of the stairs but right before you and Zena and the others found me, the weirdest thing happened. I was probably just dreaming but I could have sworn I saw Stupendo. He pushed his nose against my face, just like he used to when he was trying to wake me up in the morning because he wanted breakfast. He was right there, telling me to hang on. I actually thought I heard him say, 'Stay. Good girl. Stay.' How strange is that?'

Andrew sucked in his breath.

'You think I'm crazy,' said Tuesday. 'It was the concussion, right? Making me think he was there. You're a doctor. You can tell me.'

'I don't know. Maybe it is concussion, but . . .' Andrew paused as if to weigh his words before he let them loose. 'Tuesday, I wanted to tell you this before, but I thought you'd think I'd gone nuts. A few times since Stupendo died, I've felt as though another dog was in my house with Zena. I could hear him. I could hear the sound of a dog snuffling and occasionally groaning, just like Stupendo used to. You know the way he groaned. And when I was sitting at the kitchen table with Zena underneath, I swear I heard Stupendo's tail thump against the tiles. I knew it wasn't Zena. I recognise every noise she makes. And then sometimes I'd hear them together. Scuffling paws on the kitchen floor. Like they were playing. Too much noise to be Zena on her own. I thought it might be another effect of the accident that cost me my sight. Auditory hallucinations.'

Tuesday nodded. 'I know what you mean. I thought I was hearing things too. And sometimes, I'd glance up from whatever I was doing to see Stupendo standing right in front of me. I put it down to the grieving process and my brain translating every bit of movement it saw as Stupendo because that's what I was used to seeing. But there were other times when I would go into William's room and find him standing up in his cot, laughing at nothing. Now I think, was it really nothing? He was laughing exactly the way he used to when Stupendo was alive and he'd prance about in front of William's cot, in one of their secret games. Do you think he was really seeing Stupendo's ghost?'

'If only he could talk well enough to tell you,' said Andrew.

'One day soon,' I thought. I hoped Tuesday would believe him when he did.

After a brief visit from the consultant, of whom Andrew asked all the right questions, Tuesday was discharged. She took a taxi back to Bracken Avenue with Andrew and Zena. I sat on the back seat between them. Tuesday had the taxi drop them off at Mary's house so that she could pick up William.

'But your arm!' Mary protested. 'How will you push his chair?'

'I'll help,' said Andrew, which seemed to confuse Mary even more. 'Tuesday and I will take one handle each. Zena will guide me.'

'We'll be fine,' Tuesday said. 'With a bit of team work.'

So we made it back to number thirteen, the odd crew. VIP, broken-armed woman, guide dog and dead dog. There was still no sign of Kenton. No sign that he had been back in the house at all since we left it.

'Good,' said Tuesday. 'Because I've got a couple of things to do before I talk to that man again.'

Andrew fed William while Tuesday made a phone call to the council's refuse department. Giving her name and address got an unexpected response.

'Tuesday! From number 13 Bracken Avenue?' Zoe had picked up the call. 'How are you doing, sweetheart?'

Tuesday was delighted to talk to one of her rescue team, but there was serious business to be dealt with. She put the call on speakerphone so that Andrew could hear.

'I got this letter,' said Tuesday. 'Telling me that my van – the van I use for my gardening business – had been caught on CCTV at a fly-tipping spot.'

'Let me look into it for you.'

At the other end of the line, Zoe brought up the case number.

'Oh no,' said Zoe. She tapped on her keyboard. 'Oh, this isn't good at all. I remember this case now. I've got some stills from the CCTV here. I can see that it isn't you driving the van. It's a bloke. Brown hair. Quite tall.'

'Kenton,' Tuesday murmured. 'Are you allowed to tell me what he was dumping?'

'Are you sitting down?'

'Yes.' Tuesday took a deep breath as she waited for the answer.

'He dumped a dog.'

Not just any dog.

Tuesday closed her eyes tightly to hold back the tears. 'That was my dog, Zoe. That was Stupendo.'

Tuesday confronted Kenton as soon as he came home, which wasn't until late that evening. He denied it, of course. He repeated his story that I had run away from him during our walk in the country. But then Tuesday told him the council had CCTV footage that showed Kenton pulling me out of the back of the van and throwing me the 'dog treats' to distract me. Discarding the plastic bag the treats had come in was a littering offence in itself.

'And what did he say to that?' Andrew asked when Tuesday told him how the confrontation went.

'He told me I was mad. He said the evidence was faked. But he did it, didn't he? He wanted to get rid of Stupendo so that he could move back in without having to worry about getting dog hair on his stupid designer trousers. He always hated my lovely dog. I feel like such an idiot. I asked him to leave. Thank goodness he didn't even try to argue. He must have already had somewhere else to go lined up. He was probably with another girlfriend while I was conked out at the bottom of the stairs. How could I ever have ended up with a man who didn't love Stupendo?' Tuesday asked. 'What kind of man is that?'

'The same kind of man who wouldn't love a woman like you,' Andrew said. 'A total fool.'

Tuesday reached for Andrew's hand across the kitchen table.

'You're very sweet.'

'I'm deadly serious.'

Zena and I shared a glance.

'Shall we step out into the garden?' Zena said.

'Absolutely,' I murmured back.

Chapter Forty-Six

After Andrew and Zena had gone, I headed out into the garden again. Caligula was in his usual place, on top of the shed. These days, I didn't need to steel myself to join him up there. As soon as our eyes met, I was just there, alongside him. It felt pretty natural now.

'Kenton's gone,' I told him.

'Good,' said Caligula. 'He was a murderer.'

I nodded. 'Though he didn't know it was a taxi that would finish me off. I might as well have eaten that rat bait.'

'No. Be glad you didn't,' said Caligula. 'It's no way to go.'

I agreed, thinking of poor Emmaline.

'I'll feel much happier when that rat poison in the shed is gone,' Caligula said.

I nodded.

Caligula promised that he would make sure every critter in the neighbourhood knew to avoid it until Tuesday was able to work again and found the bait in the shed herself. It would be a difficult moment for her as she realised that Kenton hadn't just intended for me to get *lost* on my way home from the country park.

'How are you doing, Caligula?' I asked.

'My life is ruined. Now that Mary, Zoe and Derren all know that they've been feeding me, I'll never be able to get three breakfasts and three dinners again. Mary and Zoe have promised Derren they'll help him make sure I stick to my diet. They've agreed I'll get no more than one Dreamie per visit. No more tins of tuna. No more smoked salmon. No more caviar at Christmas.'

I sympathised. 'But think of how much easier you'll find climbing fences.'

Caligula yowled at me.

'That was a swear word,' I guessed.

'You're learning.'

But Caligula's misfortune brought happiness to his three erstwhile owners. Now that they had introduced themselves properly, over the next few weeks Mary, Zoe and Derren became proper friends. They exchanged phone numbers so they could keep tabs on Caligula's fitness and promised that in the future they wouldn't hesitate to help each other whenever they could. Zoe and Derren in particular were soon getting to know each other better. Then one Friday evening, Derren shyly asked Zoe whether she would like to join him for the comedy night at the local pub. At last she had a chance to get dressed up with somewhere to go.

Mary had a new friend in Tuesday too. Tuesday had invited Mary over for tea to thank her for looking after William and learned about her grandson in Australia. William was very fond of Mary. He was almost as good as I was when it came to judging character and he knew that she could be trusted. By the end of that first teatime, he had climbed on to her knee and was beaming up at her face as she talked.

'Perhaps, if you need a break, I could look after William for you. Would you like that, William?'

Tuesday agreed that it seemed like a good idea. Meanwhile, she helped Mary to properly understand how her mobile phone worked so that she never missed a video call from Kathy and Toby again. And Zoe had offered to fly with Mary as far as Australia next time she visited her own family back in New Zealand.

Emily was back in Tuesday's life too. As soon as she heard about the accident and what Kenton had done, Emily insisted on coming over. There were many tears when she heard how I had met my end. There was more sadness when Emily mentioned that soon after their falling-out at William's birthday party, she'd sent Tuesday a heartfelt letter – an olive branch – that Tuesday had never received.

'Kenton must have intercepted it,' Emily guessed.

I thumped my tail to let Emily know she was spot on.

Tuesday would never again give Kenton the benefit of the doubt. Emily shook her head sadly as Tuesday revealed that Kenton had misled her from the day they met. 'That fiancée he nursed when she was "dying of cancer"? She sent me a message on Facebook, telling me they'd been living together in the year he and I were apart. You were right that he targeted me for my vulnerability from the start.'

Emily didn't say 'I told you so.' She just opened her arms to her friend.

'Come here.'

As Emily and Tuesday hugged each other tightly, I wriggled in between them. It was almost like old times. I felt sure they would never allow a real man to come between them again.

Bracken Avenue was transformed now that the neighbours had been forced into getting to know each other thanks to the 'Night of the Alarms', as it came to be known. Caligula and I enjoyed hearing the human beings' theories about what had happened.

Some thought it was a surge in the electricity grid. 'But that doesn't explain the car alarms,' as the man at number forty-three pointed out. 'Perhaps it was the mobile phone network.' Nobody seemed to suspect the cats, the foxes and the squirrels.

Derren briefly toyed with the idea that an alien space-ship had flown low over the neighbourhood, sending all the animals berserk. He explained to Zoe and Mary how Caligula had rushed into the house and pressed 'help' on his soundboard. 'Twenty times in a row! But I ignored him.' Derren shook his head regretfully. 'The one time he was trying to tell me something important and I didn't take any notice. He must have sensed something going on that we humans couldn't see. Something extraterrestrial. I'll never ignore what he says to me again.'

Unfortunately for Caligula, this was not true. Derren continued to ignore him every time he used the soundboard to ask for a snack or plead that hunger was making him 'sad'. Meanwhile, Derren also continued to mangle Caligula's own language with a series of 'miaows' that were, in Caligula's words, 'at best, meaningless, and at worst, downright rude'. All the same, it was clear to me that Caligula loved Derren. And Zoe. And Mary. His relationships with all three may have been founded in his desire for food and his determination to stay aloof, but they had definitely grown to encompass real affection. I had discovered Caligula's biggest secret. He was a total softie at heart. One night, I even caught him using the soundboard to say thank you to Derren after he'd given him a treat.

'My pleasure,' said Derren. But then he followed it up with a yowl.

'What did that yowl mean?' I asked Caligula when he joined me in the garden.

'He said, "Put your tail down. I can see you winking."'

'Maybe that was exactly what he meant to say,' I suggested.

Caligula was unimpressed.

Life – or rather, death – for me continued as usual. I spent my days hanging out with Tuesday and William – still hoping that Tuesday might notice me and praying that William wouldn't lose his ability to do the same – and my nights following Caligula on his rounds.

Despite the conversation she'd had with Andrew in the hospital, Tuesday still didn't seem able to see me in any real way. Not like William did. But now she acknowledged the possibility that I might be there. If she came into William's room to find us playing, she would follow the direction in which William was looking and say, 'Hello, Stupendo' to a spot behind my head or over the top of my tail. That was something that made William (and me) very happy indeed.

It was a good dog's life. How could I ever leave it? Why would I ever cross the Rainbow Bridge when everything I loved was here on earth? I was certain that I would never be able to say goodbye to Tuesday.

Epilogue

As summer turned into autumn and autumn into winter and winter into spring, Stupendo remained in limbo. Emmaline the rat had bid goodbye to the earthly realm the moment she realised her purpose, which had been to help Stupendo find out how he had died. Emmaline couldn't wait to move on but Stupendo always had a reason why he couldn't leave just yet.

'It's Tuesday's birthday! It's Christmas! It's Easter! It's nearly the third Saturday in June!'

And then it was the first Sunday in July. Almost a year had passed since the Night of the Alarms and it was time for William's second birthday party. Tuesday had decided to throw a bash that would make up for the disaster of William's first, when Kenton crashed back into their lives and everything went so wrong.

It was a beautiful day – soft and warm once again – and thus the party would be taking place outside. Emily and Elvis arrived early to help, setting up tables and chairs on the patio. Then Elvis kept William amused while Emily and Tuesday worked hard/gossiped in the kitchen. There was lots to talk about. Emily and Elvis were going to be married later that year.

'Maybe you next year?' Emily nudged Tuesday hard in

the ribs as the doorbell rang. Andrew and Zena were on the doorstep.

Stupendo had been in the garden all morning, watching the comings and goings as Tuesday and her friends set out the sumptuous buffet. Caligula sat on the fence behind him, keeping him company and occasionally commenting on the food. William's birthday cake, made by Emily, was the centrepiece of the table. It was in the shape of a dog.

'Is that meant to be me? Or Zena?' Stupendo asked.

'Could be either of you,' said Caligula. 'A dog's a dog to me.'

'You don't mean that,' Stupendo replied.

He was right. Caligula didn't mean that any more.

They lapsed into companionable silence. But Caligula knew he had to break it.

There was never really going to be a 'right moment' to say what had to be said. Caligula had thought, selfishly, that it would be easier to have the conversation in the sunny garden, long before nightfall. He thought that the bright sunlight might make it better. But what words to use?

Eventually, Caligula slid off the fence to sit beside Stupendo on the lawn and said, 'You know what, dog? I think it's time.'

'Time for what?' Stupendo asked.

'You know,' Caligula said.

After a moment or two, when neither animal spoke, Stupendo blinked his big brown eyes, which were suddenly full of emotion.

'Do I have to?' he asked.

'You know you do.'

'But today? On William's birthday?'

This was going to be tough. Caligula looked around the garden for back-up from one of the other animals or birds. He was relieved when Merle fluttered down from the holm oak to stand on the grass beside Stupendo. Merle would know what to say. Napoleon and Pipsqueak paused in their chasing game to join them too. And Zena, realising what was going on, quietly padded away from the house and down the lawn to lie with her paws touching Stupendo's. Somehow Zena always knew what to do.

Ears dropping, Stupendo cast a longing look back towards the house, where all his favourite humans were together. More people were arriving. Mary, Derren and Zoe had all been invited. And there was Tuesday's father and her younger brother Henry, who were visiting from Spain. Tuesday was beaming with happiness as she and her father stepped into the garden together. William looked very comfortable in his grandfather's arms. Well, for a moment or two at least, before he started wriggling to be put down on the grass next to his favourite toy truck.

'But who will look after them?' Stupendo asked.

'We will,' said Merle.

'All of us,' the squirrels agreed.

'We promise,' Zena added.

'Then how do I do it?'

'You just have to say that you're ready,' Caligula told him. 'And mean it this time.'

Stupendo glanced at the house again. Andrew was sitting on one of the garden chairs now and William was climbing on to his knee. Stupendo's eyes softened as he watched Andrew help William settle into a comfortable position where he could reach the food on the table. Tuesday's dad sat down beside them and they were soon in conversation. Tuesday went inside to fetch a bottle of champagne. She placed it on the table for her father to open, then ruffled William's hair. And Andrew's hair too.

'They will be fine now,' Zena said. 'All of them. Look how happy they are.'

Stupendo nodded. 'Then I'll do it.'

At that, a whisper went around the garden. Soon, every animal on Bracken Avenue knew what was happening. Hundreds of shining eyes watched from the hedges and the trees.

They'd all realised what Caligula had known for some time now: for Stupendo, staying on earth hadn't just been about unfinished business or solving the mystery of how he died. Stupendo had chosen to stay, because he was a loyal dog and because he loved his people. And while there would never be an easy way to say goodbye to them, he could go now knowing that they would be OK without him. There would still be love in their lives.

'I'm ready,' said Stupendo then, fixing his own eyes on some distant horizon.

Having heard the words, Caligula, Zena and the squirrels made a semicircle behind him and looked in the same direction. None of them quite knew what they were waiting for. Though he'd told Stupendo that he was on his sixth life, even Caligula had no recollection of having experienced this moment for himself.

It was a beautiful day. One of those days that lifts every heart. The afternoon was just beginning. Up and down Bracken Avenue, people were enjoying this rarest of treats – a sunny day that coincided with a weekend. In back gardens all over the city, the humans were setting up their outdoor furniture and pretending to be on holiday somewhere exotic as they ate their lunches al fresco. There was not a cloud in the sky, which was as blue as a cornflower's eyes. Until Stupendo told his friends that he was ready, that is. Almost as soon as he finished his declaration with an affirmative nod, the first cloud appeared way up above. Just a little puff of cotton wool at first. Nothing to send anyone rushing inside. But as the animals stared up at it, the cloud started to grow and change, to grow heavy and darken until it filled half the sky. And then the rain began . . .

The humans raced inside, carrying what they could. They didn't wait long enough to see the rainbow appear just like the myths said it would. Even cynical old Caligula gasped with awe as all the colours of the spectrum poured down into the garden. Have you ever seen the end of the rainbow? It came to number thirteen that day.

Gently, the rainbow unfurled on to the grass, like a bolt of silk, coming to a stop right at Stupendo's front paws. The colours shimmered and shifted as though lit from the inside.

Stupendo looked at Zena and then to Caligula, as though for reassurance. His eyes asked what he should do next. Caligula simply nodded towards the glittering path ahead. Zena moved close behind him and gave him a little nudge forward with her nose, whereupon Stupendo lifted his own nose and tail high and walked into the colours. And in the time it took to blink, he was gone.

Afterwards the rainbow rolled itself up again like a carpet and disappeared into the cloud, which in turn dissolved into the air, vanishing just as quickly and strangely as it had come.

Those who were left behind lowered their eyes in respect. Caligula stood close to Zena. She let him lean his head against her warm, glossy flank as the sadness engulfed them both.

'That irritating puppy,' said Caligula. 'That knuckle-headed hound. That manky old mutt. My best friend in the whole world. Gone.'

'We're all going to miss him,' said Napoleon.

'I know I will,' said Pipsqueak.

'He was a good dog,' Zena observed.

'The best,' Caligula agreed. 'The very best. Stupendous.'

Tuesday tipped her head to one side as she looked out into the garden, hoping to see that the rain had stopped.

'The weirdest thing is going on out there,' she said to Andrew. 'Zena appears to be in conversation with Derren's cat and I swear the cat just leaned his head on Zena's side.'

'They're plotting to raid the birthday buffet,' Andrew suggested.

'Stu!' said William, pointing his chubby finger to where his beloved dog had stepped on to the rainbow.

Stupendo. The animals weren't the only ones who would never forget him.

Six months later

It was a beautiful day for a walk. And the perfect day for a particularly important walk. A first walk. At five minutes to eleven, Andrew called Zena into the hallway and put her into her harness. Knowing what was coming, she could not stop wagging her tail.

'Are you excited?' Andrew asked her.

Zena wagged all the harder to let him know that she was.

'Let's go then.'

Caligula was sitting on top of the front garden wall. As Zena and Andrew walked by, he slid down to the pavement and followed them, catching up with Zena and walking alongside her. This was a moment the old cat did not want to miss.

He knew exactly where Andrew and Zena were heading that fine morning. At the gate to Tuesday's front garden, Caligula hopped up on to another wall to get a ringside view. Zena paused at the gate and waited for Andrew to open it. As soon as the gate swung wide enough for her to get through, she pulled him with her, without waiting for him to say 'forward'.

'Zena,' Andrew exclaimed as he struggled to regain

control. 'What's the hurry? Today you need to set an example.'

William was first out of the door. He wrapped himself around Andrew's legs in a hug and insisted on taking Zena's lead. Dropping the harness, Andrew let William take Zena around the front garden, while he leaned against the door frame and waited for Tuesday to finish getting ready.

'Just a minute,' she called from inside. 'I'm having trouble persuading him to put on his harness. Every time I get anywhere near him he throws himself on to the floor so I can't fasten it round his belly. What do you think I should do?'

'Bribe him,' said Andrew. 'Apparently Zena was just the same when she was a pup. I swear they mess about just to get more treats. They work that out pretty quickly.'

'Yep,' said Tuesday. 'Stupendo certainly did. Murphy!' she exclaimed. 'Come back here! Murphy!'

Tuesday returned, carrying a yellow Labrador pup in her arms. His pink tongue lolled from his mouth in an expression of glee. He was having a wonderful time as he evaded Tuesday's best efforts to get him on the lead.

Andrew stepped inside and with his help, Tuesday finally managed to wrangle the newest member of the family into his little blue harness. Murphy extracted several treats for his compliance.

'Am I mad?' Tuesday asked Andrew then. 'Taking this on? I mean, it's so much responsibility. Have I got what it takes?'

'To be a puppy raiser? Of course you have. You trained Stupendo, didn't you?'

'I would never go so far as to describe Stupendo as "trained",' said Tuesday. 'He always did exactly what he wanted to do. Sometimes it coincided with my wishes.'

Hearing that made Caligula smirk.

'There.' Tuesday straightened up. 'I think Murphy's ready at last.'

'Come on,' said Andrew. 'I've been looking forward to this walk. So has Zena.'

'This is an historic moment,' Tuesday agreed.

Caligula followed the little gang to the end of the road before peeling off to spend the rest of the morning sunning himself on the roof of Mary's garden shed. Tuesday, Andrew, William and the dogs were going to the park and that was outside Caligula's territory.

Murphy the puppy zigzagged all the way there, threatening to get under the wheels of William's pushchair one minute, then coming dangerously close to tripping Andrew the next. At the crossing, Zena did her best to be a good example of excellent guide dog behaviour but as soon as Murphy felt Tuesday was ready to go, he dashed across the road, yanking her arm almost out of its socket.

Murphy had a lot of training ahead of him.

Tuesday described the regime to Andrew as they walked. 'Will he ever be as calm as Zena? He's like a wrecking ball now.'

'He'll mellow with time. The trainers at Guide Dogs know what they're doing. They wouldn't have let him get this far if they didn't think he had the potential to go all the way.'

'Will I even be able to let him go when the time comes? He's already so much part of the family. William adores him.'

'When the time comes, you'll be happy to know he's going to help someone live their best life. Like Zena does for me.'

'That's true.'

At the entrance to the park, Andrew unfastened Zena's harness. She was already wearing the bell that would help him locate her when it was time to go home. Not that Zena would ever have failed to respond to Andrew's call, no matter how much fun she was having.

Normally, Zena would have dashed straight for the centre of the huge lawn, eager to catch up with her friends, but today she waited for Murphy to be ready to join her. Tuesday had almost as much trouble getting Murphy unclipped from his lead as she'd had getting him on to it. He kept his little blue jacket on. When he was ready, Zena led the way with Murphy cantering along beside her.

All the gang were there. Zena and Murphy played a short game of tag with Zephyr the greyhound. Buster the Staffie greeted the new arrival with a jerk of his chin that made Zephyr and Zena chuckle behind Buster's back. Murphy was impressed though. He'd learn.

'Buster!' his owner called in plummy Home Counties tones. 'Come along, sweetheart.'

Worn out from all the running, Zena flopped down on to the grass. Murphy threw himself down beside her.

While Zena just enjoyed the sunshine, he rootled through the grass with his little wet nose until he found a smell that interested him. Then he rolled over with his legs in the air and his tongue flapping out the side of his mouth as he rubbed whatever scent he'd picked up all over his back and his little blue jacket. It was fox poo, of course. The most disgusting odour known to humankind. To a dog, the equivalent of something expensive and discreet by Chanel.

'Murphy.' There was something about his grin when Zena said, 'You'll have to have a bath,' that prompted a recollection. Another day. Another dog. Another pile of exquisitely disgusting fox mess.

Zena gazed back up the hill to where Tuesday and Andrew were sitting on the bench. William was fast asleep in his pushchair. Andrew was nervously patting his jacket pocket. Zena smiled as she remembered the trip they'd made to the jeweller's shop earlier that week. Everything felt just right.

Having finished rolling, Murphy lay down beside Zena again and let out a contented sigh. A familiar sigh.

'It's you, isn't it, Stupendo?' Zena asked then.

Murphy turned his big brown eyes towards her so that she could see straight into his heart.

It was all the confirmation Zena needed.

Good dogs always find their way home.

Acknowledgements

As I write this in the depths of Lockdown Three, I'd like to thank not only the people who helped me in the writing of this book, but the gang who kept me sane in 2020 and 2021. It's a long old list.

Thank you to Kimberley Atkins and Amy Batley at Hodder and to Laetitia Rutherford and the team at Watson Little. Thank you to copy-editor Sharona Selby for catching my mistakes and to Jo Myler and Fiona Purves for creating a wonderful cover.

Thank you to my family: Mum, Kate, Lee, Harrison and Lukas, and their dogs, Cocoa and Bear, who inspired many of the antics herein.

Thank you to my friends Jessica Adams, Christina Banach, Faith Bleasdale, Amanda Brookfield, Marguerite Finnigan, Mike Gayle, Lauren Henderson, Helen Lederer, Serena Mackesy, Moira Please, Alex Potter, Simon Robinson, Victoria Routledge and Jane Wright, for the book advice, the idle chats, and the Zoom calls that made lockdown liveable.

Thank you to my old pal Dr Anna Trigell for giving me a last-minute emergency briefing on how to diagnose broken bones in the foot and ankle. I hope I got it right! Or at least not very wrong.

I was inspired to write about a guide dog by real-life hero Dr Amit Patel and his beautiful Labrador Kika. Thanks are due to Amit and his wife Seema for sharing their experience of living with sight loss with me.

If you'd like to know more about guide dogs and living with visual impairment, Amit's memoir, *Kika & Me* (Pan Macmillan), is the perfect introduction. You can also follow Amit and Kika's adventures on Instagram and Twitter (@BlindDad_UK and @Kika_GuideDog).

And last but never least, dear Mark. Thank you for the tea, the wine, the love, and all the generally-being-wonderful.

When a mini-break becomes make or break . . .

Kathy Courage has never visited the famous Italian city of Florence before, so she's thrilled when she and her boyfriend Neil are invited there for a wedding. Unfortunately, with Neil's constant complaining and his teenage children in tow, it's not exactly the romantic break Kathy was hoping for.

But when a mix-up with her flights leaves Kathy stranded in the city, she decides to embrace the unexpected and stay on alone.

What follows is a life-changing few days in the Tuscan sun, as Kathy begins to question the choices that have led her here. With the help of the colourful Innocenti family, who offer Kathy a place to stay, she gradually begins to realise that there's a much bigger world out there, if only she can be brave enough to explore it.

Could Italy hold the answers to her future happiness? Or is Kathy destined to return to her old life?

Bookends

When one book ends, another begins...

Bookends is a vibrant new reading community to help you ensure you're never without a good book.

You'll find exclusive previews of the brilliant new books from your favourite authors as well as exciting debuts and past classics. Read our blog, check out our recommendations for your reading group, enter great competitions and much more!

Visit our website to see which great books we're recommending this month.

Join the Bookends community:
www.welcometobookends.co.uk

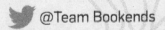 @Team Bookends 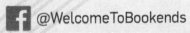 @WelcomeToBookends